TIFFANY BLUES

A Martini Munrow Mystery

J.C. Vogard

This is a work of fiction. Names, characters, places and incidents are products of the author's imagination or are used fictitiously and are not to be construed as real. Any resemblance to actual events, locales, organizations or persons, living or dead is entirely coincidental.

Publishers note: The charm recipe contained in this book is for entertainment purposes only and is to be followed exactly as written for safety reasons. The publisher does not guarantee any results from following the instructions and is not responsible for your specific condition or any other result of using this recipe or following or not following the instructions.

Copyright© 2012 by J.C. Vogard
ISBN: 9780988920316

All rights reserved. No part of this book may be used or reproduced in any manner whatsoever without written permission, except in the case of brief quotations embodied in critical articles and reviews. For information address J.C. Vogard at chocolatediner@yahoo.com.

ACKNOWLEDGMENTS

Warmest thanks and deepest gratitude go to Mike Vogel for his patient and generous technical assistance and expertise, to Sgt. Marc A. Turner (Retired) for his invaluable information and insight, to Jane de la Motte for her dear friendship, constant encouragement and astute editorial review, to The National Hotel, Frenchtown, NJ for their sanctuary and to sweet Honey, for her companionship during late night revisions. Hugs and love to Zachary, Ian and Matthew for being the amazing sons they are and for loving their crazy mom just like she is and, especially to Michael and David for their constant love and support no matter how long it took to get this written. Special thanks to Len and Tracy Coulson for their artistic connections and to Kevin McCarthy for his brilliant cover illustration.

ONE

Visibility was zero when I stepped out onto the porch of The Diner. This wasn't your, oh isn't it pretty, *Ivory Snowflakes* kind of snow. This was your total whiteout, can't see your hand in front of your face, call Rudolph, disaster in the making.

"Geez-o-pete, why didn't I wear snowshoes?" I cried out loud as I crept down the ski slope that used to be the front steps.

"Because Clara Martini, you wouldn't be caught dead in snowshoes!" the disembodied voice of Florilla Munrow, my best friend, business partner and sister by choice, shouted back from somewhere over in the driveway.

I heard the door of her Mini Cooper slam shut, then nothing. At the bottom step I waited for her while my bangs curled and my hair frizzed out of control. Hair that had taken me an hour to dry and flat iron. I finally dug my umbrella out of my bag, popped it open and glanced up at the neon clock over the door of our refurbished nineteen forties Fodero diner. Already an hour and a half late, now where was she?

It's been more than a dozen years since Flo and I first

conjured up the idea for *AstroBotanics Chocolate Diner and Metaphysical Emporium*. We spent years planning the perfect way to indulge our passions for chocolate, astrology, gardening, herbs, all things metaphysical, and sexy shoes (not necessarily in that order) and make a living while we were at it.

Six years ago, we made the big leap and opened our eclectic little boutique here in Dolly's Ferry, one of those small artsy towns on the Jersey side of the Delaware where the locals either love you or leave you alone in hopes you'll go out of business and go away. Luckily we're loved, so they just call us The Chocolate Diner or simply, The Diner. Where else can you nosh bonbons while you consult an astrologer, shop for pruning shears, or strut your stuff in sexy shoes all at the same time? I take care of the Astro and Flo's in charge of the Botanics. We both do the Chocolate.

From the bottom step, I probed for solid front walk, but my high heeled boot just sank into deep powder. How the devil were we ever going to make it to the Pub? Door to door, it couldn't have been more than a hundred feet, tops, but with the entrance on the next block facing the river it might as well have been a hundred light years away.

I was just about to climb back up the steps when the red tornado came whipping around the corner. I tried to maneuver out of the path of the quivering mass of tissue paper, boxes and gift bags but it was too late. She barreled into me, sending my umbrella flying and the two of us tumbling ass over teacup right into the snow. I landed smack on my butt. Flo was splayed out next to me, buried up to her eyeballs in birthday presents. The snowy quills sticking out all over her head were crowned with a wayward pink bow. A moment of shock and awe, then we both lost it.

"Happy birthday Sweetie." She was laughing so hard she could barely get the words out.

"Flo, you look like a gift wrapped porcupine." I

plucked the bow off her head.

"And your bangs look like curly fries." Flo sat up but flopped right back down in the snow.

I tried to push myself up with one hand, but my heel slipped out from under me.

"That's it. I'm calling Phillip," I snorted as I dug my phone out of my coat pocket, pressed *three* and waited.

He picked up right away. "Hey Coco."

"Phillip, help! Get the sled dogs! We've fallen and can't get up."

"Where are you?" Phillip asked.

I held the phone away from my mouth. "He wants to know where we are," I relayed to Flo.

"Tell him we're in heaven. Look I'm making snow angels." She stretched her arms to make wings and sent my presents flying.

Life with Florilla Munrow has been like this, literally, since the day I met her. A dozen years, three idiot boyfriends and at least a hundred bad dates ago, Flo and I were both gainfully employed by an obscure and very male dominated agency of the U.S. Government. Flo had the fun job; she was the nature guru who got paid to play in the woods. I had the job from hell; I was in charge of Human Resources.

My first day at the agency Venus was conjuncting my Mars which, astrologically speaking, should have meant that a fabulous new guy was about to enter my life. Of course it was a government job so I should have known better. The minute I walked through the door, this long-legged, red spiky-haired woman in a *Prince* t-shirt and rubber swamp boots came flying around a corner and boom, my booty was on the floor.

"Nice shoes," she said bending down to offer me a hand.

"Stuart Weitzman," I answered proudly as she pulled me to my feet. Now I'm really only five-two, but that day I was a tall, voluptuous five foot-five in my new, more-than-

I-could-afford, designer pumps. Even in those three inch heels I was still shorter than the woman in the mud boots standing next to me.

The ballsy redhead checked out my shoes again. "*Very nice*. What size do you wear?"

"Eight," I couldn't believe I answered.

"Really? Me too. By the way, do I know you?" she asked.

"You do now. I'm Clara Martini, new head of HR."

"Florilla Munrow. I do plants." She put out her hand for me to shake this time. "I can't help you with the crazy people here, but if you have any plant problems let me know."

By noon we were in the mall together searching for a chocolate fix. At twelve-twenty-seven we were standing in front of Struts, inhaling a pound of Godiva dark chocolate raspberry truffles and ogling a pair of red patent leather four inch, pointy-toed stilettos that were revolving ever so slowly on a pedestal in the display window.

"They are to-die-for," I whispered. "But how the hell are you supposed to walk in them?"

Florilla grinned like a Cheshire cat. "Don't think you have to *walk* in them."

At exactly twelve-thirty-one we bought the shoes, just one pair, and our friendship was sealed forever.

I could barely make out a jacketless Phillip Emond sliding towards us along the front sidewalk. Not an unpleasant sight. "Finally, here he comes," I said.

The day we opened for business, this half French Canadian, half Native American, free spirit pulled up on a bright red Valkyrie and parked right in front of The Chocolate Diner. He sauntered in looking for almond bark and never left. Now, when he's not on assignment for his travel magazine, he's pretty much a permanent fixture in The Diner.

Phillip shook his head, held out his two bare hands and pulled us both to our feet.

TIFFANY BLUES

"Saint Bernard at your service," he said.

"Where's your brandy keg?" Flo asked still laughing and rubbing her backside where it hurt most.

"Waiting for you at the Pub." He pointed his thumb towards the corner.

I followed his finger and noticed that the snow had miraculously died down to a flurry. The giant candy canes that were still strung across Ferry Street had stopped their wild attempts to go flying off into the river. I could even read the big faded "Pub" sign framed with red and green blinking lights. I breathed a sigh of relief while visions of filet mignon and Toll House cookie pie danced in my head.

"So where've you guys been?" Phillip's question snapped me out of it. He was doing his best to brush the snow off Flo's head and the back of her faux leopard coat.

"Good question. Ask Flo," I said checking out the status of my own derriere. I was covered.

"It's a long story," she said to him over her shoulder. "I need vodka first."

"Okay." Phillip stopped his brushing and stooped down to pick up one of my scattered presents from the buried lawn. "So what happened here? You give Clara a set of exploding presents or something?"

"Nope. Just a frozen butt." Flo picked up a gift bag that was now overflowing with snow.

I stooped to pick up one box, then another. I did a double take, and checked out the package in Phillip's arms, and the two little ones that were still in the snow. Then it hit me. None of them were big enough or the right shade of robin's egg blue.

"Flo, where's the Tiffany Box?" I asked looking frantically around us. You couldn't miss it, the box was an enormous 18 inch cube.

Flo just stood there staring down at the snow.

"Did you leave it in the car?" Phillip asked quietly. "I'll go get it." He started off towards the driveway.

"No Phillip. Don't bother." Flo shook her head.

We both looked at her and waited.

"Don't you two look at me like that. You have no idea what I've been through tonight."

"But Flo *where* is our Tiffany Box?" I asked again with a sinking feeling.

Flo sighed a huge sigh. "Let's just say it's missing."

TWO

The Pub has been a place of refuge for weary travelers since the 1770's. I know it has an official name, but no one's ever called it anything but "The Pub." The chestnut beams and massive oak bar are original. Amazing, considering the number of floods and fires that have ravaged this town in the past two hundred plus years. Nowadays, the old tavern where General Washington allegedly swigged a warm ale or two is a cross between a lively sports bar and a home style family restaurant. Cold beer on tap and comfort food. And I'm all for comfort food. The day we bought The Diner, Flo and I discovered the medium rare flank steak sandwich smothered in roasted garlic and we've been regulars ever since. Okay, so it's not the healthiest food ever but sometimes we just have to have it.

The three of us stomped the snow off of our boots and made our way single file back to the bar. A fire was roaring in the walk-in fireplace even though the place was pretty empty. Only a few locals I noticed. Not many river town tourists would come out on a Wednesday night in weather like this.

We bumped into Gertie, the Pub's original waitress, coming out of the kitchen with an armload of late night meals. Gertie's been around the block a few times and looks it. Nobody knows how old she is, the leathery skin and bleached out hair overwhelms any hint of her real age. Hard to tell by looking at her now, but from the wild stories she tells, there's no doubt she was a hot mama in her day.

"Hey Gertie," we said in unison.

"Hi Clara. Hi Florilla," she said to us. She cocked her head at Phillip. "I see you rescued them. Gorgeous, why'd you go out there without your jacket? You'll catch your death."

Phillip adjusted the pile of presents in his arms to make enough room for Gertie to get by us. "You worry too much Gertie," he laughed.

"Darlin' take a load off, go put those packages down on that table over by the kitchen," she drawled.

Gertie pushed her heavy tray of dinner entrees up over her head as she squeezed past us and nodded towards the bar. "He was waitin' for you ya know."

Sure enough, a Jack and Ginger on the rocks, half a Black and Tan, and a martini with three green olives were already set out on the bar in front of three empty stools. The beer was Phillip's. I drink the Jack, easy enough to remember, but Flo's was way more complicated. She could never just order a simple martini. No it had to be a vodka gimlet, served up, in a martini glass with a splash of olive juice and at least two big green olives, please. Phillip knew us too well.

"I thought you were going to be here at seven. If you would've called me sooner, I could have met you guys at The Diner," he scolded as he helped us out of our damp coats and hung them on the back of the barstools.

He pulled out the stool on the right for me and as I hopped up, he leaned in close. "I was beginning to think I was going to have to celebrate your birthday without you,

Coco."

His nickname for me. *Coco. Chocolate.* In the world according to Phillip, one and the same. "Chocolate," he says, "is irresistible." I'm not quite sure if that makes me irresistible too, but I'll take it.

Phillip slid onto the stool next to mine, shook out his shoulder length hair and pulled it back into a ponytail with the ever-present rubber band on his wrist.

"Sorry Phillip, it was all Oz's fault." A sheepish grin crept across Flo's face as she climbed up onto the barstool on Phillip's other side and wriggled her butt all around to get situated. Finally she added, "Well, you know, Oz may appear to be a mild mannered history professor..."

"From a great metropolitan university," Phillip finished the adage for her, having heard it a million times.

Flo nodded and added one more line of her own, "but once I saw those long, gentle supple fingers, I sure as hell knew better."

We all half-laughed and half-groaned but the next words out of Phillip's mouth were serious.

"You know Flo, you and Oscar are like two peas in a pod. The man's asked you to marry him a dozen times. Why won't you give in?"

Flo just shook her head, smiled and kept silent. I knew she didn't want to marry Oscar because she was afraid it would ruin their relationship. Ten years ago Flo had bumped into Oscar Stern in the map room of the Library of Congress, spilled her bag and watched in horror as a dozen super plus tampons went rolling under the Louisiana Purchase. Oscar didn't bat an eye. He got down all fours, crawled under the map table, and retrieved the wayward feminine products. They've been together ever since.

Personally, I think Flo's out of her mind. Oscar is sweet and funny and he makes her laugh. Not to mention the fact that he's a tenured professor who just happens to own a wonderful prewar apartment a stone's throw from

NYU in the Village. And there's a lot to be said for a man who after all these years still loves to surprise the woman he calls "Red" with candlelight suppers, rose petal strewn beds and, like today, impromptu afternoon delight.

Phillip let it go. "Okay, so, is Oz coming tonight?"

"I think he already did," I murmured and took a sip of my Jack and ginger.

Phillip looked confused and I didn't bother to explain. I leaned across Phillip's back so I could talk to Flo.

"So what's the story with our Tiffany box? Did it spontaneously combust in the heat of passion?" Knowing those two, anything was possible.

Phillip immediately picked up on the tone in my voice and tried to change the track of the conversation. "Flo, I forget, wasn't that your mom's Tiffany box, I mean before you and Clara started trading it back and forth as your birthday present box?"

Florilla took a long sip of her gimlet and answered Phillip's question instead of mine. "Actually, it was my grandmother's. When Cody and I were born, nobody was expecting twins. So Grandmom took her crystal punch bowl out of the box and filled it with enough little pink and blue outfits to last our whole first year. I found the box up in the attic when... you know, when my mom died." Florilla tried to fix the crack in her voice with another sip of vodka.

Phillip put his arm around her shoulder and reached for his fresh beer, "Hey Flo, sorry. That was one hell of a big box. You could've fit a Hummer in there." Phillip shot me a look that said, "I need a little help here."

Geez-o-pete, just one birthday without some drama or disaster would be nice. Clearly the party goblins that had sabotaged most of my childhood birthdays were on the prowl again. There'd been a blizzard almost every year followed by some kind of disaster. Like my twelfth. My ingenious father thought it would be a great idea to hide my present, purported to be a mother of pearl ring, in the red butter cream rose on the Italian rum cake he bought at Logucci's but he forgot to tell anyone. Only my Aunt Camille and my mean little cousin Richie from around the corner showed up for the party. Aunt Camille cut the cake, Richie ate the rose and the ring was never seen again.

"Sweetie, did you look out in the little house?" I asked as helpfully as I could. The little house is the old stone well house behind Flo's cottage where she stores her garden stuff and holiday decor. "Maybe it fell behind the Halloween decorations."

"Of course I looked there," Flo frowned. "Oz and I spent the whole day, well most of the day, searching high and low for it. It's not anywhere."

Flo pulled her drink napkin out from under her martini glass. "*Bpllllewh*," she blew into the napkin. "As a matter of fact I even made him go back to New York to look and see if it was at his apartment for some bizarre reason which, by the way, is why Oz is not here wishing you a Happy Birthday now."

She finally took a breath and composed herself. "I think somebody stole it."

"What? That's crazy. Who would climb all the way up your hill, wade through all those raspberry picker bushes and dig through a pile of pumpkin heads just to steal our empty box?" I asked.

"I don't know. I can't think about it anymore." Flo turned to Phillip and raised her martini glass. "Welcome home Phillip. We're really glad you got back in time to celebrate."

"Thanks Flo, I wouldn't miss this for anything," he said in response, but his eyes were fixed on mine.

Kevan, our favorite bartender, wiped down the bar and placed napkins and utensils in front of us.

"Hey C, hey Flo. Phillip said you were on your way. The hot crab dip'll be out any second. You want menus or the usual?"

"It's C's birthday, tonight we want the house special!"

Flo rubbed her hands together with gusto.

"But, no shrimp on my salad, balsamic dressing. And medium rare on my filet.", I reminded Kevan.

"I know, and you want black olives and a baked potato, no sour cream."

"Absolutely." I tipped my glass to him.

"And I *do* want the shrimp. And my filet's medium *well*. The rest is the same as C's, except..."

"Except you want the sour cream. You got it." Kevan humored us. He'd taken the same artery clogging order from us at least once a month for six years. He knew it by heart.

"Damn, it's really too bad you're married," I teased him and got a wink in return. A wink is a funny thing, you're never sure if they are agreeing with you or feeling sorry for you.

"Hey, Kev, I'll have another black and tan while you're at it. Thanks," Phillip said.

"You got it." Kevan answered and started the beer tap. "So C, what birthday is this anyway?"

"Don't ask. It's an "F" word," I whispered.

"Fifty and Frumpy," Phillip teased and ducked as Florilla crumpled her napkin and threw it at him.

"Okay, okay, she's forty... and rockin!" Phillip leaned over and kissed me softly on the mouth. A warm tingly sensation rippled through me.

As far as Phillip and I go, it's so thick you could cut it. Has been from the start. Flo likes intellectual and interesting. I appreciate intellectual, have to have interesting, but I always seem to crave a little bit of that bad boy mixed in. At first Phillip seemed to have all the right ingredients. The man is mad sexy and has a huge heart of gold, but long term security is not part of his repertoire. Short lived serial relationships, especially with six foot tall, triple D, twenty-something blondes, were really more his style.

Still there's some kind of karmic connection between

us and he knows as well as I do, what it's like to fall in love with idiots.

Kevan placed a crock of hot crab dip surrounded by an entire loaf of fresh, warm Italian bread in front of Phillip for us to share.

Flo ripped off a chunk of bread and dipped it in the bubbling appetizer. "Mmmm…" She closed her eyes. "This is absolutely orgasmic."

Phillip tore into the bread and dive bombed it into the dip. "I'll have what she's having." Did I mention he's seen *When Harry Met Sally* at least 10 times? Voluntarily. He tried to swallow the hot crab dipped bread and talk at the same time. "So Coco, did you hear from anyone in your crazy family today?"

I held up my finger as I finished off my first mouthful of the yummy appetizer and swallowed. "All of them. Spencer texted me, *Happy B'day Mom, love me and the band from somewhere between Texas and California.* He didn't even know where the hell he was."

"At least he remembered your birthday, C," Flo said.

"He's my only child, he better remember my birthday! Anyway, my brothers called. Christopher was nice enough not to make me speak to Melissa and Chase told me he was sending a huge vase of roses from The Monaco. We'll see if I get any. And Dad and Ginny sent me a card they made on their computer. It had a picture of them on a golf cart and it said, *Hope your birthday's a hole in one.* Oh and they sent me forty singles, one for each year."

"And what did your mother have to say?" Phillip asked.

"Oh that was the best. Delores sent me an email at midnight which said, and I quote, *Did you ever in your wildest dreams think you'd end up single and alone on your 40th birthday? Happy Birthday, dear. P.S. I'm off to play with Brad Pitt. All my love, Mother.*"

"She did not!" Phillip looked at me in disbelief.

"Oh yeah, she did. Delores never disappoints."

"Off to play with Brad Pitt?"

"She managed to get a part as an extra in a movie he's making on the Amalfi Coast. She'll probably never even see him." I polished off my Jack. "Imagine a seventy-two year old woman, living on her own in Italy, partying every night and auditioning for every bit part that comes along, still hoping for her big break so she can relive the fifteen minutes of fame she had when she won that avocado refrigerator on the *Price is Right* back in 1973."

Phillip raised his glass to toast. "To Delores, she's having a blast. You've got to give her credit."

"Yeah, you *would* think it's great. She's not your mother." I clinked my empty glass with his then offered it to Kevan for a refill.

Florilla shook her head in agreement and leaned forward on the bar so she could talk to both of us. "So Phillip, tell us all about the Seychelles. Did you write a glowing review?" she said.

"Oh man, exquisite beaches, pristine coral reefs, pulchritudinous women. Didn't want to leave." He mumbled as he stuffed another piece of bread into his mouth.

"Pulchritudinous women? Did you actually use the word pulchritudinous in your article?" I asked.

"Damn right I used it. It's a great word isn't it? Means having great physical beauty."

"I am pea green with envy, Phillip Albert Emond. You're the second man in my life who went to the most exotic islands in the world without me." Flo shook her martini glass in his face.

"And who was the first?" Phillip asked with mock indignation.

"My dad. Ever the ornithologist, he traveled halfway across the globe just to catch a glimpse of the paradise flycatcher for his life list."

Flo dug the last olive out of her glass and waived to Kevan for another gimlet.

"Life list? They have a life list, like the hundred places

to see before you die? The hundred birds to see before you die?" I asked.

"It's more like a list of all the birds you've ever seen in your life. It's a birder thing, Sweetie," Flo answered.

"I guess so."

"I forget what island the flycatcher nests on. Did you get to see one?" she asked Phillip.

"Praslin," Phillip answered. "It's the second biggest island in the Seychelles, but I didn't really go bird watching there." He turned to me. "However, I did find the Garden of Eden." He was grinning from ear to ear.

"Oh really, did you run into Eve?" I asked.

"No, but in the Valee de Mai, they've got these palm trees called Coco-de-Mer. Made me think of you. They grow these big mother coconuts the locals say are the forbidden fruit from the Garden of Eden." He spread out his hands like he was holding a giant beach ball. "Have you ever seen one?"

Flo and I had our mouths full of crab dip and just shook our heads "no."

"It only grows on Praslin, nowhere else in the world. It's shaped like a particular part of the female anatomy. The best part," he winked. He whipped out his digital camera and clicked through the pictures until he found it.

Phillip turned to me. "I was going to bring one back for your birthday, but they're protected and you have to have some special permit to buy one. So the best I could do is a photograph."

We both leaned in to get a better look. "Holy cow, it's even got pubic hair!" Flo choked.

I took a gulp of my Jack, "Well that's some birthday present all right."

Phillip's face flushed. "Yeah, it's a wicked aphrodisiac. All you gotta do is look at it."

"Aphrodisiacs." Flo blurted the word so loudly that the old guy across the bar from us smiled and winked in her direction.

She lowered her voice. "Phillip did we tell you we're going to the Metro Botanical Gardens tomorrow?"

He shook his head and waited while she popped an olive in her mouth and chewed it thoughtfully. "That's if the trains are running in this weather, but the Weather Channel says it's supposed to clear up before midnight so I don't think it'll be a problem by morning..."

Phillip cut her off, "And this is related to aphrodisiacs how?"

"We're going to hear Dr. Duncan McPherson give a lecture about medicinal herbs and Oz arranged for us to meet with him afterwards. We're going to pick his brain about aphrodisiacs for our new product line."

"Oh yeah? What new product?" Phillip asked.

"Scorpio Moon, for passion. It has to be ready to go for Valentine's Day," I answered.

"Awsome idea. It'll fly off the shelves. How did Oscar get you a meeting with this doctor guy?" Phillip yanked the rubber band and shook his hair out again.

"Well he used to be a botany professor at Cambridge and now he's a visiting Dean at the Gardens," Flo answered. "He's an old friend of Oz's."

"Oscar went to Cambridge?" Phillip asked, surprised.

"No, he went to Cornell, but he did some of his postdoc in England. Oz met Duncan when he was working on a journal article on the D-Day Invasion. He needed to know something or other about the vegetation along the coast of France and McPherson helped him out. They've been friends ever since. Oscar says, and I quote, 'He's a card that oughta be dealt with', whatever that means," Flo smiled. "But I've never met him."

Kevan finally appeared with two sizzling steaks and placed them in front of me and Flo.

"Watch out, the plates are hot," he warned.

I didn't care. I cut into my two inch thick, perfectly grilled, medium rare filet mignon and was just about to take a bite when a pair of cold hands slipped over my eyes.

TIFFANY BLUES

"Happy Birthday to you," a breathy voice sang behind my head.

"Abbs," I guessed. I'd know that sultry voice anywhere.

I turned in my seat and she hugged me tight, letting her armload of helium balloons go flying up towards the ceiling. Phillip jumped up and caught them, then tied them to the back of my barstool.

Abigail Stone is a twenty-six year old local dogsitter by day, a rock singer with a band called Blu by night and an employee of The Chocolate Diner on the weekends. Abby is in an on again off again long distance relationship with an up and coming glass artist, Akio. His name means "bright" in Japanese and demand for his pate de verre castings and custom lamps skyrocketed after his work was featured in the annual *New York Times* Home Fashion Magazine. Their only problem is that he lives in Austin, Texas.

"Hi Flo. Hey, Phillip, welcome back to New Jersey. Sorry I'm so late, it was a bitch walking over here." Abby hugged them both and handed me a little golden box tied with golden ribbon. "This is from both of us. Well, Akio made it. I wrapped it," she said kind of bouncing up and down.

I pulled off the sparkly bow and opened it gently. Inside was a hand blown golden glass ornament of the sun hung on a blue satin ribbon.

"It's beautiful!" I said.

"To celebrate this important solar return," Abby smiled.

Now it was my turn to choke up. "I don't know what to say. It's perfect."

"Okay. Okay. Enough." Abby waved her hands around. "You're not supposed to cry on your birthday. Change of subject. So what did Flo put in the Tiffany Box?"

I looked at Flo who had turned her stool back to the bar and was dipping her beef ever so slightly into the béarnaise sauce.

Phillip made a cutting motion across his throat and answered for both of us. "The box is M.I.A."

"Oh no, that's not possible. That's your special box." Abby looked from me to Flo and back again.

Flo put her fork down and spoke for the first time since Abby had walked into the Pub. "Abby, that gives me an idea. C, you think we could just go to Tiffany's and buy a new box?"

My mouth was full of steaming baked potato. I swallowed and chugged some of Phillip's beer before I could speak. "No way. Tiffany's guards those boxes like they were ten carat Lucida rings. We'd actually have to buy a large object to get box as big as your mother's."

"Well, how hard could that be? Let's just go buy a soup tureen. That should score us a big box."

"Tiffany's doesn't sell soup tureens."

"How do you know they don't sell soup tureens?"

"Because they don't," I said. Flo rolled her bullheaded Taurus eyes at me.

"Okay," I relented. I pushed aside the veggies on the plate and offered a piece of filet to Phillip. He shook it off. "I'll look online, but even if they do it'd probably cost at least three hundred dollars. Do we really need a three hundred dollar Tiffany box and what would we do with a soup tureen anyway?"

"Make soup. I have to go to the bathroom," Florilla suddenly announced as she jumped off her barstool.

I watched her make her way through the mostly empty tables to the back. She stopped to hug Jason and Louis, the middle aged couple who own Jason Louis Interior Design, the home decor boutique a couple of doors down from us. She pointed to me and they raised their glasses and blew kisses my way.

"She's too much. Before you know it, everybody in here is going to know it's my birthday," I sighed.

"Yep. That's Flo." Abby said as she flipped her long

TIFFANY BLUES

Superman colored hair over her shoulder.

She slipped her wispy body into the space between the stool to my right and the bar and for a second I longed to be in my twenties again. Her multiple earrings and the butterfly tattoo on her collarbone, reminded me of myself twenty plus years ago. Of course I wouldn't have been caught dead wearing purple plaid pajama bottoms and black lace up combat boots but I could relate to her extreme fashion statements.

At eighteen I was dying my then waist length hair jet black and serving Saturday detention with Sister Dominic at Our Lady of Perpetual Hope High School for passing around my *Cosmo Bedside Astrologer* during Theology class. It didn't help that I kept trying to get away with wearing things like *Madonna-Like-a-Virgin* toile over my plaid skirt and a bustier on the outside of my blouse. My mother took the rebellion in stride so long as I was a Madonna in Bass Weejuns. Like she always said, "It's important to always have the right shoes honey. The shoes make the woman." No wonder I was so messed up.

"So Abbs, we need to ask you a favor. Flo and I are going to the Metro Gardens tomorrow. I know you're scheduled to work on Saturday, but is there any way you could cover The Diner for us tomorrow?"

"Oh Clar, sorry, no can do. The Birdwell's golden retriever, you know, Honey, just gave birth to ten puppies. Everything's good there, but I've got to be with them all day tomorrow. You should see them, they're this big." Abby held her palms about four inches apart.

"Aww, I'd love to see them, but it's going to have to wait 'til after tomorrow," I said.

"Are you sure you want to go to Metro Gardens? You heard about the woman they found drowned didn't you?" Phillip asked.

"What woman?" I asked.

"It was just on channel six news tonight. She was a researcher at the Gardens. Didn't show up for work

Monday and they found her this morning, frozen in ice, at the bottom of a waterfall."

"That's horrible," Abby put her hand on my shoulder. "Maybe you shouldn't go."

"Don't worry, we're not going near any waterfalls. We're going to a lecture, inside. So Phillip, darling, could you please watch The Diner for us tomorrow? Since you're home?"

Phillip shrugged. "Sure, no problem." He leaned his head back and took the last swig of his Black and Tan.

He's a true Pisces; artsy, obsessive and anal. Lucky for us Phillip takes better care of The Diner than we do and he loves to help women try on shoes. "Anything special you want me to do?"

"No, we've got a prosperity workshop on Friday but we can get ready for that tomorrow night." I put my knife down having vaporized everything but the broccoli and carrots on my plate. "We'll be gone all day. The lecture's in the morning and now we apparently need to stop at Tiffany's on the way back."

I noticed Flo talking to Gertie outside the ladies room door. Sure enough, thirty seconds later *Hot Hot Hot* was blasting through the bar. A conga line of maybe twenty or so of our local friends, business acquaintances and all the waitresses and even the two busboys emerged from hiding in the kitchen and snaked through the bar in my direction. Gertie led the line carrying a whole Toll House cookie pie heaped with vanilla ice cream, whipped cream and chocolate sauce. A burning candle was stuck right in the middle.

They pushed the tables away and wiggled their way into a semi circle around me. I cringed as they sang "Happy Birthday" in sync with the rhythmic *boomba boom boom boom* of that eighties disco tune. Then Gertie held the lit pie up to my face with both hands. I glared at a beaming Flo and blew out the candle making my perennial wish to the universe to bring me my perfect mate.

TIFFANY BLUES

Everyone clapped and cheered.

"A round of Toll-House Cookie Pie on me, Gertie! Oh, and Tofutti for Abbs." I shouted.

After lots of hugs and kisses, we all settled down and finally dug into the pie. Florilla leaned in front of Phillip and raised her chocolate filled fork at me. "Are you *sure* Tiffany's doesn't sell soup tureens?"

THREE

"**W**ant one?" I smiled, flicking open Elvis Presley's head with my thumb like I was going to light a cigarette.

Flo grinned from ear to ear and held out her hand. "I couldn't wait to give you those. Elvis Pez dispensers, who knew? When I saw the set included both the old *and* young Elvis I just had to get it for you."

"Of all the presents, these were the best. They might even make up for the Tiffany box." I dropped a little pink candy into her open palm and examined the dispenser. "Where'd you find them?"

"Where do you think? At Tice's…" The last part of Flo's answer was drowned out by the din of squealing brakes on metal.

"The Flea Market? I shoulda known," I shouted over the racket.

We gave up trying to talk as the subway clamored to a stop at the MBG station. Bright green and white Metropolitan Botanical Garden signs were plastered all over the platform: *Green Living Starts Here, Winter is Greener Than You Think, Got Green?*

Nope. Not today. There wasn't a green thing in sight

when we came up out of the subway. The sky was overcast and the icebergs pushed up on the curbs by the overnight plows were already turning grimy black and starting to melt.

"Green my ass," I griped as we zigzagged our way across the street to avoid the puddles of dirty slush.

"Don't worry Sweetie," Flo linked her arm through mine. "The tea leaves tell me the grass is way greener on the other side of that wall."

Reality warped the instant we passed through the wrought iron entry gates; like being teleported into a winter wonderland postcard from the early twentieth century. Along the narrow lanes, evenly spaced giant oaks stood guard over the rolling white landscape, their branches covered with sugar frosting.

"Okay, this is better," I said.

"C, just look at the Oak Allees. They have to be a hundred years old and they go on forever."

I unfolded the map the guard gave us when we came in the gate and studied it.

"It sure seems that way. They lead to the administration building. A half mile up that hill." I nodded towards the path on the left. "And, the Bartram Auditorium is *behind* the administration building. And we're wearing high heeled boots," I said with dismay.

"Oh it's not so far," Flo said cheerfully.

"Yeah, right. Like in Newport."

"You can't still be mad at me for that, are you?" she said and started up the hill ahead of me.

Last October we had gone to Newport for a girl's only weekend. Actually it was Flo's idea to help me get over the Royal Supreme Idiot. I'd caught him cheating on me with, count them, not one, but two, other women in the span of one week. Everyone told me I was paranoid until the day he left his text messages open by mistake. The whole thing was there in cartoon bubbles full of x's and o's and kissy hearts from both of them. Turned out it had been going on for almost a year right under my nose. I threw my engagement ring into the toilet and swore off men for the rest of my life. After a week of not wearing anything but his ratty old *Eagles* Football jersey, Flo decided I needed a little help from the Universe to get on with my life. A change of scenery and a New Beginnings spell was just the ticket. Hence, the girls weekend in Newport. The first morning there, Flo shook me awake before dawn and dragged me out, without so much as a glass of juice, for a brisk walk on the Cliff Walk so we could burn the *Eagles* jersey and throw the ashes into the ocean.

"Oh, it's not so far," she had said.

I figured we'd stroll by a few mansions, barbeque the shirt and turn around and come back to the inn for some breakfast. Two and a half hours and seven miles later, I was unable to speak, limping and craving French toast and bacon. How can we be friends?

After what seemed like more than a seven mile trek uphill towards the administration building we stopped to catch our breath. I wiggled my toes to make sure they were still there.

"Look!" Flo threw her arms out towards the building across the street. "The Hall of Botantists. How cool is that? Think we have time to go in?"

"Oh yeah, way cool." Was she kidding? "Maybe next trip. We have to keep moving or I'll have to have my toes amputated." I pulled her the rest of the way up the hill.

We finally found the warmth of the Bartram Auditorium and made a beeline for the ladies room in the lobby. Once we were sufficiently thawed and beautified, we calmly made our way into the intimate hall and were taken off guard by the sheer volume of people already there.

"For once we're early," I said.

People were milling about the small auditorium, taking off coats, finding seats, and chatting in small groups.

I turned to Flo, "I don't see a whole lot of women

TIFFANY BLUES

here, never mind in high heels."

"True," answered Flo, "but there are a lot of interesting men. I thought there would only be crazy botanists here. Look at all the suits. What do you think? Doctors? Rich corporate CEO's?"

"Doubt it. Whoever they are they're probably all married."

"You might catch one in-between wives," Flo said seriously. "What about that guy in the third row?" She pointed to a man with salt and pepper hair in a disheveled grey suit. He looked a lot like Albert Einstein with round wire rimmed glasses. "He looks interesting."

"Are you serious? He's a crazy botanist if I ever saw one." Which I hadn't.

"How do you know he's a crazy botanist?"

"Because he has fungus growing out of his ears," a deep male voice answered over my shoulder.

We both turned around and Flo's eyes widened with recognition. The voice had large, wide set brown eyes which seemed odd with his sharp nose and angular face. He wasn't very tall, maybe five-eight or nine. His brown hair was short and curly with just a hint of gray at his temples. He was casually dressed: blue denim button down shirt, khaki pants and brown lightweight hikers. He grinned at Flo.

"Blaine Winship?" she said incredulously.

He reached for her hands with both of his and I noticed that there were no rings on his smallish fingers.

"Flo Munrow! What are you doing here? You're not still slogging around the swamps in the Pinelands, are you?"

Flo pulled her hands back quickly and replied "No, after I got my master's, I traded in my hipwaders for garden boots." She turned to me. "Clara, this is Blaine Winship. Blaine, this is…"

"That's Doctor Blaine Winship," he interrupted, slightly annoyed.

Flo cleared her throat, "As I was saying, this is Clara Martini, my business partner."

Doctor Blaine Winship did not even reach out his hand to greet me. He just sort of nodded, obviously taken with Flo. She, on the other hand, looked like she might throw up.

'So Doctor Blaine Winship, you did finally get your doctorate. You were on the ten year plan weren't you?"

Ignoring her remark, Blaine reached into his shirt pocket and pulled out a business card and handed it to Flo. She glanced at it and gave it to me, holding it between her thumb and first finger like it was something nasty. It was a simple white card with green print. *Blaine Winship, Ph.D. Specializing in Exotics,* his phone number and email address. Could have been the very well educated owner of a strip club.

"Seems like Rutgers was a lifetime ago, doesn't it? The days of the lowly graduate student are long gone," he said, rolling up the sleeves on his denim shirt.

Flo leaned her head down towards me and whispered, "Thank God."

Blaine continued, "Did you know I just finished a stint as a consultant to the International Congress on Biodiversity? Headed up a two year research project in Madagascar." It was a more a statement than a question.

"What is it you do?" I asked.

"Oh my specialties are *Nepenthes, Dionaeas, Droseras.* I sell them for mega bucks to collectors in Japan, Dubai and the UK."

I looked at Flo for help. I didn't have a clue what he was talking about.

He was losing his patience. "You know, carnivorous plants. I have my own specialty nursery. I'm a grower. Hy-bri-di-zer." He enunciated every syllable like that would help me understand. "I have several carnivorous patents under my belt."

I looked down and thought that was just about all he

had under his belt.

"Excuse me Dr. Winship." The interruption came from a young guy wearing a Brazil world cup soccer tee and jeans under his unbuttoned white lab coat. He cleared his throat and swept back his long bangs with one hand. "Doctor McPherson sent me to see if you were able to bring the delivery today."

Blaine looked annoyed. "Andrew. Of course. It's in my truck. Maybe you could help me unload it later, after the lecture?"

"I'd be happy to." He nodded and his long sandy brown hair fell back into his eyes. He brushed it again awkwardly with his fingers. "Thank you, I will let Doctor McPherson know." He smiled at us and left the auditorium through the side door.

"Who was that? Nice smile. Sounds European." I asked.

"He's a research assistant in pharmacology doing his postdoc here at the Gardens. Ph.D. from Copenhagen. Good kid."

"So you're just here to deliver something?" asked Flo.

"No, Duncan and I go way back and I haven't seen him in a while. I want to hear his lecture. Pharmaceutical companies are paying a lot of money for new botanicals. You never know where the next cure for cancer is coming from. And you?"

We looked at each other and said in unison, "Aphrodisiacs."

"Aphrodisiacs?" Blaine's mouth dropped open.

Flo quickly continued, "We're meeting with Doctor McPherson after the lecture."

Just then, an announcement was made for everyone to take their seats. "Maybe you girls could fill me in later. Let's talk after," he winked. "Where are you sitting?"

"We already have seats. We'll see you later." Flo tugged at my sleeve and headed up to the second row.

I whispered in her ear, "So, what's the story?"

She groaned at me, "I knew him in grad school. We were both doing our research in the Pinelands. He was looking for rare orchids that grow in the bogs down there and I was mapping their locations."

"And?"

Flo bit her lip and carefully put her coat over the back of her seat. "He was a big mistake, huge. Talk about your fungus, the man's a slime mold. I'll tell you about it later."

We sat there people watching while we were waiting for the lecture to begin. The audience was mixed. Mostly scientists, obvious graduate students, and a lot of foreign accents. Dr. McPherson had an international following.

Flo enjoyed pointing out potential mates for me. She just doesn't get that I don't want a professorial type like Oscar. I'm too easily bored. Idiots were never boring; painful, but never boring.

Suddenly Flo pinched my arm and I yelped, "OWWW! What was that for?"

She nodded to a place behind my head. "Clara, Sweetie, I think your birthday present just walked in the door."

I reluctantly turned around in my seat and saw him. This was no Einstein look-a-like. He was about six feet tall, with short, well styled dark hair. He was dressed impeccably in a very expensive looking dark blue suit and yellow tie. A black coat was folded over one arm. This was too good to be true. Had to be married with one on the side.

"Where did he come from?" I whispered. "What do you think? Thirty-six? Seven?"

"Nah, he's at least thirty-eight. No ring." Flo had a better view of him. "He's taking a seat in the back."

He sat down about a dozen rows behind us.

An Asian woman in a gray suit and black ballerina flats began introducing Duncan McPherson, "*Dr. McPherson is a visiting professor from Cambridge University and holds the newly created position of Associate Dean for Applied Botanical Research*

TIFFANY BLUES

here at the Center. He is a world renowned ethnobotanist and author of the most authoritative sources on medicinal botany available today. His newest book is entitled A New World Apothecary."

Flo was excited, leaning forward in her seat. "Look at him--he's so sweet. He has a cane. Neatly trimmed silver beard. Tweed jacket. He's even got a plaid bowtie!"

I had turned in my seat to look at the stranger again. "He's not wearing a bowtie."

"C, I'm talking about Dr. McPherson. I bet his bowtie is for his clan," Flo said as she shook my knee. "Listen to his brogue. Doesn't he remind you of Sean Connery in Indiana Jones?"

"No, more like Pierce Brosnan as Bond, James Bond."

"Oh, never mind, I'll fill you in later."

And she turned her full attention to the podium where Duncan McPherson was saying *"The plant kingdom provides the world with chemically active compounds which are inherently medicinal in nature. I want to speak to you today about the evolution of medicinal methods and materials that led to the discovery of these botanical compounds..."*

The lights went out and McPherson started showing slides about the history of pharmacology and the connection between plants and modern day drug synthesis. I craned my neck, but I couldn't see the back of the room in the dark so I tried to pay attention.

He began with some of the most well known examples of medicinal plants; Opium Poppies (the modern day source of morphine and codeine), the Cinchona Tree, (quinine to fight malaria) and Foxglove (the heart drug digitalis).

Next was a slide of Dr. McPherson standing next to an enormous coffee mug and huge aspirin tablet.

"I want to personally thank mother nature for coffee beans and willow trees. How would we get through the day without our jolt from caffeine and our acetylsalicylic acid?" he asked.

That got a hearty laugh.

"The Chikasaw were using root infusions of the willow, *Salix alba*, to treat headaches eons before the little white pill was developed in the early 1900's. But what is it about salicylic acid and the other botanical compounds that makes them medicinal?" he continued.

At that point he started talking about carbon molecules and glycosides and my mind wandered to the back of the auditorium.

Forty five minutes later, McPherson was saying something that sounded like "*cleanseth the boil and will ripen and breaketh*" and the lights came back on. He ended with an Old World story about Scottish thistle being used for protection around villages in Scotland. Apparently, attacking armies, who were barefoot in skirts, would be torn to shreds by the thistle and their screams would alert the villagers. That brought me back to full consciousness.

"He didn't even mention aphrodisiacs. But he had such fascinating material about bloodletting and leeches though," Flo said matter-of-factly. "Were you paying attention when he talked about how the Native Americans used willows to treat headaches?"

"Yes I was paying attention. I could use an aspirin right about now," I yawned. Getting up, I stretched and twisted around to scan the back of the hall. I found 007 standing near the doors in deep conversation with a middle aged woman in a navy suit.

"Think I could meet him?" I asked.

"We're going to meet him right now. Maybe we should just go up there and introduce ourselves," Flo said.

"I can't just go up there and introduce myself!"

Flo looked confused. She turned around and followed my gaze to the back of the lecture hall.

"Oh. I'm sorry Sweetie, introducing yourself to James Bond is just going to have to wait." She handed me my coat. "Maybe we'll run into him again after our meeting with Dr. McPherson.

"Seriously doubt it," I sighed.

TIFFANY BLUES

"Oh no, here comes Blaine. Let's get moving before we have to talk to him again." Flo nudged me and we quickly made our way up to the podium.

I peeked over my shoulder and realized Blaine didn't want to talk to us, he was trying to get Dr. McPherson's attention. They made eye contact and McPherson nodded. With that, Blaine gave him a little salute goodbye.

Blaine winked at me and pointed his forefinger and thumb like it was a pistol. "Later," he mouthed and grinned broadly as he turned to leave.

"He's gone," I said.

"Who, 007 or Blaine?"

"Unfortunately both." I watched the two of them leave the auditorium with the rest of the crowd and turned my attention back to the man at the podium.

Duncan McPherson was closing up his laptop and chatting with a few of the other attendees. As we approached him he looked up at us and I swear his eyes twinkled. We waited until the small group around him dispersed. Flo walked up to him with her hand out, "Doctor McPherson, I'm Florilla Munrow, Oscar Stern's..."

"Ah, I'm delighted! Please, call me Duncan," he answered in that distinctive brogue. "And what is a beautiful woman like you doing with a rogue like Oscar Stern?"

"Well, he does have his charms," she smiled. "I'd like you to meet my business partner, Clara Martini."

As I shook his hand, he twinkled again and mentioned that he needed to drop off his papers and laptop in his office and asked us to walk with him.

It was a short walk. His office was in the building attached to the auditorium. Two men in raincoats were waiting outside his office door.

"Oh, looks like I have visitors. Can I help you gentlemen?" Duncan asked.

"Doctor McPherson? I'm Detective Carlton. My

partner, Detective Mooney."

Mooney was chewing a candy bar and just nodded. "We need to ask you a few questions, sir." Carlton said.

"I'm terribly busy right now and I have a lunch appointment. Could it possibly wait until this afternoon?"

"No problem, we have others to interview. How about two o'clock?"

"That's dandy. Two o'clock then."

When the detectives were out of earshot, Duncan whispered, "Terrible, terrible tragedy. One of our own, a research assistant, a lovely lass, was found drowned. Right here at the Gardens. Poor, poor Tracy, so sad." He shook his head and his voice trailed off as he unlocked his office door.

The office was small, cluttered with piles of papers everywhere. Scientific looking books marked with colored paperclips were stacked, some on his desk, some on the floor. On a small table in the corner by the only window was a Wardian Case. Inside was a beautiful pink tropical orchid that looked like a ballet slipper.

I moved in for a closer look. Duncan noticed. "Ah, *Paphiopedilum glaucophyllum.* Loosely translated, 'Venus' Slipper' or 'lady slipper', exquisite isn't it?"

He turned his attention back to Flo. "So Oscar tells me you've chosen a vocation that is botanical in nature."

Duncan began clearing piles of papers off the two chairs in the room.

"My education is in botany. I used to map wetlands in the Jersey Pinelands. Mostly cedar swamps and pitch pine lowlands."

"Ah, fascinating landscape. The land of McPhee's Pine Barrens. Those pygmy plains are extraordinary." He motioned for us to sit down. "They think it's partly the thousands of years of fire history that keep those pitch pines so small. Great place to study Cypriprediums."

I looked questioningly at Flo. She mouthed the word "orchid" to me when he wasn't looking.

TIFFANY BLUES

He continued, "I've been on many field outings there. Have you ever had the pleasure of the curly grass fern?" He asked her as he continued to rummage around the room.

"Yes I've seen it," she said, "but that's a long time ago now. It's not what we came to see you about…"

"Oh I know, I know," he clapped his hands together. "Oscar has told me about your current venture; AstroBotanics is it?" He was grinning. "I understand you ladies are in the business of making love," he paused, "spells? How can I be of service?"

"Well, it's true, we do make some serious mojo." Flo answered.

I quickly jumped in, "Yes, but *AstroBotanics* isn't just about love spells. We like to think of ourselves as spiritual motivators. Teachers."

"Life coaches with a twist," Flo added. "*Astro,* *f*or the spiritual, *Botanics* for the herbal. We help people create their own magic."

"I'm the A*stro*. Astrology readings, energy balancing, holistic counseling things like that. Flo's the *Botanics*. Horticultural consulting and garden design." I quoted.

"But my real passion is herbs," Flo jumped in. "I'm fascinated by the lore, you know, what the ancients thought of as their 'magical' properties. I grow some specialty herbs for the business."

Duncan raised his eyebrows at her.

"Not those kind of herbs!" She shook her head, slightly flustered. "We sell chocolates too."

Duncan stroked his beard and peered at us over his half glasses clearly amused. I thought he was going to say, "You can't be serious," but he surprised me.

"I'm something of an astrologer myself you know, fascinating subject. You can't truly understand plants without studying the stars and planets as well, now can you?"

"That's how we feel about it," I agreed.

"Right now we're creating a whole new line of products. We call it Magical Intentions," Flo said. "Starting with a client's astrology chart, we customize blends of herbs for them."

I continued, "Depending on their needs, we might add crystals, florals, or candles to the recipe."

"Then they add their own intentions to the mix and use the kit for increasing prosperity, achieving well-being, getting over old boyfriends...you know, things like that." Flo finished the explanation.

Duncan laughed out loud. "Very resourceful," he chuckled kindly.

"Anyway, our new product line is really taking off and we're looking for new ideas. That's where the love spells come in. We really would like to pick your brain for our latest project, Scorpio Moon," I said.

"Scorpio Moon?" he seemed very intrigued by the name.

"It's the herbal charm that we're putting together for Valentine's Day. To help bring passion into your life. That's really why we're here.", Flo said.

"Is it now?"

"I mean. Umm. To learn more about aphrodisiacs. From you. For Scorpio Moon."

"Well, my bonnies, I can certainly teach you a thing or two about that subject. I'm a Scorpio myself, you know."

Then he added, "What you're really looking for are plants ruled by Venus and Mars."

Flo was relieved. "Exactly."

We were interrupted by an attractive mocha skinned young woman who popped her head in the door. She looked to be in her early twenties, with wavy brown hair and striking green eyes. Her khaki pants, green turtleneck with pushed up sleeves, and Birkenstock clogs told me she was probably employed there.

"Oops, I'm sorry Duncan, I didn't know you were busy. I just wanted to let you know that I'll be in the lab if you need me," the woman said.

I couldn't place her accent. Definitely British, with something else thrown in.

"I always need you, Slip," Duncan responded with a wink. Flo and I exchanged knowing glances. "Clara Martini, Florilla Munrow, let me introduce Samantha Rousseau, one of my bonnie research assistants," Duncan said as he waved his cane towards her.

She stepped into the office confidently, obviously comfortable with the professor.

"The man needs all the help he can get," Samantha remarked jokingly. The ten or so silver and crystal bangles on her thin wrist jingled as she extended her hand to us. We exchanged hellos.

"These lassies are here to pick my brain about aphrodisiacs," Duncan explained.

"Well then they've come to the right place." Samantha answered. I wasn't quite sure about the tone of her voice. "Don't let me hold you up. I'll see you later, Duncan. Nice to meet you."

She smiled warmly at us and disappeared out the door. Two seconds later she stuck her head back in. This time she was frowning.

"Excuse me Duncan. I forgot to tell you. There were two detectives here looking for you. They've been interviewing our department all morning. Want to know all about Tracy," her voice trailed off.

"Yes I know. They're coming for me at two. We'll talk about this later, alright?"

"Okay Doctor." With that Samantha Rousseau was gone.

"Samantha's a bright lass, that one. Lots of brain in that beautiful head. She's doing her postdoc here. BS from Princeton, PhD from Columbia." Duncan looked down. "I don't know what I'd do if anything happened to her."

He paused a minute then began rifling through the piles of books and papers on his desk. "I wonder how much time we have," he mumbled. He continued to sort through the clutter. "Where's my blasted calendar?"

While we waited, Flo spotted a small stack of books on the floor in the corner of the office. She nudged me and pointed to them. They were copies of *New World Apothecary*. I saw the wheels turning in her head.

"You know Duncan, I think your book is incredible. The photography is so vivid and the herbarium sheets really look like freshly pressed material."

I shot her a look but she ignored me. I knew where she was going with this. She wanted an autograph. To get that she needed a book. To get that she was kissing ass.

Duncan fell for it. He gave up looking for his calendar and maneuvered his way over to the corner. He casually picked up two of about ten copies of the coffee table sized books from the pile and handed one to Flo. She hugged her book and grinned at me.

Duncan held the other one out to me but I protested, "Thank you Duncan, that's very sweet but Flo's really the herbalist. She'll share hers with me."

"All righty then," Duncan said and he threw the book back on the pile. "We probably don't have too much time. Why don't we take a stroll through the conservatory and see what we can find for you." Duncan glanced down at our feet. "'Tis a bit of a walk if you think you can manage in those... galoshes."

When he turned to reach for his cane we looked at each other and mouthed the word "*galoshes?*"

Duncan slipped his arms through ours, "To Oz?" he said. With that we headed off down the yellow brick road for another long trek to the conservatory.

***

The gray day had given way to almost blinding sunshine. The Gardens were magnificent in the snow.

As we walked we learned some more about Duncan's work. He explained that pharmaceutical companies are

TIFFANY BLUES

spending millions trying to identify new prospective drugs. Now they have a huge interest in revisiting ancient herbals and medical texts to rediscover what was common knowledge a couple of centuries ago. He was both pleased and annoyed at the amount of attention his research was getting. It turns out that Duncan had suddenly become a hot commodity.

As we neared the end of Snowdrop Way, we caught sight of the enormous conservatory dome sparkling like a jewel in the sunlight. I'd been to the Gardens on several occasions before but each time I see that Victorian glasshouse I'm blown away. It's a crystal palace, especially in the winter light.

Duncan was still talking as he held open one of the tall double glass doors for us.

"You know it used to be a physician was part herbalist, alchemist, and yes, sorcerer," he said.

I smiled to myself when he said "sorcerer." I liked this cute little man. We passed through the doors and were suddenly in the tropics. We peeled off our coats and Duncan offered, "Let me take those for you."

He walked up to the coat-check lady. "Here you are Tildy, take good care of these for me. Must be 85 degrees in here today."

"Yes, Professor, just like always," Tildy answered.

Ahead of us was a large round tropical pool with floating lily-pads surrounded by all kinds of palm trees. The galleries opened up to the right and left and ahead of us. We followed Duncan to the right into the Tropical Rainforest. He immediately began pointing at different plants with his cane and mumbling latin names like *Busera simaruba* and *Piper methysticum*.

I was thinking this was not going to help us much when he turned to us and said, "*Theobroma cacao*. The food of the gods! So valuable in Mayan culture, the beans were used as currency. Now that's an aphrodisiac."

Flo leaned down and whispered in my ear,

"Chocolate."

Duncan kept walking slightly ahead of us and the mumbling continued. I was still fixated on the chocolate when he stopped suddenly and I almost walked right into him. His cane was pointing to the sign that said *Passiflora incarnata*. Passion in the Flesh.

"Passionflower. Now you'd think with a name like that it would be great a sex inducer but here, look."

We crouched down with him under the archway where the thick vine was growing rampantly across the gallery to look at the deep purple flower.

"The passionflower first got its name from Spanish missionaries in South America who saw symbols of the Passion of Christ in the flower petals. They failed to mention the pentagram formed by the anthers, which frankly, I believe is much more obvious. Crucifix or wiccan symbol? Either way it's not an aphrodisiac. The pharmas are showing a great interest in this one however. Might be useful in fighting cancers," he explained.

From our crouched position, Duncan pointed his cane up towards the palm trees ahead of us. He shouted gleefully, "Now there's what you're looking for!"

I glanced at Flo. She was in heaven and furiously taking notes in the back of her book. I couldn't tell one tree from the next. I was hot and my bangs were curling up. Duncan was headed towards a tall tree that looked like a palm but with fatter leaves and hanging down from it were the biggest bananas I'd ever seen. Now we're talking sex-inducers.

"*Musa sapientum*. Ruled by both Venus and Mars. The flowers are hermaphroditic, both male and female." He actually reached up and picked a banana and handed it to Flo. "The perfect ingredient for your magic potions."

With a grin she wiggled it right in my face and I smacked it away.

This went on for almost an hour, Duncan pointing out the "lust provokers" as he called them. Things like fenugreek, basil and even onion, were all used to provoke lust. Seemed like every damn plant in the place was an aphrodisiac and by the end I was pretty provoked myself. We had circled around the entire conservatory and I thought we were done when Flo piped up.

"We didn't see any orchids."

"I was saving the best for last. Follow me." Duncan said.

"She's got to be kidding," I thought. "It's almost one o'clock." My stomach grumbled in protest.

Of course we followed Duncan back into the rainforest.

Flo practically danced while I trudged over to the spot where Duncan was standing. Spiraling around an obviously artificial tree trunk was a thick, long vine with large glossy leaves. Duncan stood at the base of the trunk and held his cane low and erect in front of him. He was grinning, pleased with himself. We followed his wooden pointer to a creamy white and yellow blossom just above our heads. Now it was Flo's turn to impress.

"*Vanilla planifolia*," she said proudly.

"The ultimate aphrodisiac," said Duncan. "The Vanilla Orchid. Do you have any idea what it takes to get a bean for America's favorite ice cream? The vine blooms once a year with up to a thousand flowers but each flower lasts only one day. The male and female part of the flower are fused so it can't self pollinate. The job must be done by hand."

He paused and turned to look at us, "Did you know orchid is the latin word for testicle?"

I couldn't look at Flo. I knew we were both thinking the same thing. Vanilla was definitely going into Scorpio Moon.

"Then of course we have the Venus Fly Trap. The black widow of the botanical universe." Duncan sounded irritated as he looked past us towards the gallery entry. "She eats the males that come in contact with her. Poor suckers."

We followed his gaze. Walking towards us in functional flat shoes was a tall, thin, pinched looking woman with ash brown hair recently highlighted. She was wearing an ivory cashmere sweater and navy wool skirt mostly covered by a white lab coat. She looked a lot like the woman I saw talking to my mystery man in the lecture hall. Fiftyish maybe. Could be younger and just looked older. A freshwater pearl eyeglass holder with black half-glasses was hanging around her neck.

"Ladies, may I introduce Doctor Janice Pearl, my associate." Then he leaned in close to me and whispered "She's after my job."

Doctor Pearl scowled at him and ignored us. "Have you forgotten the lunch with Zylanica?"

Duncan answered, "You go on ahead, I'll join you as soon as I escort these lassies to the Garden's gates."

"I'm not letting you out of my sight or you'll never show up," she said as she latched onto him, patting him gently on his arm. Duncan rolled his eyes.

"'Tis true lassies. I am behind my time and I suppose I must go. 'Tis amazing to me that the pharmaceutical industry insists on my presence at these luncheons. I trust you can find your way back to the gates."

Flo was looking panic stricken as she clutched her book to her chest.

Duncan noticed, "Oh, of course, I almost forgot, let me have the book. Would you happen to have a pen handy?"

Janice Pearl was getting impatient and her grip on his arm visibly tightened. He peeled her hand off his arm and reached for the book and the pen Flo had quickly dug out of her handbag.

"Is that a double 'L'?" he asked looking up over his glasses at Flo. She nodded. He wrote something and snapped the book shut. Handing it back to Flo, Duncan peered at us over his glasses and smiled.

TIFFANY BLUES

"'Tis been a pleasure ladies. Good luck with your aphrodisiacs." He winked and added, "That Oscar's a lucky boy. Please give him my best."

With that he took Flo's hand in his left and mine in his right and kissed them both.

"Nice galoshes," he murmured ever so softly. Hmmm, I thought, never underestimate the power of a man in a bow tie.

We gathered up our coats and all four of us walked out of the double doors into the bright sunlit gardens. Doctors Pearl and McPherson headed off to the right. I checked my cell phone for messages. Nothing.

"What do you want to do now?" Flo asked.

"Let's go downtown, get something to eat and go to Tiffany's for dessert."

"How about dessert first?"

"Works for me, but let's get a cab back. I can't deal with mass transit again."

Outside the Garden's gate we hailed a taxi.

"Tiffany's" we said in unison.

FOUR

"Holly Golightly you are not," I said as I paid the cab fare. "You don't even know the words. It's *mile*, not *the Nile*." The dazed taxi driver nodded his head furiously in agreement.

"It is? I don't believe it," Flo sang her own version of *Moon River* to the doorman in the double breasted long coat, black gloves and Tiffany blue scarf.

"Good afternoon ladies. Welcome to Tiffany's," he smiled and held the door open.

I headed straight back to the bank of elevators at the rear of the store and scanned the directory on the wall.

"Okay Flo, looks like china and tableware is on four."

A little man on my right said, "I'm not going to China."

"Oh, sorry." I did a one-eighty and swept the room. She was still talking to the doorman. I couldn't yell to her so I had to walk all the way back and get her.

"Did you see the doorman's scarf? Tiffany blue, just like the boxes. I need one of those. Think they sell them?" she whispered as we made our way back to the elevators.

"No they don't and I'm telling you they don't have soup tureens."

TIFFANY BLUES

"They have to have soup tureens."

"Nope, no soup tureens," I said pointing to the directory. "How about a very large crystal bowl? That might get us a big box. They're on the third floor, see?"

"China and Crystal."

"How about we take a detour to the second floor first?" Flo begged.

"Engagement rings? Why on God's earth would I want to look at engagement rings?"

"Come on, let's just pretend we're filthy rich." Flo pressed the up button and the number two elevator door opened.

We were the only ones in the elevator, well except for the elevator operator. That's one thing I love about Tiffany's. They still have elevator operators, like in the old days, except now all they do is push a button, which we're totally capable of doing ourselves. The ultimate luxury, someone to push your elevator button for you. This someone was a young man in navy blue suit and striped tie.

He very formally said, "Welcome to Tiffany's. What floor, please?"

Flo ignored the question. "Didn't your uniforms used to look like marching band uniforms, with a little pillbox hat, you know, with a strap?" Flo's index finger drew an imaginary smile under her chin.

He raised his eyebrows and shook his head in disbelief.

I stifled a laugh and said quietly, "Second floor please."

The doors opened to the second floor, a portal to a world that screamed opulence, tempered by impeccable taste. Three floor to ceiling mirrored columns, at least three feet wide, perfectly reflected the sparkling glass cases surrounding them. There were several customers but the floor was very quiet.

"I think I need my Hollywood shades," Flo said a little too loudly.

"Shhh!" I scolded.

We strolled nonchalantly around the perimeter of the burled wood paneled room.

"Flo, look," I whispered. "Legacy rings."

"Holy tamoly! Look at this one," Flo pointed to a large cushion-cut surrounded by bead-set diamonds. Could have been an estate jewel.

"That's it, if I ever get another one. That's the one I want. Wonder how much it is," I said.

"Well, I'm going to find out," Flo answered as she walked away to the next case where a young couple was with a salesman trying on a ginormous fancy solitaire with baguettes.

I watched her sidle up to the couple, lean over and crane her neck sideways to look at the woman's hand.

"That's fabulous on you." I heard her say.

Next thing I know, Flo was trying on the ring. She waved me over. There was no way I was getting sucked into this and I headed for the elevators.

Flo met me just as elevator number three opened.

"I'm going to have to settle for the knock off on the Shopping Channel. That ring she was trying on was ninety thousand dollars. And, she didn't like it! And the Legacy ring, guess how much."

"I don't want to know, I'm depressed. Fourth floor please," I told the elevator operator. "We came in here for soup tureens."

"Two and a half carats..."

"It doesn't matter! Nobody's getting engaged."

An hour later we walked out of Tiffany's carrying a four hundred fifty dollar hollow porcelain pig nestled in an eighteen by eighteen by eighteen inch Tiffany box and three white paper hand towels with the words "Tiffany & Co." embossed in blue that Flo swiped from the ladies room.

"I told you they sold soup tureens," Flo said adjusting the unwieldy box so it sat on her left hip.

"They don't sell soup tureens, they sell porcelain farm

animals the size of a VW Bug!"

"Hey we got the box didn't we?"

"What are we going to do with a giant pig?"

"Make a lot of soup. Speaking of soup, if we don't eat soon, I'm going to die." "It's already after three."

"How about Zen? It's close by. Between the book in my bag and this box I can't walk too far," Flo replied.

"No, it's too early for dinner at Zen and too late for lunch." I turned my head to scan the stores down Fifth Avenue. "Oh-My-God, look!"

"What?"

"Coming out of Trump Tower. It's 007 from the lecture. He's walking towards us."

Flo frantically turned in circles trying to see around the box. "I can't see him. I can't see anything."

"Damn, he's crossing the street, he's jaywalking. He should have come down here to cross at the corner."

"Keep your eye on him. We'll follow him," Flo said smacking into me.

I took Flo's arm and led her across Fifth Avenue. He was walking toward Central Park. "Can't you go any faster? We're going to lose him."

"I'm wearing heels and I'm carrying a big pig," Flo was out of breath. "I'm going as fast as I can."

"Here, give me your bag," I said and yanked the tote bag off her shoulder.

We scurried after him for two blocks when he made a left and headed towards the Plaza Hotel. We stopped for a second to catch our breath.

"I think he's going into the Plaza," I told her.

"Then we're having tea at the Plaza."

We cut across fifty-ninth street and ran after him up the steps. The entryway was full of tourists taking pictures. I caught sight of him heading toward the Palm Court, the grand courtyard dining room in the heart of the landmark hotel. We quickly followed him onto the line of guests waiting to be seated for tea.

"Look at this place. Doesn't it just make you want to don a bustle and a peacock plume? La Belle Epoque," I said.

The room was elegant, all blues and golds. Tall graceful palms and tables set with soft ivory linens were reflected in the floor to ceiling arched mirrors. The crowning glory was the restored rose patterned laylight, the stained glass ceiling which had been hidden from view for more than fifty years.

"He's next," Flo nudged me out of my Edwardian daydream.

Our prey was at the front of the line having a word with the maitre d'. He pointed to the back of the restaurant and we followed that finger to a cozy table for two in the corner.

"Damn, he's pointing to that gorgeous blonde," I said.

"Where? I can't see her."

"She's under the palm tree in the back. You can see her face in the mirror. She's all in black. Ultra thin, not a stitch of make up."

"I can't see a damn thing with this box. Is she young or old?"

"Maybe thirty. Hard to tell."

007 leaned over and gave the woman a peck on each cheek.

"May I help you?" The maitre d' asked us.

Flo peeked around the Tiffany box and said "Tea, for two."

The maitre d' coughed slightly, "Yes, do you have a reservation?"

"No, never mind we're not staying," I said.

Flo's eyes bugged out. "Oh yes we are, my arms are going to fall off if I can't put this down."

The maitre d' coughed again and examined his reservation book. "Ah, I think I have something Madame. Would you like to check your coats and your... um, package?"

TIFFANY BLUES

"You can take our coats but I'm not letting this box out of my sight," Flo answered.

He showed us to a tiny table in the middle of the room. There was barely enough space for our legs under the table, never mind the farm animal. I couldn't see 007 behind me but Flo had him in direct sight. I opened my tea menu and gulped.

"He's talking to her. Her left hand is up. Wait. No ring!" Flo whispered loudly.

"Ok, so she's not married or engaged, she's probably his girlfriend, that's worse," I whispered back.

"I don't know. He's not touching her hand or anything. They aren't playing footsie under the table. He doesn't seem to be gazing soulfully into her eyes. Looks like they're just eating."

"Which I don't think we can do."

"What? What do you mean?"

I pointed to the menu. "We just paid a fortune on a porcelain pig we didn't need and now we're about to spend more money we don't have, just to watch a man who has an uncanny resemblance to James Bond have a tete-a-tete with a gorgeous blonde. This is nuts!"

Flo looked down at her menu. "Holy tamoly, you're right."

"It'll be less if we share," I said.

"Well, looks like it's a lot of food. There are five sandwiches on here, but I don't like smoked salmon."

"Neither do I and then only one of us gets the tea. Besides, look at this, there's tea from Zimbabwe, there's tea from Malawi, tea from Kenya and Egypt. This is incredible."

"How many scones you think we get?"

"I have no idea, probably two. But we get pastries too. Not a lot of chocolate though. Maybe we can substitute."

A waiter approached our table. Flo asked, "Is it possible to substitute some chocolate covered strawberries for the lemon tea cake?"

The waiter leaned over and turned Flo's menu page. "If you're interested in chocolate, you might like our Chocolate Tea?"

I scanned the Chocolate Tea menu. Chocolate fondue, chocolate scones, chocolate everything. This was a no brainer.

"This is perfect, but is the fondue milk chocolate or dark chocolate?" Flo asked.

"It is exquisite rich chocolate," the waiter answered.

"Alright, never mind. If I get the New Yorker, could I still get some dark chocolate covered strawberries in lieu of the lemon curd?"

We were assured that although it wasn't usually done he would see what he could do for us. We went ahead and ordered one New Yorker with sandwiches and one Chocolate Tea with the fondue to share. Before we could even check out what was happening behind me in the corner, the waiter placed china plates of tiny finger sandwiches in front of us.

"This isn't enough food for a hamster!" Flo said.

"For heaven's sake Flo, this is tea, not an all you can eat buffet. It looks yummy. And there's still dessert."

"I guess we can always stop at Aunt Annie's in Penn Station for pretzels later," she answered.

As I nibbled our cucumber sandwiches Flo gave me a blow by blow of what was happening across the room.

"Maybe it's just business," she said, picking the truffled quail egg off my plate and popping it into her mouth. "It really doesn't look romantic. Oh, wait a second, she's getting up. She's putting on her coat. He's handing her a big envelope, legal size. She stuffed it in her tote bag. Ok, she's leaving...look. No kiss."

I turned to watch the woman walk briskly up the aisle and out the door.

"What's he doing?" I asked.

Flo looked around. "He's up. He's coming this way. He left his whole plate of dessert. Damn, he's talking on his

TIFFANY BLUES

phone."

We watched him walk right past us towards the lobby. Our sandwich plates were replaced with a chocolate fondue pot, pastries, sweets and two big beautiful chocolate covered strawberries.

I bit into my cupcake. "Do you think he's coming back?"

"His coat's still here and he didn't pay the bill." Flo went for her profiteroles. "This is divine," she said. "I think profiteroles are aphrodisiacs."

"Too bad we can't put them in *Sorpio Moon*. Oh, no, here he comes."

"Stop him and talk to him," Flo said.

"Yeah, right, what am I going to do trip him?"

"Great idea." Flo nudged the Tiffany box into the aisle and a second later our desserts and 007 were splayed across our table. His nose was almost touching mine and I was staring into a sea of cerulean blue. His warm breath smelled like chocolate.

Without missing a beat, he moved his gaze to the spot between my breasts. With one hand, he plucked the chocolate covered strawberry that had landed there and popped it right into his mouth.

"Are you okay?" I asked, mortified.

"I'm... overwhelmed," he answered chewing and smiling.

He pulled himself upright and brushed powdered sugar off his expensive suit.

Flo was grinning from ear to ear but said with a sincere voice, "I'm so sorry about the box. Didn't see you."

"That's quite a Tiffany box you've got there. What'd you buy? A soup tureen?"

I shook my head in disgust.

He looked down at me, "Have we met before?"

"No, not actually met, not in this lifetime anyway," I answered.

"Huh, you look so familiar. Oh, I know," he smiled.

"You were at the lecture at the Botanical Gardens today. You were sitting up front. I remember your face."

Probably because I was the only person there staring like a lunatic at the back of the room instead of paying attention to Duncan. I wanted to crawl under the table. Flo was happily collecting all the pastries off the tablecloth and putting them on her plate but looked up when she heard 'Botanical Gardens.'

"Yes, Duncan McPherson is a friend," Flo chimed in. "After the lecture he graciously gave us a personal tour of the conservatory."

"Really? So, you're personal friends of his, Dr. McPherson?"

"No, he's actually a friend of a friend of mine. We were there to do some research for our company. I'm Florilla Munrow and this is Clara Martini."

"Pleasure to meet you. Quentin Adams."

The three of us exchanged awkward handshakes.

"We were there looking for aphrodisiacs," Flo blurted. I glared at her. "And...other things," she added sheepishly.

"Exactly what sort of business are you in?" he asked, looking directly at me.

"It's a bit complicated. Let's just say it's metaphysical. I'm an astrologer and uh..." The blue eyes were getting to me.

"And I'm an herbalist of sorts," Flo jumped in trying to help me. "We make custom herbal products based on a person's astrological profile."

"The aphrodisiacs are for our new product line," I said finding my voice again.

"Were you at the lecture for aphrodisiacs too?" Flo flirted.

Quentin grinned and shook his head. "I'm in pharmaceuticals and my company is interested in McPherson's research. They sent me as a rep."

"Would you like to join us?" Flo asked. "There's still

TIFFANY BLUES

one more strawberry."

"Sorry, I can't. I'm already late for an appointment, but thank you."

Flo kicked me hard under the table and mouthed "Give him your card." Without thinking, I reached down and dug through my bag and pulled out an old business card which looked a little worse for wear. I found a pen and scribbled my cell phone number on the back.

"Well, Ms. Martini, Ms. Munrow, this has been an unexpected pleasure. I'd love to learn more about aphrodisiacs and astrology." He turned to me, "Too bad I've got to go."

I held my card out to him. That's when I noticed his hands. Masculine, thick long fingers but very graceful, perfectly manicured.

He brushed my fingertips ever so slightly as he took the card and read out loud, "AstroBotanics Chocolate Diner and Metaphysical Emporium. Interesting. Dolly's Ferry? I'm in New Jersey too, not that far from you. I might just have to make an appointment."

With that, he put the card in his breast pocket, winked at me and went back to his table to fetch his coat. We watched as he took three bills out of his wallet, left them on the table and came back towards us.

"I'll call you," he said touching my shoulder as he walked by. Before I knew it he was gone.

"He said he'll call you!" Flo said, pleased with herself.

"Yeah, that's what they all say. Just broke every rule in the book. I'll never see him again. Can we please just go home?"

We gathered up the big blue box, unchecked our coats and slipped the hotel bell captain a five to flag down a cab for us. We made it to Penn Station just in time to grab two cinnamon pretzels and run for the five-thirty train. Out of breath, we were lucky to find two seats together in the rush hour madness.

"Phew! We just made it," Flo said flopping down in the

two-seater, biting off a chunk of her pretzel.

"What a day. I'm exhausted." I closed my eyes, resting my head back on the uncomfortably straight New Jersey Transit seat.

As the train slowly pulled out of the station Flo and I looked at each other horrified.

"The Tiffany Box!" we said in unison.

FIVE

I was still half asleep when I got to The Diner on Friday morning. The local weather forecast blaring from the back told me Flo had beaten me in.

"Flo, what are you doing here so early? It's not even nine yet," I yelled as I hung my jacket up on the stainless steel hooks in the vestibule. Although the diner has undergone some major changes over the years there were still remnants of the original art deco décor. A couple of booths with their individual juke boxes that still played a song for a nickel, a portion of the laminated counter and three stools still remained.

Young Elvis was curled up in a black ball on an overstuffed chair in the meditation corner. He opened one eye, stretched his back and jumped down to greet me. Meowing incessantly, he circled around my legs until I reached down to scoop him up in my arms. I kissed his nose, scratched him under his chin and held him like a baby, like I did when he was a kitten.

Flo and I share two cats, both named Elvis; Phillip rescued them from the animal shelter. They spend the day at The Diner and we take turns with them at night and on the weekends. The Elvi are fraternal twins. One's big, fat and white. Old Elvis. The other is small, sleek and black. Young Elvis.

"Whadaya think El?" I sighed. "Is she still as upset as I am?"

He purred loudly as we headed through to the kitchen and peeked in. It was empty except for the hunky weather forecaster on the small flat screen in the corner of the Formica countertop. He was smiling and pointing to a big yellow sun over a map of New Jersey. Flo and her Weather Channel, it was like Valium for her.

I carried Elvis into the enclosed back porch that served as our potting and storage room.

"I couldn't sleep so I came in to get ready for the workshop," Flo said without looking up.

Bright sunlight poured in through the tall windows and warmed up the room. In the summertime we replace the windows with screens and the aromas from the herbs mixed with the sweet smells of summer make it one of my favorite spots in The Diner. Flo was framed in the light, specks of herb dust floating all around her flaming red head. She was wearing her short blue jean skirt, black tights and a lime green sweater.

"I guess she's not a happy camper," I whispered into Elvis' soft fur. "That sexy guy is on the Weather Channel now if you want to catch him," I said cheerfully, hoping she'd brighten up.

Ignoring me, she pulled the lid off a clear glass apothecary jar and filled a measuring cup with dried rose petals.

"Are you mixing *another* batch of prosperity herbs for the workshop? What, are we trying to win Mega Lotto or something?" Elvis pushed his head against my hand and I rubbed him hard behind the ears.

"No, I'm not mixing more prosperity herbs," she frowned at me. "When I got here this morning, the studio was already set up for the workshop. Phillip must have done it yesterday. Everything was already out; charm bags, recipes, and candles. Even the table's all set. So I figured I might as well start pulling together the herbs for Scorpio Moon."

"Did he remember to take the aventurines out of the crystals chest?" I asked. "How about the astrology charts, did he put those up?"

Flo nodded yes to both. "We're ready to serve good fortune for eight. All we still need is the basil and the laptop," she added.

"So... what've you got in there so far?" I asked peering over her shoulder into the speckled enamel tub already filled with herbs. I took a deep breath in through my nose. "Mmm... lavender."

"Well there's lots of *sex inducers* in here," she said imitating Duncan McPherson's Scottish brogue. "The lavender's for passionate liaisons and I added cinnamon, basil, and rosemary for lust. I'm throwing in some rose petals too; wouldn't want to leave out the possibility of true love. The herbs 'll go in those red bottles."

Flo nodded to a row of ruby glass bottles lined up on the pine farm table. She poured the rose petals into the bowl. "But I'm thinking we should use vanilla oil instead of rosemary oil to make it stronger and put a vanilla candle in each kit," she added.

I let Elvis jump down to the floor and tried in vain to pick the black hairs off my white sweater and jeans. I put on an apron that stated I was a "tree hugger," chose one of the red bottles, took a handful of Flo's herbal mixture and began filling the bottle.

"So what do you want to do?"

"Do about what?" she asked concentrating on the herbal concoction in front of her.

"You know what."

"We'll just have to save up four hundred fifty dollars and go back to Tiffany's. What else can we do?"

"Ooookay. I think you're right, the vanilla will be

perfect. Think we should put a banana in there too," I teased.

Flo glared at me out of the corner of her eye, but her mouth twitched. "How could you leave the box?" Flo cried chewing the inside of her cheek.

"Me? I didn't leave the box. We were both in the cab."

"Never mind, I don't want to talk about it." She changed the subject, "I hope George brings the black velvet boxes today. We need them. Scorpio Moon has to be ready before Valentine's Day."

"I hope he brings the Sno-Caps."

"Yep, we definitely need those too," Flo sighed.

The chimes on the front door rang.

"It's coffee time," Phillip announced from the front of the Diner.

We dusted off our hands and followed the aroma of hazelnut coffee into the kitchen. Phillip had placed three cups in a straight line on the nineteen fifties chrome table. I slumped down onto one of the red vinyl seats and took the cup with the tea bag.

"Hey Sweetie, thanks for getting the studio ready for us. You're too good," I said.

Phillip blew me a "you're welcome" kiss as he took off his leather biker jacket and hung it around the back of a chair. He handed Flo the hazelnut coffee.

"Where are your mugs? I couldn't find them. I hate this foam--it's a crime," he said.

"They're in the dishwasher," Flo answered. She moved in front of the television and gazed intently at the weather map for a few seconds. "They're dirty."

Phillip shook his head disgustedly and walked to the dishwasher and took out two mugs, one with "Good Witch" written in pink and one with "Bad Witch" written in black. He held them up and looked at me.

"Which one are we today?"

Florilla snorted, "She lost the new Tiffany box. What do you think?"

TIFFANY BLUES

"What new Tiffany box?" He looked at me confused as he donned yellow rubber gloves.

"I didn't lose the box, we both left it in the cab," I protested. "Flo can you please turn off the TV?"

"I just want to see the local radar."

"Look out the window, it's sunny."

Flo answered with a sharp click of the remote.

"What cab, what are you talking about?" Phillip picked up a sponge and furiously scrubbed the mugs in the kitchen sink.

We took turns filling him in on the details of the previous day. Every once in while he asked for clarification, like, "Now who's this Blaine guy?" and, "Duncan was wearing a bowtie?" He dried our mugs, found a mug for himself, and transferred the hot drinks for all of us.

"There," he said handing us back our caffeine. "That's better. So did you hear anything more about the dead girl?"

Before I could tell him about the detectives the door chimes announced a customer. The three of us fell over each other trying to squeeze through the kitchen door at one time.

I popped out first. It was only George, thank goodness. George is our new UPS delivery man, a young, hard-bodied mahogany masterpiece. As Abby says, "He's crunk."

"Hello my lovelies" he chirped, then added, "Oh, hey Phillip."

I tore off my apron and tossed it back into the kitchen. George stacked three big boxes in a pile in the doorway. "I've got three more in the truck."

I held the door open for him, while he went back outside. Flo watched him intently through the showcase window. Phillip unpacked.

"Your velvet boxes for Scorpio Moon are here," Phillip noted as he ripped the tape off the largest carton. "I guess we'll need to get started on the window display for Valentine's Day. I'm thinking about draping a pink toile background... we'll add dried roses, some black lace, and maybe a red teddy with garters..." He knew he was talking to himself.

George brought in three more large cartons and put two down next to the others. He handed off the third to Flo.

"More high heels," he said grinning at her. "You ladies do have quite a collection." He nodded to *Stilettos*, the shoe display in the far corner of The Diner.

Flo ripped opened the box and held up a pair of gorgeous black velvet pumps with four inch silver metallic spike heels.

"Now, that's what I call candy," George smiled.

"Speaking of candy, did you bring our Sno-Caps and Raisinets?" Flo asked, stuffing the shoes back in their box.

"Five cases. What's up with that? I thought AstroBotanics only sold fine Belgian chocolates," George said as he checked out the big glass confectionary case.

"Oh they're not to sell," Phillip answered over his shoulder holding up a box of Sno-Caps he'd just unpacked.

"It's January, we're starting the diet," I answered.

At that moment, as if on cue, all nineteen pounds of Old Elvis fell out of one of red vinyl booths. He lumbered over to us and plopped himself at George's feet.

"There are a hundred and ninety calories in a quarter cup. That equals about eighty Sno-Caps or forty Raisinets. Every morning we count out either Sno-Caps or Raisinets," Flo explained. "You know the Raisinets are bigger so you don't get as many."

"We divide them in half and put them in two dishes, one for each of us," I added. "That's our allowance for the day. Anytime we need a chocolate fix we get to eat one from the dish."

Flo snatched the box of Sno-Caps from Phillip and

shook it like a maraca, "It's a bitch when you eat them all before ten am."

"You are one fat cat Elvis. Maybe you should try this diet." George blew up his cheeks like a blowfish. Elvis took a swipe at the brown chinos with his huge white paw and rolled over.

"Oh, don't listen to him." Flo bent over and covered the cat's ears with her hands. Old Elvis thumped his tail and struggled to push himself up off the floor. He strolled away indignantly, ears back, belly wagging. We all laughed and George looked at his watch.

"I've got to keep moving," he said.

He handed me the UPS thingy to sign and gave us a little wave as he opened the door. Flo and I both ran to the window. He took the porch steps two at a time and strutted back to his truck. I let out an audible sigh.

"Don't you two witches have a workshop to get ready for?"

Flo threw the Sno-Caps in the general direction of Phillip's head. His left hand snatched it midair. He ripped open the top, chugged a mouthful, crumpled the rest, and slam dunked the box into the trash can across the room.

"I feewl ten pow wighter albeady," he mumbled. With that he picked up some cartons and sashayed back to the potting room.

"Where's my coffee?" Flo asked shaking her head.

"In the kitchen with my laptop."

Flo immediately disappeared into the kitchen, but I stopped to grab a box of Raisinets on the way. When I pushed open the swinging door, the television was on again and she was about to nuke her cold coffee.

"It's still sunny," I teased. I reached around her to get my laptop off the counter and put it down on the table. "You want a Raisinet?"

Flo held out her hand. "Give me four, I'm depressed."

"Me too." I opened the box and counted out four each.

We both popped them all at one time. I tapped the icon for the astrology program and brought up my daily planetary transits.

Flo retrieved her coffee from the microwave and gathered the big basil plant from the greenhouse window over the sink.

"Your planets haven't moved in the last 3 hours. I know you checked them as soon as you got out of bed," Flo said.

"I haven't had a chance to look at them for two days. The laptop was here. I just want to see what yesterday was all about. There's probably something going on."

"There's always something going on. If it's not Mars, it's Uranus wreaking havoc. I'm going to take this to the studio," she said gesturing to the basil. "We'll use fresh basil since this one's so healthy. Works better than dried for prosperity. Hurry up and bring the laptop when you're done." She pushed her butt against the door and disappeared.

I clicked off the television and looked at the computer screen.

"Damn! I knew it," I complained to the refrigerator. "Bad enough Mercury's retrograde. Look at this. Yesterday afternoon I had Uranus conjuncting Venus exactly *and* Mars squaring Venus at the same time. How'd I miss this? That explains it!"

"Explains what?" Phillip asked as he came back into the kitchen.

"Q, the Tiffany box, everything."

"Q? What's a Q?" Phillip asked. He moved over to the sink and lathered his hands with the cucumber melon soap.

"Q is a Quentin. We met him at the Plaza after Tiffany's."

I told him the rest of yesterday's events--the trip to Tiffany's, following Q to the Plaza, my encounter with him and of course the price of afternoon tea.

"It's New York, what do you expect? Does he have a last name?" Phillip rinsed his hands, opened the drawer next to the sink and pulled out a clean red and white checked dishtowel. He flicked it open with two fingers. A drop of water landed on my nose and I twitched. He gave me a sexy smile, walked over and casually wiped it off with the towel.

"I think it's Adams or something. I really wasn't paying attention. We just call him Q. It doesn't matter, no way I'll ever hear from him again. Phillip, the man was wearing cuff links," I drooled.

Phillip moved back and leaned against the cabinet. "Coco, what would you do with a guy with cuff links anyway?"

We were interrupted by the front door again.

"Geez-o-pete, who's that? It's too early for the workshop. I haven't even finished my tea yet," I moaned.

Phillip peered out. "It's Oscar." He neatly folded the towel, tossed it into the dirty laundry bin and pushed through the door.

Just as I came out of the kitchen, Florilla jumped into Oscar's arms. "What are you doing here?" she squealed with delight.

All six foot three inches beamed back at her. There was that smile again. Oscar's dark green down jacket was unzipped and I could see the taupe cashmere scarf Flo had given him for Christmas. I was used to seeing him in professorial mode, but he looked good in his stonewashed jeans and hikers.

"Well, you didn't want to take the train into the city. So, I cancelled my class to come out and get you." He unwrapped himself from Flo and came over to me, leaned down and pecked me on the cheek. He was a saint.

"Hey Phillip. Hi, C ," he said. "Hope you had a good birthday. Sorry I missed it. And sorry about the box."

"Thanks. The birthday was perfect. The box is another story."

Florilla laced her fingers through his and led him over to the seating area in the corner. Oscar lowered himself into one of the faux fur comfy chairs and pulled Flo down on his lap. She wiggled around as she adjusted her skirt. When she was settled, Oscar rested his hand on her thigh and gave her squeeze. I caught Phillip's eye and pretended to stick my finger down my throat.

"How did it go yesterday?" Oscar asked as he squirmed out of his jacket.

"Oh, Duncan is quite the renaissance man! He gave me a copy of his book and he autographed it for me," she bragged. "The conservatory tour was phenomenal. You're going to love Scorpio Moon. We're putting vanilla in it." She lightly tapped Oscar on the tip of his nose, "We'll have to be the guinea pigs."

I sat down opposite them.

"Oscar, thanks for setting up the meeting with Duncan. He's a pretty amazing character." I said.

"Did he ask you to sleep with him?" Oscar joked.

"No, I don't think he needs us. Do you know about his 'bonnie research assistant', Samantha Rousseau?" I asked.

Oscar hesitated. "No, but I'm not surprised. The man is incredibly charming and does like the ladies, young and old."

"Speaking of young ladies, you never answered me before, did you hear anything else about the dead girl?" Phillip asked.

"What dead girl?" Oscar took Flo's chin in his hand and turned her face towards his.

"They found one of Duncan's research assistants frozen at the bottom of the waterfall in the Gardens. Two detectives came to grill everyone while we were there. That's all we know," I said.

"Her name was Tracy something or other," Flo added.

"Do they think it was an accident?" Oz asked.

"Well, NYPD sent two detectives to investigate so who

knows."

"Duncan was pretty upset about it. I guess he's fond of all his research assistants," I said.

"Speaking of ladies' men," Flo said to Oscar, "I didn't tell you. After the lecture we went to Tiffany's. We had to buy a giant porcelain pig to get a new box. Then, as we were coming out of the store, C insisted on following this guy who was at the lecture."

Oscar looked lost but Flo just kept talking.

"He looks like 007, not the new one, the one before him, and we ended up having tea at the Plaza. Do you know they actually serve a Chocolate Tea? But then C lost the box…"

Thank God the phone rang.

SIX

"*AstroBotanics Chocolate Diner and Metaphysical Emporium,*" Phillip answered like he owned the place. "Whom may I say is calling?" he asked looking directly at me. His eyes widened and pointing to the phone he mouthed, "It's a Q!"

"Q?" I shrieked without making a sound. Flo sat up straight on Oscar's lap.

"Who?" Oscar was confused.

"The guy from the lecture," Flo answered.

Phillip handed me the phone and I moved over to the shelves by the apothecary jars to try to get a little privacy. I could see Flo whispering to Oscar out of the corner of my eye as I turned my back.

"Hello?"

"Clara? It's Quentin Adams. We met at the Plaza yesterday."

"Oh, yes. Hi," I took a deep breath and let it out slowly to keep from hyperventilating.

"I was hoping to see you again, for a reading I mean. Can I make an appointment?"

"Of course, when would you like to come?"

"How's Monday, around five?"

"Let me check my calendar." I held the phone to my chest and counted to ten. Like I wouldn't cancel an appointment with the Queen of England if I had to. "Monday at five is open. I'll need to get some personal information from you first."

"Personal? Okay, I'm six feet tall, have a thirty four inch waist and I hate broccoli."

Hmmm, a sense of humor. "Really? Me too...the broccoli I mean. I don't do green food."

"No green food? You mean like no green vegetables?"

"No vegetables period. We'll I eat salad. Oh, and spinach and celery in my Chinese food. But that's it."

"Do you eat meat?"

"Of course. But right now, I need your birth information, time, date and place."

I motioned frantically to Phillip to get me a notepad. He took his time and finally found one near the register. It was the Frank Lloyd Wright Fallingwater notepad I got as a souvenir when I toured the house last summer with the Royal Supreme Idiot. I should have known it was never going to work when he said, "How could anyone live here? The water is too damn noisy." Idiot.

"Clara, are you there?"

"Oh, sorry. Could you repeat that again? My pen ran out of ink." I scribbled everything down, said good-bye and hung up.

They all looked at me expectantly.

"He's coming here Monday at five for a reading," I squeaked. My mouth was so dry I could barely talk.

"Awesome!" Flo said.

"Yeah, awesome," Phillip went back to unpacking.

Flo got quiet and narrowed her eyes at me. "Wait a minute. When's his birthday?"

"July 27th," I answered nonchalantly inspecting the cantilevered house on the notepad cover.

She threw her arms up. "Oh no C. Not another Leo."

Oscar rolled his eyes and patted Flo on the butt.

"Maybe he's got a Libra rising," I said hopefully. I already knew he didn't.

"I sincerely doubt it's a Libra he's got rising. C for pity's sake, how does this always happen?"

"May I remind you that you were the one who tripped him?"

Oscar bounced Flo on his lap and gave her a nudge. They stood up and he wrapped his arms around her shoulders like he was putting her in a straightjacket. "Red, you have a workshop in a few minutes, you better get busy. Tell you what, I'll go over to the Cottage now and pack some things for you. I'll come back to get you later. We'll leave for the city from here."

"But-"

Oscar turned her to face him and put his index finger on Flo's lips. "I'll be back around one." He bent to kiss her. Kisses interruptus by a huge commotion on the front porch.

"They're here!" Phillip sang.

Oscar opened the door and was nearly knocked to the floor as Bobo and Bosco bulldozed their way into The Diner. Lucille Carlisle was desperately trying to hold on to their leashes with her right hand while her left arm cradled a quivering white puff of fur also known as Blanche. A five foot tall, ninety-eight pound woman with a seventy-five pound long haired mutt; a ninety pound chocolate lab; and a six pound Havanese you can carry in your purse. What was she thinking?

"Bobo, Bosco! Ah, bonjour." Lucille, royal blue beret and poncho askew, made her entrance. "I hope we're not late."

Bobo and Bosco pulled her around the room as they came to greet each of us, tails thumping wildly. She gently put Blanche down on the floor and brushed her jet black chin length hair away from her face.

"We had to stop at the gallery to drop off more of my

photos, they've sold out of almost everything." She looked up curiously at Oscar.

Flo reintroduced them. "Lucille Carlisle, you remember my, umm..., Oscar Stern."

"Oh, of course." Lucille said.

"Hi." He shook Lucille's free hand then dropped down to one knee. "And how are these big guys?" Oscar asked alternately rubbing Bosco's enormous chocolate head and Bobo's chubby belly. Blanche ran circles around them and yapped incessantly. He tried to give the little white fuzz ball a pat, but she ran to hide between Lucille's legs.

Lucille chastised her, "Blanche, don't be so rude."

Oscar laughed and stood up. He turned to Flo, "I'm sorry but *your* Oscar Stern really must be going."

Bobo and Bosco pushed against him, begging for more attention.

Flo waded through the dogs, "I'll walk out with you."

"Nice to see all of you." He gave a little wave as they backed out the door trying to keep the panting pack at bay.

"Sit. All of you sit! Asseyez-vous!" Lucille was exasperated. "Henri, God rest his soul, never had these problems. That Frenchman was the alpha dog."

We relive this scenario, with slight variations, on a daily basis. Lucille Carlisle and her "children" come for chocolates every day. She is always the first to try a new product and probably now owns at least one of every item we have ever sold, except for the high heels. I've never seen her in anything but red wellies in the winter and garden clogs spring, summer and fall. Lucille is, in her words, "an artiste". She's actually a successful landscape photographer and we occasionally sell her river scenes on consignment. She doesn't need the money though; Henri left her millions. Henri was from a small town outside Paris. They had been married for 25 years and Lucille honored his memory by attempting to speak French often, but just a bit off kilter.

"Was that Oscar's adorable little red BMW outside?

Henri had a black one but his brother wanted it. Henri always said the Six Series was *la plus jolie femme dans le monde*, the most beautiful woman in the world," Lucille reminisced.

"Oscar thinks so too." Flo came back in closing the door behind her.

"Lucille, let me take the kids to the kitchen and give them a drink," Phillip said. "I'll babysit them while you're in the workshop."

"Oh, merci Phillipe," she relinquished the leashes. Phillip scooped Blanche up off the floor and the yapping faded into the kitchen. It was suddenly quiet.

Lucille looked at us a little confused, "Which workshop is this today? Did I take it already?"

"We're making prosperity charms, Lucille," Flo reminded her. "We're going to take some Mars herbs like basil for wealth and mix them with some Sun and Jupiter herbs like cinnamon and nutmeg for success. Then everyone will add their own intentions for increasing their good fortune. I don't think you took this one yet."

The chimes announced a stream of more attendees; four giggly college roommates and three of Flo's garden clients

Just as we were about to lead the group to the studio, the chimes rang again. Abby stood right inside the door, her nose red and eyes swollen.

"I'll take them in and get started, you go see what's up with Abbs," Flo whispered in my ear.

Abby wasn't moving so I went to her.

"I'm so sorry Clara, I forgot about the workshop, I didn't get any sleep. I really need to talk to you."

"What's wrong?"

"Akio."

"Is he alright?"

"Oh, yeah, he's fine. But Austin isn't temporary anymore. He decided to stay and he wants me to move there...like soon." She started crying again.

TIFFANY BLUES

I hugged her. "Well, do you want to go?"

"I don't know!" she wailed. "Everyone I know is here… I've never even been to Austin. It's great for him, what if it's a terrible place for me? For us together?"

"Look, why don't you come back after lunch and we'll talk about it. Hey, we can even sit down with your astrology charts, look at where Venus and Jupiter are and do some astrological locality mapping. We'll see if Austin's a good place for you to be."

"You can tell that from my chart?" Abby sniffled.

"Sure, we can get a good idea. Who knows, maybe your Venus line is going right through Austin. Either way, we'll figure it out."

"Or not."

"Let's try and be positive okay?"

Abby hugged me, "Okay. Thanks Clar. Text me when the workshop is over?"

"I will, promise."

***

For me the workshop was a total blur. I was the only one not focused on prosperity, oblivious to everything except the voices in my head. Abby. Austin. *Q. Quentin. Quentin Adams.* The names rolled around and around in my brain.

"Yoo hoo, Earth to Clara." I heard Flo calling from someplace far away.

I looked around the corner of The Diner we had curtained off as workshop studio space. Candles were lit and a bowl of green gemstones sparkled in the middle of the table. The bowl that had been filled with the mix of prosperity herbs was empty. The ceramic dragonfly plate with the pile of shiny pennies was empty too. Each of the eight women at the table was holding a little cloth pouch filled with coins and herbs in one hand and a gold ribbon in the other. They all looked at me in anticipation.

"The intention C. We're waiting for you to read the prosperity intention out loud so we can finish the charms," Flo said very precisely like an annoyed schoolteacher. The college girls stifled their giggles.

"I was just meditating," I lied.

Flo raised her eyebrows at me and handed me the scroll with the magical words *"Herbs and coins, bring money that is needed. Prosperity, luck and good fortune be speeded. So be it and so it is."*

I read it out loud and everyone repeated the words as they tied their little pouches closed with the golden ribbons. "Okay everyone, take one adventurine and keep that with you all the time. It will work best if you put your charm bag in a special place and focus on your intentions for prosperity at least once a day. And remember, the magic comes from you!" I said.

The workshop was finally over. I stayed and cleaned up while Flo went to man the cash register. When I came out everyone was done shopping except for Lucille.

"Flo, sorry about that. I just zoned. How'd we do?" I asked.

"Great. They loved the workshop, which, thank you very much, I now realize I can do all by myself, and they all signed up for the Scorpio Moon workshop next month."

"Did anybody buy anything?"

"Two of my clients bought garden books and a pound of lavender. Keisha and Monique bought astrology calendars and a pound of chocolate truffles each."

"Really?"

"What was up with Abbs?", Flo asked.

"Akio decided to stay in Austin permanently and he wants her to move there."

"To Texas?"

"She doesn't know what to do."

"Mon Dieu! Those two are always having some kind of crisis," Lucille spat. "Many nice young men come to the gallery. Abigail should come this weekend, she could meet a new beau there. She shouldn't move halfway across the country for a man. If he really loves her he should come back. Clara, the same goes for you too."

I've been to three of Lucille's gallery exhibits. Not once did I meet a man, much less a nice man.

I just nodded my head.

"Magnifique! Now, before I go, I need a quarter pound of dark chocolate raspberry jellies and, of course, some of those delicieux poochy treats for the children," she said pointing to the bottom shelf of the glass case.

"Of course, we'd never forget the children," I said as I reached into the case and pulled out the trays of chocolates and faux chocolate doggy treats. Truth be told, we stocked the doggy treats pretty much just for Lucille.

"Speaking of the children..." Flo was interrupted by chaos coming through the swinging door of the kitchen.

Bobo and Bosco were in the lead pulling Phillip along behind them. Blanche was trembling in the crook of his arm. She almost leapt into the air when she saw Lucille.

"Oh my darlings." She tenderly took the shivering Blanche away from Phillip and hugged the little powder puff to her. Bobo and Bosco wrapped themselves around her legs. "Mon chouchou, did you miss Mama?"

"Oh, they were so good. They had drinks and treats and naps and I took them out," Phillip said.

"Merci Phillipe. I must say the workshop was superb. These two women are a font of fascinating information and always so... tres amuse."

She reached under her poncho and pulled out her little sparkling pouch tied with gold ribbon.

"See Blanche, Mama is going to sell all of her photos at the gallery and we'll take a lovely holiday to the beach. What do you say to that?"

Blanche yelped loudly. Bobo and Bosco just panted and drooled.

I handed the bag with the chocolates and doggie treats

to Lucille and she tucked it underneath Blanche in her arms.

Phillip slipped on his jacket. "Tell you what, I'll walk you home Lucille. I need to go over to my place anyway."

Phillip owns a hundred year old duplex two blocks away from The Diner. He lives on one side and rents out the other side to Freddy, his auto mechanic. Freddy is the only person I know who could match Phillip's obsessive compulsive tendencies. Even with Phillip's bike, SUV and 1965 classic Vette, they keep the detached garage so neat and clean you can eat off the floor. His house wasn't really on the way to Lucille's, but he knew she would welcome the assistance. Those dogs were a real handful.

"Did you hear that Bosco? Phillipe is going to walk us home. My old boy is going deaf you know."

Florilla opened the door for them. "Poor old Bosco," she bent to rub Bosco's ears. "He doesn't seem to mind though."

"Okay, off we go. Au Reservoir."

It's always *reservoir* instead of *revoir*. It used to drive Henri crazy. Lucille waved with her free hand as she and Blanche stepped onto the porch. Phillip took hold of the two big boys and followed right behind her. The chaos was gone.

"Whew," I said as I sank down into the closest chair. I slipped off of my shoes and rubbed my sore feet.

"Okay, so what do you think?" Flo asked from behind me.

"I think it went great, Sweetie. They all learned something, they all bought something, and they all left happy. I also think I'm not going to make it through this weekend. I think I'm going to have an apoplexy before Monday gets here."

"No, that's not what I mean. Look. I'm talking about these. Which one should I take this weekend?"

I looked over my shoulder to the back corner of the Diner. Flo was standing in *Stilettos* holding a pair of red patent leather pumps in her left hand and the new black velvets in her right. "Which one?"

"What outfit are you wearing?"

"Well, I have the red lace teddy I bought for our tenth anniversary trip to Vegas, or I could do my black patent leather thing."

"Does it really matter? He'll have you naked in thirty seconds anyway."

Flo giggled and her face turned the color of her hair. "No, the shoes stay on. Oz says, and I quote, *'High heels are one of the finest inventions of mankind. They're right up there with fire.'*"

"Well, in that case it doesn't matter."

She shrugged her shoulders and put both pairs back on the shelf. "Sweetie, you'll make it through this weekend just fine. Your brother's taking you out for your birthday dinner tomorrow night, right? Where's he taking you anyway?"

"Geez-o-pete, I almost forgot. No, we changed it to brunch on Sunday because The Monaco is having a televised celebrity poker tournament tomorrow and he needs to be on the property. He made reservations at Chez Pareo. But maybe I should just cancel."

"What, are you kidding me? How'd you get reservations at Chez Pareo? They're booked for brunch like a year in advance."

"You know Chase. He knows everybody. He's got connections."

"You don't cancel reservations at Chez Pareo. It's just not done," she said.

"But you know what it'll be like. I love him dearly but he'll be schmoozing with the owner and the chef and I'll end up eating alone most of the time. He can't help himself, he's always working it."

Chase, the younger of my two older brothers, worked his way up the resort hotel industry ladder. He started as a front desk clerk on the night shift at the Holiday Inn in

Secaucus and now he's the General Manager of The Monaco, the newest over-the-top casino hotel in Atlantic City. The lobby features a two story spiral aquarium, three thirty foot waterfalls and a tropical rainforest. As far as I know he's not working for the mob and he's never met Donald Trump. He's forty-seven, single, with no apparent desire to change his status. Think George Clooney.

"It'll be fabulous, just go."

"Just wish it could be Monday already so I can get this over with."

"The weekend will fly by, you'll see. Hey Sweetie, by the way thanks for holding down the fort here so I can leave early with Oscar."

"No problemo. I'm thinking about closing early so I can work on Q's chart but I promised Abby I'd talk with her and look at her astrology maps this afternoon. She'll be back any minute. Austin. Can you believe it?" I shook my head.

"Well now if we didn't like Akio, you could tell her that none of her planets were aligned anywhere near Austin on the day she was born. But tell her that her Venus and Jupiter lines run right through Austin this very minute and she'll be out of here. Then we'll have to look for a new employee and we'll have a hard time finding another Abby."

"True, but I'm just going to tell her whatever I see about her planets and we'll deal with it."

"Of course you will," Flo sighed. "Speaking of honesty, I really hope that you're going to be honest with yourself about Mr. Quentin Adams. Yes, he's gorgeous and he wears cuff links; but the man's a Leo. Be careful."

"Two out of three's not bad."

Flo shook her head and came over and sat down on the red lacquer coffee table in front of me.

"Look C, you know I love you, but it's just not healthy to lay on the tracks when there's a freight train coming. All I'm saying is…"

TIFFANY BLUES

I could see Oscar parking his Beemer out front through the showcase window. "Uh-oh. Oscar's here. You gotta go."

Flo jumped up and made a beeline for Stillettos.

"C, help!"

She pulled both pairs of shoes off the rack again and held them up against her trying to decide. I pointed to the red and she put the black pair back on the rack.

"Sweetie, are you going to pay for those?" I asked her.

"I pay for them every day darling," she answered stuffing the shoes into her tote bag. "I'll talk to you tomorrow. Give Chase a hug for me." She blew kisses at me from the doorway and danced out of the shop.

SEVEN

I made my way, barefoot, down the two flights of stairs to my front door. My naked body was barely covered by a *Flying Guitar* tee shirt, souvenir from the Green Parrot, the first and last bar on US 1 in Key West.

The last time Flo and I visited her brother Cody we practically lived at the Green Parrot, a one-of-a-kind open air saloon that's been around for more than a century. Hey, when in Rome. One particularly sweltering afternoon, in between shots of tequila, Flo reached over the bar and snatched a maraschino cherry.

"Can I feed the parrot?" she had asked the bartender.

"You can try but he's already stuffed," the bartender answered.

It wasn't until Cody held her up to the taxidermied mascot that Flo fully understood the futility of her mission. I smiled at the memory and put it away for a future daydream. Right now I needed my newspaper.

I pressed my nose on the etched glass of my front door searching for my *New York Times*. Reading the Sunday *Times* was a non-negotiable ritual and any man I finally settled down with would have to understand that the first two hours of the morning was reserved for my leisurely perusal of The Paper. Sure, I could e-read it but there's nothing like the feel of good old fashioned newsprint. I mean, it's *The Times*.

My expedition through the paper always follows the same route. The first stop is the Tiffany ad on page three. I don't linger for long because the Style Section awaits me. The weddings; Saturday weddings, Sunday weddings and the special featured wedding. If you pay attention, every once in a while, you can find the wedding announcement of someone noteworthy or their offspring. Next stop, the advice column; guaranteed laughs. The columnist makes short shrift of the often sophomoric quandaries presented by readers but gives sage advice nonetheless. When I'm done with Style, I skim the front page, then the Metro section, Arts and Leisure and the Book Review. I usually save the magazine section for later in the week.

Luckily, the paper guy had landed it right on the top porch step, a rarity lately.

Someone called my name as I opened the door. It was Ed, my weird neighbor in the Victorian across the street. He was doing his daily morning aerobics which involved running up and down the six steps of his townhouse for a half an hour. It was January so he was wearing his winter warm ups: a turquoise velour running suit with white stripes down the sides. Thank God it wasn't summer. As soon as the temperature gets above seventy, he "works out" in nothing but a Speedo and black crew socks and sneakers. He gave me a big smile and waved. I nodded and closed the door. Waving and nodding was all he was getting from me.

My patch of real estate is just like Ed's, in fact the house itself is a mirror image. Three floors, two small bedrooms and bathroom on the top floor, kitchen/dining area on the second and a living room with a fireplace and French doors leading to a postage stamp backyard on the ground level. Ours and the twenty other identical houses on Franklin Lane were built in the 1880's. For the last five years, I'd been renovating to bring it into the twenty-first century complete with Zen garden. We're far enough out of town to be away from the tourists but still close enough to walk in on a warm spring day.

Where I grew up there was no such thing as walking to town or anywhere else for that matter. My family moved to a subdivision carved out of a dairy farm about forty-five miles west of New York City when I was only three years old. I was too young to remember the cramped apartment we left behind in Hoboken so the only house I ever knew was a 1960's bi-level.

It was all done up in kitschy Mediterranean. The black wrought iron rails, walnut paneling and my father's naugahyde recliner never changed. My brothers had to share a room, but I, of course, had my own girly girl bedroom complete with a white canopy bed, eyelet curtains and a pink shag carpet. It was my private sanctuary where I dirty danced with Patrick Swayze, flying off my bed into his arms. If anyone ever needs my DNA all they'd have to do is track down my old bed post. I'm sure there's enough trace saliva on there for a million positive ID's, none of them Johnny Castle's.

I plopped the paper on the kitchen island and put the pot on for tea. "Well, there's always Ed," I sighed to the cats who were waiting patiently for their breakfast. The Elvi moaned pitifully. "You're right," I said as I gave them each a handful of dry food. "I'll never be that desperate."

I rummaged through the bread drawer for my breakfast. Multigrain bread--I could toast that and slather it with butter and raspberry preserves. Or, I could open the box of chocolate chip Fat-Away muffins that had been sitting there for the last two weeks. Who was I kidding, Quentin Hunkasaurus was coming at five tomorrow. The Fat-Away won.

I knew I really had to start working on his astrology chart. I'd managed to avoid it all weekend, but it would

TIFFANY BLUES

just have to wait until I'd had my way with the Times. The teapot whistled and I poured a large mug of green tea, grabbed the muffin and the paper, turned on some Japanese flute music and headed downstairs.

Snuggling into the sofa, I sipped the steaming tea and checked out the Tiffany ad. A filigree diamond pendant necklace. Pretty. Someday. I began flipping through the endless paper looking for the *Style* section. *Business. Travel. Metro. Real Estate.*

"What the...? No *Style* section! Geez-o-pete!" I complained to Elvis.

I rifled through each section back to the front page. Still no *Style*, just boring headlines. *Secretary of State in Talks with Middle East.* What else was new? Scanning down to the bottom of the page another headline caught my eye. *Botanist Dead at Botanical Gardens, Crime of Passion?*

I spit out a mouthful of muffin into my napkin to keep from choking and frantically searched under the papers and in the cushions for my phone. Where the hell was it? A blind swipe under the sofa produced one mega dust bunny and two thoroughly chewed catnip mice but no phone. *Close your eyes, take a deep breath and pray. Saint Anthony, help!* When I opened my eyes the phone was right in front of me on the black ottoman. Swear it wasn't there a second ago. I unlocked it and pressed Flo's smiling face.

"Hi, this is Florilla Munrow, I can't come to the phone now, but please leave a message and I'll get back to you as soon as I can."

"Flo, call me back, *now*! Read the *Times* front page and call me back."

I hung up the phone and it immediately beeped back at me. "Missed 1 call 11:31 am." I glanced at the clock on the cable box, eleven thirty-two. How'd that happen? I looked again, saw it was Flo and checked the message.

"C, call me back, *now*! Read the *Times* front page and call me back."

It'd be so much easier if we were just in one body. I

pressed *two* again.

"C! ...read it? I can't ... dead!"

"Flo, I can't hear you. You're breaking up. What'd you say?"

"Duncan's dead!"

"Did you read it?"

"Not all of it."

I began reading aloud to her.

Dr. Duncan McPherson, world renowned ethnobotanist and Associate Dean of the Botanical Research Center at the Metropolitan Botanical Gardens was found dead in the conservatory at the Botanical Gardens early Saturday morning. Dr. McPherson, 69, was discovered in the tropical plant gallery by one of the gardeners upon his arrival at six am. He was pronounced dead at the scene. The immediate cause of death is unknown; however a police spokesman said that a passion flower vine was entwined around his neck. It is not known if the vine could have been used to strangle him.

"What do they mean 'It's not known'? Of course it's known, he was strangled. He had a vine around his neck!" Flo interrupted. She picked up where I left off.

Dr. McPherson's is the second death reported at the Gardens this week. On Tuesday, Miss Tracy Bennett, a researcher on Dr. McPherson's staff, was found, apparently drowned, near the waterfall area of the Gardens. The NYPD is calling both deaths suspicious and an investigation is underway according to Detective Sergeant Hector J. Cordova.

The gardener, who has worked in the Botanical Gardens for thirty years, was taken to Presbyterian Medical Center with chest pains after the discovery. 'The vine was ripped right off the tree, it was a good 40 to 50 feet long. I got closer and saw the poor Doctor slumped up against the mahogany tree with the passion flower vine wrapped around his neck. He was dead wood alright. Poor guy, he was always very nice to us,'the unidentified gardener told the police.

Samantha Rousseau, one of Dr. McPherson's research assistants was distraught by the news of his death, "He was a gentle, sweet, brilliant man. He was like a father to me. I can't believe anyone would want to harm him. First Tracy, now Dr. McPherson. How could this happen, especially here?" The office of the Director of the Gardens was contacted but had no comment.

Dr. McPherson was a professor from Cambridge...

"...blah, blah, blah... Now the rest is all about his career accomplishments. Where are the obituaries? Look and see if it's in there."

I paged through the rest of the paper and found the obituaries. "He's not in here yet. I can't believe this. Who would want to kill him? He was so sweet."

"Dr. Pearl, in the conservatory, with the passionflower vine."

"Ya think? She was frigid but do you think she'd want him dead?"

"I think she wanted him any way she could have him, it's stiffer that way," Flo cracked back but her voice was muffled and I could barely hear her.

"What are you doing? I can't hear you."

"I'm crawling under the bed. I'm missing one of my red high heels."

"What does Oscar think?"

"He hasn't seen this yet. He's still drooling on his pillow from last night. This wasn't exactly how I was planning to wake him up. Hold on a second." I could hear heavy breathing while she crawled out from under the bed. "Okay. I'm back in the living room, now I can talk."

"You might be right about Dr. Pearl. But why would she want that Tracy girl dead?"

"Who knows, maybe she was jealous. Maybe Duncan was messing with her too."

"Or maybe Samantha was ticked and off'd them both. Father figure, huh? I don't think so."

"I still can't believe he's dead. Oz is going to be so upset. How am I going to break this to him? I've got to go. I'll call you back later."

"OK Sweetie, good luck. Bye."

I read the article three more times in disbelief. Duncan was a devilish man but harmless. Who would want to kill him? I couldn't think about it anymore. I piled up the paper and threw it in the recycling box. All I wanted right now was to take a steaming hot shower and let the water pound on me until I forgot all about Duncan McPherson. I had to meet Chase in two hours. Q would have to wait.

EIGHT

Q was still waiting Monday morning. Nothing short of a ruptured spleen could keep me from my second Monday of the month hair appointment. Everyone knows not to mess with my eight-thirty a.m. touch up, but if they're *really* desperate to talk to me, they can find me at Etoiles with my head in a sink.

Etoiles Salon and Spa was a godsend for us. The same year we opened The Diner, Ilyana Kovalenko, a recently naturalized, wise-cracking, Ukranian set up shop directly across from us on Ferry Street. She converted what had once been a women's hat shop into a trendy salon and day spa that fits right in with the rest of our quirky river town. The décor she chose was ultramodern. Stainless steel, shiny black leather, and floor to ceiling mirrors that melt ten pounds off a body instantaneously. An unlikely backdrop for the bizarre collection of retro mannequin heads sporting felt fedoras and colorful pill box hats displayed like hunting trophies on the walls. Ilyana discovered the bodiless heads underneath a pile of dusty hatboxes in the store's ancient basement during the renovations.

"Okay, put your head back and relax now. Ve can talk more after I rinse you out," Ilyana said. I had just spent nearly an hour retelling the entire story of the last four days while she touched up my roots. She adjusted the water temperature and tested it on my head. "Ees it too hot?" she asked.

"No, it's wonderful, thanks," I answered, shimmying around in the chair until I was comfortable. I closed my eyes and let the warm water massage rinse out the pain in my third eye along with the excess haircolor.

Five seconds later the water shut off abruptly. "What the..?" I said as I opened my eyes. The cover of Duncan McPherson's *New World Apothecary* surrounded by a halo of spiked red hair was two inches away from my nose.

"Look!" Florilla ordered. She opened the book and stuck it back in my face. Ilyana leaned over the sink to look too.

"Vat are ve lookink at?" Ilyana asked turning the water back on.

"It's the book Duncan gave to Flo, the one I told you about," I explained trying to focus my eyes on the page in front of me. Damn, it wasn't going to be long before I needed reading glasses all the time. I could barely make out the words. Gray hair and reading glasses, what's next?

The page read *Chapter 6: Dionaea, Drosera, Utricularia and other Unusual Carnivores*. The title was printed over what looked like an antique sketch of a Venus Fly Trap. *Ladyslipper, 4/11/1940, LA, 1200P* was scribbled in blue ink across the leaves of the plant. At least I thought that's what it said.

I sat upright in the chair with my hair dripping.

"Vait a meenut, I'm not done rinsing yet," Ilyana complained trying to catch the drips with a black towel.

"Sorry, but this is an emergency," Flo said shivering. She hadn't even bothered to put on a coat to cross the street even though it was freezing again this morning.

"Are you sure that's Brazilian Coffee?" Flo asked

inspecting my head.

"Better be," I said.

"Looks darker than usual."

"It's wet."

"Still seems darker to me."

"It's the same kolar as alvays," Ilyana said turning the water back on.

"So what's the emergency already?" I asked.

"*Just look.*" Flo held out the book.

I looked. "Okay, so?"

"So, this is *my* book. Duncan must have written this. Why?"

"Well, he took it off that pile on the floor, maybe he wrote that in all the books."

"I think it's a clue."

"A clue to vat?" Ilyana asked.

"His murder, that's what," Flo answered.

"I need to finish rinsing you Clara, your hair vill be jet black if eet stays on much longer."

I leaned my head back into the sink. Flo was standing over me, her mouth moving a mile a minute but I couldn't hear a word she said other than a faint "my book" here and there. She gave up and plopped down next to me in the only old-fashioned hair dryer chair in the salon. The book lay open on her lap. I closed my eyes.

When the water shut off this time Ilyana was saying, "Absolutely ees. One hundred percent."

"One hundred percent what?" I asked as Ilyana wrapped my head in a dry towel.

"Ilyana's got it all figured out," Flo informed me.

"It absolutely ees. What is the word? Jealous. Death by jealous lover. One hundred percent," Ilyana repeated.

"Let me see that book again." I got up from the sink, took it from Flo and settled myself into a leather and chrome chair. I read out loud. "Ladyslipper. Four Eleven Nineteen Forty. LA. 1200P. Well, Four Eleven Nineteen Forty is obviously a date. 1200P could be a time or a code."

Flo rolled her eyes and shifted in her seat. "And Ladyslipper is an orchid. Like the one in Duncan's office."

Ilyana frowned at herself in the mirror. To my surprise she yanked her platinum blonde ponytail right off her head, pulled her own hair back and up and re-clipped the ponytail. She nodded, satisfied with the adjustment. "Ladyslipper ees not orchid. Ladyslipper ees jealous lover!" Ilyana insisted.

Flo and I looked at each other. "Janice Pearl?" we said in unison.

"Who ees Janice Pearl again?" Ilyana asked parting my wet hair down the middle.

"Ice queen." I checked out my hair color in the mirror. Same as always. "Good candidate for jealous lover."

"She's a colleague of Duncan's. She acted like she owned him," Flo added.

"How old she ees? The date in the book ees April eleventh, Nineteen-Forty?" She started to trim my already curling ends.

"She's probably in her late forties, fifty maybe. Can't be her birthday. We don't know that Duncan actually wrote that. Maybe he didn't know it was there," Flo said.

"None of this makes any sense." I flipped to the front of the book. "Sweetie, look at Duncan's handwriting in the front. It's the same." I held the book out for Flo to see. She took it back from me.

"Okay, so Duncan wrote it. Nineteen Forty. Maybe it's his birthday." Flo sank back down on the dryer chair and folded one leg up underneath her.

"The year's about right, the paper said he was around seventy. But he said he was a Scorpio, remember? April eleventh is Aries. And what's an orchid got to do with it? Maybe he was just writing a note to himself and it doesn't mean a thing."

A blast of January morning air ripped through the salon and we all cringed from the surprise attack. In the mirror I watched Phillip and two large vaguely familiar men, with long open overcoats entering the salon behind me. Phillip! We hadn't told him about Duncan's murder and he never reads the newspaper. I swung the chair around.

Phillip was wearing his worry face. He knew.

"These gentlemen insisted on seeing Flo right away," he explained apologetically. Flo was now hiding under the hair dryer. The hood down over her face and her hands folded in her lap on top of the closed book, like a terrified schoolgirl.

The pudgy guy walked over to the nail polish rack and started fingering them one by one reading the labels. He wrapped his pasty white fingers around a red bottle.

"*Used to be a Ho.*" he read out loud to no one in particular. "Huh?"

Ilyana catwalked over to the nailpolish rack in her turquoise platforms and grabbed the bottle out of his hand.

"No, it ees not your kolar!" She put it back on the rack and folded her arms across her overflowing chest, angry that her sanctuary had been invaded.

"New York City P.D. Detective Darnell Carlton," the other guy said holding up his badge. He nodded to his companion. "This is Detective Tom Mooney."

Mooney casually held up his own badge as if he was ticked that he had to prove who he was. Now I remembered. They were the same guys we ran into at Duncan's office.

Detective Carlton continued, "We're investigating Duncan McPherson's death. Are you Florilla Munrow?" he asked looking at me.

I shook my head and grinned. Ilyana pointed her scissors at the hair dryer.

Carlton walked over to the dryer chair and lifted up the hood. "Ms. Munrow, we're here because your name was in Dr. McPherson's appointment book for Thursday morning." The detective looked toward me. "I believe we saw you both with Dr. McPherson that morning." Then back to Flo, "You might have been one of the last people to see him alive."

Flo opened her mouth but nothing came out.

I quickly answered for her. "Yes, we ran into you outside Duncan's office." I held out my hand. "I'm Clara Martini, Florilla's business partner." They just stared at me.

"We'd like to hear from Ms. Munrow please," Mooney said.

When Flo finally started talking she couldn't shut up. "Well, Clara and I went to the Gardens to hear Duncan's lecture, didn't we Sweetie?" I nodded. "At first we weren't going to go because of the snow and it's such a pain to go in on the train and have to take the subway from Penn Station, you know? But then it started clearing up so I said let's go because Oscar went to all the trouble of setting up the meeting with Duncan to talk about aphrodisiacs and we figured we'd never get a chance like this again."

"Who's Oscar?" Mooney interrupted from over by the product shelf. Before Ilyana could stop him, he had taken the Vanilla Musk for Men hand lotion tester off the shelf and squirted a blob into his palm. Yuk.

"He's my Oscar. Anyway, after the lecture Duncan took us to his office, that's when you saw us. Then he gave us a tour of the conservatory to show us the best aphrodisiacs to use in Scorpio Moon. That's our newest product. You should come back around Valentine's Day and buy some, it's pretty powerful stuff."

Phillip had his head in his hands rubbing both of his temples. My guess was by this point the two cops were mighty sorry they ever set foot in Dolly's Ferry.

"Excuse me Ms. Munrow." Carlton turned to me hopefully, running his left hand over his brown bald scalp. "Ms. Martini, is there anything you can add that's... of value?" Flo looked relieved.

"Not really. We took the tour of the conservatory and left. Duncan had to go to a luncheon with some pharmaceutical company. That was the last time we saw him."

"Did you meet or speak to anyone else while you were there?" Carlton asked.

"Oh yeah, Doctor Blaine Winship was there alright," Flo said. "The slimemold," she muttered under her breath.

"Did you say slimemold?" Mooney sniffed his fingers and wiped his hands off on his overcoat.

"Bad date from college, nevermind. He was at the lecture."

I jumped in. "Well, the only other people we spoke to were Duncan's research assistant, Samantha, and he introduced us to a Dr. Pearl when she came to get him to take him to the luncheon. She was a little, um, cold. Right Flo?"

"Downright frigid. It was pretty clear he didn't like her though, he called her a Venus Fly Trap." Flo shot me a look.

Ilyana started on my bangs. "Show the detectives de book."

"Wha fook?" Mooney mumbled. He had found the gourmet chocolate chip cookies on the ever present snack table. He was covered with crumbs.

"Book? What about the book?" Phillip asked. Ilyana put her arm around him and whispered something in his ear.

"This book." Flo held it up for them to see. "Duncan signed it for me when we were there." She laid it in her lap and opened the cover. *"To My Bonnie Florilla, Save me some Scorpio Moon! Best Wishes, Duncan,"* she read out loud.

"Can I see that?" Carlton asked. Flo ignored him.

"Then, yesterday after I read about his murder, I was looking through it and found this." She flipped back to the carnivorous plant chapter and showed Carlton the handwriting. "Do you think it might be a clue? We think it's a clue."

"I don't know Ma'am. But we'll certainly check into it. We'll have to take this though." Carlton reached out to take the book.

"No way! I don't think so. Can't you just write down what it says in your little notebooks?" Flo protested.

"We don't have little notebooks," Mooney answered, now trying to pick cookie bits out of his teeth with his pinky nail.

"How about if we make a copy of this page and the one he signed? Do you have a copier?" Carlton asked.

"Ve don't have copier here," Ilyana answered.

"We have one back at The Diner," I offered.

"Want me to take them back and make a copy for them?" Phillip asked.

I nodded. Flo jumped up and hugged the book against her chest. "I'm coming with you. I'm not letting this out of my sight."

Carlton raised his eyebrows at her and fished around in his pocket. He pulled out a card and handed it to me. We made eye contact. He had nice eyes. "Just in case you think of anything else, Ms. Martini," he smiled.

The detectives followed Phillip out of the salon with Flo trailing behind them. She turned around and stuck her head back in. "Hurry," she begged and slammed the door behind her.

"Idiots!" Ilyana spat, hands on hips. She stood at the front window and watched as they navigated the morning traffic to cross the street. She turned shaking her finger at me.

"Clara, I tell you thees one time, and one time only. Dun't poke comb of bee. Eet's not always honey you find."

"Tell me about it," I answered as she turned on the blow dryer.

NINE

By the time I got to The Diner the detectives were gone. Flo was folded sideways in a chair with her legs hanging over the arms and Old Elvis purring loudly in her plaid lap. She was reading to Phillip from Duncan's book.

Darwin wrote a friend that carnivorous plants were more important to him than the origin of all the species. In fact, Darwin called the Dionea, or Venus Fly Trap, the 'most wonderful plant in the world.' In Venus Fly Traps, it has been determined that it is a spark generated by static electricity that shuts and holds the trap closed. An acidic enzyme dissolves the soft tissue of the insects trapped inside, converting them to nitrogen which is used by the plant for nutrition. All that is left at the end, when the trap reopens, are skeletal remains.

"Are we talking about Janice Pearl again?" I asked.
"Not very flattering is it?" Flo answered looking up.
I started to unbutton my fleece jacket, but changed my mind and kept it on. "I can't get warm this morning. Wish we had a working fireplace."

Phillip leaned over from his chair to scratch Old Elvis behind the ear. "You don't need a fireplace. You have nineteen pounds of feline fur to keep you warm as toast."

With that, Old Elvis uncurled himself, stretched, turned himself completely around, then flopped right back down again. He began softly kneading the hem of Flo's red poodle knit sweater and turned his purring machine volume up to its highest setting.

"So what happened after you guys came back here? You find out anything else from them? Any idea what Duncan's message meant?" I asked.

Phillip answered. "Nope, if they knew anything they weren't talking. They just took their copies and rode off into the sunset." He eased himself out of the comfy chair and headed to the kitchen.

The front door chimed. Abby came in quietly, her long Superman hair now had a neon green stripe down the left side. She was wearing a very mini green skirt over black leggings with the combat boots.

"Hello Abigail," Phillip sang from inside the kitchen.

"Hey guys, I can't stay. I'm on my way to watch the puppies," she said loud enough for Phillip to hear, then made herself at home on the edge of the round coffee table.

"Are you feeling better?" Flo asked.

"I don't know, I'm still confused. Clara, you were a big help. At least now I know my Mars line doesn't go through Austin and if I do go it won't be a disaster but I just don't know…" her voice trailed off.

"All will be revealed in time, don't worry," Flo said.

Abby leaned in close and whispered, "That's not why I stopped in though. I have to ask you guys, is something weird going on here that I need to know about?"

"What do you mean, something weird?" I asked wrapping my jacket tight around me. I curled up in the soft chair, still warm from Phillip.

"Well, yesterday afternoon, there was a call from the

TIFFANY BLUES

New York Police Department, Detective Somebody. I wrote the name of the guy down, it's over by the cash register. He wanted to talk to Flo."

"It's okay Abbs, they showed up here this morning," Flo said.

"But what's going on? You rob Tiffany's or something?"

"No, it's worse. Remember we went to the Botanical Gardens last week to meet Oscar's friend, Dr. McPherson? Turns out they found him strangled to death with a passionflower in the conservatory. NYPD checked his appointment book and we were in it the day before. They just wanted to ask us some questions," I said.

"No way!"

"Way," Flo said.

"Strangled?" She pretended to strangle herself with her hands. She was wearing black nail polish.

"I know, it's awful. He was a nice man. We can't believe it," I said.

"Yuk. Two dead. Same place. Do they think there's a serial killer on the loose?" she asked.

"Doubt it. Serial killers usually kill the same kind of people, like dark haired women or people who like creamy instead of crunchy peanut butter," Flo said.

"Maybe this one's killing people who are into aphrodisiacs," Abby offered.

"Sure hope not. We'll keep you posted when we know more," I said.

"Sweet." She popped up like a jack-in-the-box. "Okay, I gotta go, I'm late. Ttyl. Bye." With that Abby was gone.

"The whole thing is bizarre," I said. "NYPD showing up here. How'd they even find us?"

"They probably just Googled us," Flo guessed. "When I Google myself, I get two whole pages and The Chocolate Diner is at the top. But my master's thesis is on there and so is my lavender cookie recipe. Hell, they even have the pictures of the Lambertville Petscarade two Halloweens ago when I finally won first prize."

"Technology's going to be the death of us."

"Remember? I was Glinda the Good Witch. Made that big mylar crown with pink toile and glitter all over it."

"You're always Glinda the Good Witch."

"But that year I dressed up Young El as the Bad Witch with that little witch cap and the little bitty black satin cape and Old El made the best..."

"Flying monkey." Phillip finished her sentence as he came back in and handed me a hot cup of tea. "This'll warm you up."

"Oh, nice. Thanks." I took a long sip. "Mmm, Plum Berry."

"You know Flo, maybe they checked out your Facebook page," Phillip laughed. "Looks like you might have a couple new friends. You should invite them in."

"Not funny. That Mooney was groaty, cookie crumbs everywhere," Flo said.

"The other one, Carlton, wasn't so bad. He had nice eyes," I said.

"C, maybe you should invite him into *your* cyberlife," Flo said.

"He's married. Wedding ring," Phillip was quick to point out.

That was the story of my life. The good ones were always married. If they weren't married they couldn't quite grasp the concept of a monogamous relationship. Just when you think you've got the real thing you find a text message to, *"Sugar Britches"* that says *"Can't wait to see ALL of you tonite,"* the night he was supposed to be in the studio rehearsing with his all male rock band. I had a feeling Q was going to be different. He had to be. He had a Libra Moon, like me. And like Oscar. Oscar couldn't be the only decent single man left on the planet.

"So Sweetie, I never talked to you again yesterday. How'd Oscar take the news?" I asked.

"I had to make him a drink just to calm him down.

He's a mess. He just kept walking in circles repeating, 'Who would do such a thing?' over and over."

"Did you show him the book?" Phillip asked.

"After the second screwdriver. He doesn't have a clue about any of it either. So Clara Martini, I guess we're just going to have to figure this out."

"How are *we* supposed to do that? This whole thing is just creepy. We don't know anything about what's really going on here."

"Maybe not, but the Universe plopped this in our laps and we don't have a choice," Flo said. "Besides, you think Dick Tracy and Mr. Vanilla Musk for Men are going to solve this on their own? This is about plants, they don't know a damn thing about plants." She sat up and Old Elvis let out a pitiful moan at the imposition.

She was right. I didn't have a lot of faith in that dynamic duo either. "Okay, fine," I said. "How about tomorrow you and I sit down and start solving McPherson's murder. But I can't think about that now. I've got to get Q's chart done by five."

Phillip had his jacket on and looked ready to leave. "Are you leaving?" I put my teacup down.

"I've got a meeting in Philly to talk about my next assignment. They want to send me to Greenland."

"Hope it's still there by the time you get there, I mean global warming and all," Flo said.

Phillip nodded. "I think that's actually part of the assignment, the global warming angle." He leaned down, gave me a peck on the cheek and blew a kiss to Flo. "Try to stay out of trouble girls," he said and made his way out the back.

"Speaking of trouble Sweetie, what *do* the stars have to say about your Q man?" Flo asked.

"I'm still working on it. First Duncan, then I had to have brunch with Chase, I'm not even close to being ready."

"How was your brunch anyway?"

"Like I expected. He was preoccupied the whole time but the food was fabulous. He may get a job with the Monaco in Vegas."

"We are so there! Did you get the flowers he promised?"

"No. Have you seen my laptop? And I could use some Sno-Caps. All I had so far today is a cup of green tea at seven o'clock this morning and this." I held up my cup.

"Me too. I mean I had my coffee, but I've only had one cup so far. How about I go make us some breakfast and open a brand new box of candy for dessert? I think Phillip had the laptop in the kitchen. I saw it when we went to make the copies."

Flo, Old El and I headed for the kitchen.

***

Before I checked my emails, I noticed I had a new text message on my phone. Spencer sent me a message at 4 am from Tijuana. Apparently Cicada took a detour on the way to LA.

Hi Ma, In Mexico. Don't panic. We took detour to Tijuana. Everything's kewl here. Talk 2 U soon. Luv u.

Mexico? I texted back, *BE CAREFUL!!!* and put the phone down. I couldn't think about it and refocused on my email. Ten offers for miracle erectile dysfunction cures and deals on foreclosed real estate. Chase had forwarded me a ridiculous video about a giant crab. I clicked open my astrology program. Mars was squaring my Venus today. Not good. I couldn't think about that either.

I had just started working on Q's birth chart again when Flo handed me a dish of nonpareils and half of a whole grain bagel with cream cheese. I raised my eyebrows.

"Don't worry, its fat free." She took a sip of coffee and put the mug down on the desk next to my bagel.

"Where's your bagel?"

TIFFANY BLUES

"I already ate it."

I went back to the computer screen. Flo leaned over my shoulder and stole some Sno-Caps out of my dish. The "crunch, crunch, crunch" in my ear was deafening as she popped one after another into her mouth.

"*What?*" I turned to her and my nose almost made contact with her right molars.

"I'm not seeing a Libra rising here, Sweetie. Darling. Not only is he a Leo, he's a *double Leo.*"

"Yeah, but look at his Venus. It's conjuncting my Sun in his seventh house. Marriage and partnerships. It's karma."

"Warning! Warning!" Flo flailed her arms in all directions like the robot on that show she watches on RetroTV, almost spilling coffee all over my head. She stopped suddenly, wrapped her free hand around the mug and gazed into it as if it were a crystal ball.

"I don't see karma. I see emotional roller coaster coming soon to love life near you." Her fortune teller imitation sounded a hell of a lot like Ilyana.

"How can you say that? Just because he's got a little Leo in him." I shrugged and turned back to the computer.

Flo sighed. "Maybe tripping him was a big mistake afterall." She wrapped her arms around my shoulders and sat her chin on top of my head. "Sweetie, I hope he's different, but you and Leos just don't work. Every single Leo or Leo rising, never mind a *double Leo*, you've ever been with has broken your heart."

"That's not true. What about the guy with the bright yellow Chevy Avalanche. I dumped him."

"Yeah, because he was a Leo with a bright yellow Chevy Avalanche. First there was Spencer's father who just walked away when you were pregnant. Idiot. Then what about whatshisname, the married guy who lied and said his wife was dead when she was only on assignment in Japan for two years. And of course, last, but certainly not least, the Royal Supreme Idiot and his Sugar Britches, both of them. The wedding was a month away for heaven's sake!"

"At least he paid for you and me to take the honeymoon to St. Barts."

"True, but he should have paid a lot more than that."

Flo's poodle sweater pocket began to vibrate against my back followed by a full orchestra blasting the cyclone crescendo from the Wizard of Oz. I nearly jumped out of my skin. She pulled her cell out of her pocket and her eyes bugged out when she saw the caller I.D.

She mouthed, "SHIT!" to me, but said very calmly into the phone, "Oh, Mrs. Case. I was just about to call you. I had to make a few minor changes to the border that runs along the drive. I have the plans in my hands and I'm on my way right now. I'll be there soon."

She tapped at the screen in frustration and flew out the kitchen door.

"I totally forgot I'm supposed to be doing a garden design for Jacqueline Case over in New Hope forty-five minutes ago," she yelled to me. "What time did you say Q's coming?"

"Five, why?" I yelled back to her as I followed her laptop in hand.

"Then I'll be back by four-thirty." The front door chimes echoed for a long time after she was gone.

***

By four thirty I was in big trouble. "This chart is impossible," I said out loud and threw the laminated astrology chart down on the round corner booth table. It just missed the sticky Chinese food containers stacked in the middle. Disgusted, I picked up the little white cartons and the empty aluminum tray. The forgotten fortune cookie fell out onto the table. I cracked it open hoping for a clue from the Universe. The little white strip of paper revealed my destiny: *Wow! There's a secret message from your teeth!* Now what the hell was that supposed to mean?

I was just scraping my plate into the kitchen garbage

when the door chimes did their thing. My stomach clenched and a noisy bubble from my semi-digested chicken with garlic sauce popped out of my mouth. "I'm not ready. Please, don't let it be him." I cracked the door and peeked out. It was only Flo.

She flung her red parka over a counter stool. "He's not here yet?"

"Not yet. Good thing too, his chart is driving me crazy."

"I don't think he's going to give two hoots about his chart when he sees you. Look at you all in black with those red Jimmy Choos."

"Does it look okay?"

She shook her head. "Too good. Bubble, bubble, toil and trouble," she sniffed. "I smell Chinese food. Any left? I'm starving."

"Not much Sweetie." I walked past her to look out the front window. "There are two scallion pancakes if you want them and some rice. Oh, and all the broccoli that I picked out of my chicken." I always order number fifty-three without broccoli. I don't know how they always mess it up. "But it's cold. I had it for lunch."

"You read your fortune? Anything about mysterious strangers?" Flo asked.

"Only if they're in my teeth."

"What the hell does that mean?"

"Who knows." We went back to the kitchen together.

"I'm absolutely famished." Flo rummaged through the containers and took a bite of a cold scallion pancake. "Jacqueline Case offered me brie and a glass of wine but I didn't want to take it."

"So how'd it go with Jackie C. anyway?" I looked for my Sno-Caps. The bowl was empty. I looked at the clock. Four-fifty!

"Really great. She loved the idea of a hummingbird garden next to her pond. And guess what. She just bought a hundred acre estate in Vermont and wants me to come up and help her with the landscaping in the spring. How's a trip to Stratton in May sound?"

"Springtime in Vermont. Sounds wonderful especially since we don't ski. We can just sightsee and eat."

The front door opened again. I held my breath. This time it was Phillip.

"What are you doing back here?" I asked. "Didn't you go to Philly?"

"There and back again. I didn't want to miss your mysterious Q man." He made little quotation marks around the 'Q' in the air with his fingers. Phillip's eyes traveled over me, head to toe and back again. "You going to dinner or giving an astrology reading?"

"You don't like it?"

"I didn't say that." Phillip popped the last scallion pancake into his mouth.

"How's my hair?" I was panicking now. I grabbed my makeup bag out of my purse and hurried to the bathroom to check my hair and fix my face. While I was reapplying my red *Hot Flame* lipstick I heard Flo say loud enough for me to hear over the fan, "She's powdering her nose." Damn, he was here!

I burst out of the bathroom catching the hem of my new sweater on the door knob. It pulled me back and smacked me head first into the adjacent wall. I fell with a thud and laid in a lump on the cold tile. *Please floor, open up and swallow me now.* My right temple throbbed.

"Whoa. That red lump on your forehead goes perfectly with your shoes." Flo was standing over me. Q and Phillip were on either side of her.

I moaned and tried to get up. Q reached out and took my left hand in his to help me. Phillip quickly grabbed my other hand and both men guided me to the corner booth and eased me onto the end of the curved bench seat.

"I'll get you some ice," Flo offered.

"Are you okay?" Q was standing in front of me with his hands in his pockets.

TIFFANY BLUES

I got my first good look at him. Nobody had eyes that color. Had to be contacts. Strong jaw line and faint five o'clock shadow. If it weren't for a few very faint scars he could have been a GQ model.

"I'm fine, thanks. You know, I don't fall for every man who walks through the door."

Flo reached around Q and smashed an ice pack onto my head. "OWWW!" I cried.

Q was smiling. "We have to stop falling like this. It could be dangerous," he said with a sensual voice I didn't remember. "Are you feeling up to doing this now?"

"I'm fine, really." I put the ice pack down on the table next to me. "Besides, I've already done all the work. I have your chart and all the interpretations right here. I'm ready to go."

"So you know all my secrets now?" Q teased. He took his phone out of the inside pocket of his charcoal suit jacket, tapped the screen, glanced at it and slipped it back surreptitiously.

I stood up and picked up his chart from the table, "Don't worry. Your secrets are safe with me." Flo shook her head in disbelief. She was right. What an inconceivably corny thing to say.

Phillip cleared his throat. "OK, well, I'm outta here. Have to stop at Rum Runners to pick up some Guinness. Jason and Louis are starting a Monday night hockey thing. They just got a new sixty inch flat panel. Should be interesting." Phillip gave Q a good once over, puffed out his chest, and nodded. "Have a good reading. She's the best."

Flo had planted herself behind the cash register. I caught her eye and motioned for her to leave. She made a stinky face, "I'm just going to fix myself something to eat. I'll be in the kitchen…if you need me." She moseyed as slow as molasses to the kitchen.

I turned nervously to Q. "Can I get you something to drink? Tea? Water? Seltzer?"

"Water would be great, thanks." He slid into the booth and watched me as I headed back toward the kitchen. I prayed I would make it without smashing into anything.

"If you want, I could just stay and eat with you while you do his reading," Flo offered. "It's too dangerous to leave you alone with him."

"Just stay in here and don't listen," I whispered through my teeth. I grabbed two bottles of water out of the fridge and scurried back to my lion in waiting, dangerous or not.

Q was in the corner booth with Young Elvis curled up in his lap, purring like a motorboat. His right hand softly massaged the cat's back while he flipped through the jukebox selections with his left. He liked cats. Ten points.

"So you've met Elvis. He loves being stroked like that." I said.

Q looked up, "Who doesn't?" He sighed and scanned the room. "Herbs, astrology, chocolate, stilettos...quite a volatile combination don't you think?"

"Well, we sell garden tools too." I smiled and offered him one of the bottles.

"Thanks." He grinned, took the bottle and turned his attention back to the tabletop jukebox. "Does this work?" Q dug around in his pocket.

"Do you have a nickel?" I answered.

The kitchen door swung open and Flo backed out carrying a heaping plate of steaming broccoli and a Diet Coke. I shot daggers at her and she turned right around and made her way ever so slowly back to the kitchen.

Q popped a nickel in the jukebox, pushed some buttons and patted the seat next to him.

I slid into the booth, my leg accidentally brushing against his. Young Elvis must have felt the electricity too because he leapt off Q's lap. The real Elvis started to croon.

"Interesting choice." I pressed the low volume button and *Stuck on You* became a garbled whisper. "Let's go through your astrology chart step by step," I said trying to speak normally.

"Can you really read all these hieroglyphics?" Q took out his phone again, checked the screen and put it away quickly.

"Sure can." I took a deep breath and started to explain astrology. "It's really based on the energies of the planets and how they influence our lives," I told him. "As I tell all my clients, it's not about fate. The stars incline, they don't divine."

Q nodded his head. I had the sense that he wasn't listening. I followed his gaze across the room to *Stilettos*.

"A birth chart is like a map of where the Sun, Moon and planets were in the sky when you were born. It's a circular chart divided into 12 sections called houses. See, it's like a pie," I pointed to the chart but Q had slipped out of the booth and was heading towards the shoes.

He picked up a black patent leather four inch pump off the shelf and examined it carefully. "Nice. How much are they?" he called out.

I cleared my throat and took a sip of water. "We don't carry them in your size."

He smiled, returned the shoe to the shelf and came back toward me. Instead of sitting with me, he sat on a counter stool in front of me. There were crow's feet around his eyes but there wasn't a speck of gray in that full head of hair. Maybe he colored it. I struggled to keep things professional. "I can see that you must have bounced around a lot as a kid, living in more than one place. Now you live in New Jersey?"

"Princeton. I take the train to the city when I need to go in. My lab is out here," he answered. "But you're right on about moving around a lot as a kid. My father was a diplomat. We lived in Australia, India, British Columbia. It was a different kind of life. You know, rank and privilege. Australia was the best."

"A whole British Empire thing going on there." I

opened the laptop and clicked on the mapping link. "How about if we make a locality map of your birth chart? If we look at where the planets were in the sky when you were born in relation to where you've lived, we can see what influence they had on you in each place."

"Are these the aphrodisiacs?"

I looked up. Q was up again, leaning across the counter reading the labels on the apothecary jars.

"Aphrodisiacs? No. Oh, do you know? Did you hear about Dr. McPhearson?" I had his attention now.

"Hear what?"

"It's been all over the news. He was murdered."

"Murdered? You've got to be kidding. When?"

"Friday night apparently. They found his body Saturday morning."

"I've been holed up at Zylanica all weekend working on the end of year report. I didn't hear anything. How'd it happen?" He did the phone thing again and came over and stood in front of me.

"Strangled. They don't know who did it yet." I looked up at him. "You work for Zylanica? Duncan was supposed to have lunch with Zylanica reps after the lecture. Did you go?"

"I was invited but I had another meeting. Besides, it's not really my thing. I'm on the research end. The lunch was more for the PR guys." He sat back down in the booth, this time his leg brushed mine.

Yeah another meeting all right, with the anorexic blonde, I thought. "How well did you know Duncan?" I asked.

"I didn't really know him at all. I was only at the lecture as a rep from the clinical side of things. The other day you said Duncan wasn't a personal friend of yours either, how did you know him?" We made eye contact. I looked away first.

"We just met him the day of the lecture." I concentrated on his chart in front of me. "Flo's boyfriend knew him pretty well. They worked together when Duncan was at Cambridge."

"Flo's boyfriend?"

"Well, for lack of a better word. Doctor Oscar Stern."

"Oh. I still can't believe Duncan's dead. What an awful way to die," Q shook his head.

"I know, it's creepy. Two dead people at the Gardens in one week. You know NYPD actually came all the way out here to talk to us this morning because we were in his appointment book the day before he died. They'll probably go talk to your people since they had lunch with him after we left."

"NYPD? Came all the way out here? Do they actually think you're suspects?"

"Geez, I never thought of that. No, they just asked a lot of questions about our meeting with Duncan, what he talked about, did we notice anyone or anything suspicious."

"Did you?"

"No, not really. We told them we were there for aphrodisiacs. That kind of threw them for a loop. We showed them a book Duncan gave Flo. They made a copy of it."

"The whole book?" he asked. "An aphrodisiac book?"

I laughed. "No, his book, you know, *New World Apothecary*. He signed the inside cover for Flo but she found something else written in the middle of the book. They copied the page that's all. I doubt it means much of anything at this point." I shivered thinking about the whole thing. "How about we get back to your reading?" I shuffled the papers around to find his chart.

He leaned in close to look and I could feel his warm breath on my neck.

"Here's your tenth house, career. Looks like you just started a new venture. Mars entered your tenth house about six months ago."

"I started at Zylanica six months ago. Before that I

worked in Chicago."

"Uranus is going to enter your tenth house this week. It could turn things upside down. What are you working on now?"

"I can't really talk about it but we're testing new vaccines. It's not easy...finding new sources of drugs, creating them, clinical trials and getting them approved. If we're successful it could be very lucrative for Zylanica. Do you see me getting any bonuses?" He laughed a deep genuine laugh.

"Well, looks like you're getting some kind of money. Jupiter's in your eighth house. That's about benefiting from other people's resources, or maybe even an inheritance." I didn't want to tell him there was a small possibility it could also mean mass quantities of sex. "You're not just in this for the money are you?" I asked.

"No, but when you have it, everything is so much easier."

"True, but..."

"Look, I know the drug companies get a bad rap but we really do a lot of good. You know, you haven't said anything about my love life." He tickled my pinkie with his index finger. "Any hope there?"

"I can't believe that you have any problems with your love life."

"I'm a workaholic, it's hard to find someone who'll put up with me."

"Well, Jupiter could spice up your love life too."

"That's good news." Our eyes locked for a second time. He changed the subject by pulling the phone out once again but this time he tapped the screen twice. I was dying to see who or what was so important that he had to check his phone four times in one hour.

Q rested his hand on my knee. "I'm really sorry but I have to go, something's come up. Looks like I have to drive into the city tonight."

"But what about your reading? We haven't finished

yet. Don't you want to know about Pluto?"

He moved close to me, our noses almost touching. He grinned. "I thought Pluto wasn't a planet anymore."

"It still counts. It's the energy that matters."

"How about you tell me about Pluto over dinner tomorrow?" he asked. "I know a great little restaurant just down the river."

"Um...tomorrow? Um..." I hesitated.

"Oh, I didn't think to ask. Are you seeing someone?"

"Someone? Oh, no, I'm not dating anyone in particular right now," I answered, making it sound like it was my choice. It was mostly true.

Q got up and leaned over me. His baby blues were smiling.

"So what do you think? A supple Shiraz, a crackling fire, dinner for two? You bring the stars."

Was he serious? I couldn't believe it when I heard myself answer, "Make it a perfect Pinot and you got a date Mr. Adams."

"Not a problem, they have an extensive wine list. I'll pick you up around seven?"

"Sure, seven's fine but pick me up here." Flo was not going to be happy.

Q handed me twenty dollars more than the reading cost and refused to take it back when I protested. I gave him a hug, like I do with all my clients, and I tried hard not to get too close. He kissed the lump on my head, "I hope your boo-boo is all better." God, he was good.

He drove away in a silver Carerra. Very good.

Flo yelled from the kitchen, "Well?"

"He's very nice. I'm having dinner with him tomorrow night." I tried to change the subject. "So what were you doing in there besides listening to our conversation?"

"I wasn't listening." Flo plowed through the swinging door. "But I know that look Clara Mercedes Martini. He's got you sucked in but good."

I collected all the papers on table and put them back in

the folder marked "Q chart". "Geez-o-pete, it's just dinner."

"Okay, dinner's fine but just don't fall in love with *Mister* Adams," Flo warned me. "At least not tomorrow night. C, I'm telling you, he's a player. Interesting that he works at Zylanica though, don't you think?"

"Weren't listening huh? What else *were* you doing?"

"For your information, I was researching Venus Fly Trap."

"So what did you find out?"

"Well, a lot. Venus Fly Trap was named Dionaea, by a British botanist, John Ellis, after the Greek goddess of beauty. He and his botanist friends nicknamed it Tipitiwitchet, or Tippity Twitchit.

"Tippity Twitchit?"

"Yeah, like honey pot, coochie, vajayjay."

"Are you kidding me?"

"Think about it. Two fringed lips, sensitive to touch…snapping gyro as Oz would say."

"Ewww. Did you learn anything important?"

"Maybe. They've just discovered that fly traps contain some compounds called naphthoquinones which may have some kind of therapeutic value, but also have high toxicity. Doesn't seem like they were ever used as aphrodisiacs, but with a name like that just having them around could bringeth on the boner. There's tons of information out there on carnivorous plants. I don't have a clue about what the date means though or the link to Duncan."

"Wait a sec. Carnivorous plants, Duncan… Blaine Winship, duh?" I closed the blinds on the front window.

Flo deliberately changed the subject. "We don't need to settle the cash drawer right? You didn't have many sales today did you?"

"Don't worry I'll do it tomorrow morning. So back to carnivorous plants…"

"You think Dr. Slimemold knows what the scribbles in the book mean?" Flo interrupted.

TIFFANY BLUES

"Well, there's one way to find out," I answered.

"Oh, no, no way. I'm not calling him, not a chance." Flo grabbed her parka.

"He was at the lecture. He's a carnivorous plant *expert*. Come on. Call him and tell him you want to see him. Maybe he knows something or at least can help us figure out what the date in the book is about. Make up some excuse, like Duncan referred us and we want to talk about his plants for our next project or something."

"We have to actually go see him? Can't we just talk to him on the phone?" Flo was giving in.

"You should go see him in his natural habitat. You never know Flo, maybe he'll entice you with his Exotic, what was it? Exotic Aquatics," I teased.

"When pigs fly. Look I'll call him. But that's it." She reluctantly took her phone out of her pocket and looked lost for a minute.

"You put his card in your bag," I reminded her.

"Damn!" She took her time fishing it out of her purse, dialed the number and disappeared into the potting room.

I turned off most of the lights and checked and rechecked the thermostat and the alarm. A minute later Flo reappeared looking slightly nauseous.

"Okay, so, you're going down there tomorrow. He says you *need* to be there by noon." She headed for the front door. "And, he can't wait."

"Me?"

"Yes, you. Somebody's got to stay here, we can't close the store again."

"We'll call Abby, and you're coming," I said. "Flo, that means we'll have to leave here by ten at the latest."

"Okay, but don't say I didn't warn you." She opened the door to the frigid air and stepped out. I followed behind her.

"Maybe we can take Phillip's SUV, it's four-wheel drive. The roads are icy and we may need that down there," she said.

"I'll call him when I get home and ask but you know how he baby's that Range Rover. I'll let you know. I'll call you first thing in the morning." I gave her a peck.

"Well tell him we won't be gone too long. I don't want to spend any more time at Exotic Aquatics than is absolutely necessary."

TEN

In spite of the fact that New Jersey is only one hundred and fifty miles long, if you're a native you know that the Garden State is divided into three distinct regions, North, Central and South. In the North, when I was growing up, you listened to New York radio. In the South, it was Philly. Who knows what the people in between did, probably just got a lot of static.

In 1980 South Jersey actually voted in a non-binding resolution to secede and form its own state. At ten thirty Tuesday morning that's where we were headed, in Phillip's SUV, doing thirty-five on a mostly two lane road that probably started out as an Indian trail. The speed limit is really fifty but when you get stuck behind a minivan full of kids with the mother talking on her cell phone, you're screwed.

To get away from her we had to stop at the Vincentown diner. After French toast, home fries and bacon we got back in the Rover and sailed across the "border" into the New Jersey Pine Barrens. There is no real border, but you know you're in them when all you can see for miles are pitch pines, scrub oaks and burnt trees;

the trunks charred from recent fires. The Pinelands cover almost a quarter of the state and are dotted with forgotten places like Ong's Hat and Mt. Misery, farm stands, canoe rentals, authentic general stores and people who like to be left alone. And of course, there are the cranberry bogs. There's a good chance the jellied sauce that gets stuck in the can on Thanksgiving got its start from cranberries grown right here.

"Turn left!" Flo shouted out of the blue. "The GPS says turn left here."

"There's a sign for Wharton State Forest, are you sure?"

"No, but the stupid GPS thinks it's around here somewhere. I'm shutting the blasted thing off."

I turned onto a narrow side road. About a mile and a half in we passed a mailbox with a barely legible sign that read "Exotic Aquatics".

"Stop!" Flo yelled. "That was it. Oh well, too late, never mind I guess we might as well keep going."

I said nothing, did a "K" turn and headed back to the black mailbox and turned.

"This isn't a driveway, it's a dirt trail," I said. It was just two tire ruts of sand with some tufts of grass growing here and there. A loud bang startled us both. The ruts had potholes. "This is going to kill the suspension."

"Damn, never mind the suspension, I hope we don't end up with two flat tires out here," Flo said.

"I think we need to be more afraid of Phillip right now than flat tires."

Scrubby woods lined the narrow drive and the branches of the pine trees scraped the side of the Rover. We bumped along for about three quarters of a mile crossing a stream with water the color of black tea. The forest became dense and dark as the pines gave way to cedar trees. I was glad we were making this trip during the day.

Suddenly the trees ended and off to our left was a vast

cranberry bog. It was flooded and frozen this time of year. To our right were acres of naked blueberry shrubs planted row upon row as far as you could see. The lane wound around and ended up at a white trailer. Behind it there were about a dozen greenhouses. The place seemed deserted except for a red pickup truck and a bright yellow Hummer parked next to the trailer. Looked like the trailer was the office. Above the door was a green sign with black lettering "EXOTIC AQUATICS".

"Houston, we've reached the lunar base camp," Florilla moaned.

"Where should we park?" I asked Flo. She just waved her finger in a circle pointing towards the back of the trailer. I noticed the tire marks that led around the trailer and followed them. We parked in the back next to a grove of twisted pitch pines.

"Now remember, don't get too close to him," Flo warned me, "And you do all the talking."

"How can I do all the talking? I don't know anything about exotic aquatics. I won't know what to ask." I switched off the ignition.

"Well, I don't either."

"Okay, look, we'll tell Blaine we need aphrodisiacs for Scorpio Moon, and that Duncan told us we should talk to him about Venus Fly Traps. We'll see where it goes from there." I got out of the car.

Flo didn't move. I sighed and walked around to her side and opened the door. "Get out." Flo put one leg out of the car and looked up at me.

"So help me, if he tries anything he's carnivorous plant food."

"Just come on. Let's get this over with." I turned and started off toward the trailer.

We walked around to the front and opened the trailer door. No one was home. It was your standard trailer business office. A desk with a late model laptop, a white board on the wall with what looked like a production schedule of some sort. Several topographic maps with red circles marking various spots were laid out on a drafting table. A Doctor of Philosophy diploma from Rutgers was hanging on the wall behind the desk. Sitting prominently on the desk was a huge red mug with the words, "*I thought I was wrong once, but I was mistaken.*"

The door flew open behind us and Blaine Winship burst in swearing under his breath. He was accompanied by a very large German shepherd. Blaine's hair was still in a ponytail but today he was wearing a plaid flannel shirt and well-worn jeans with muddy hikers. He stopped short when he saw us and his mood changed instantly.

"Two hot women on a cold January day, what more could I ask for?" His arms opened in welcome. The dog went right up to Flo and started sniffing her crotch. "I have to admit, Flo, I was hoping our paths would cross again soon. But I am surprised you'd trek all the way down here."

Flo shooed away the dog and Blaine opened the door. "Out, Pyxie," he said.

"Pyxie?" Flo mouthed to me.

"Doctor Winship, thanks for seeing us," I said quickly.

"Blaine. Please. Call me Blaine."

"Okay. Blaine, when we met with Duncan McPherson he said that we should talk to you if we wanted to get some information about more unusual aphrodisiacs."

"He did, did he?" A grin crept across Blaine's face then quickly disappeared. "Poor Duncan. It's awful, such a waste. The man was brilliant." He was quiet for a second then continued, "Did you hear how he died?" He went over to the drafting table and started rolling up the maps and putting them in cardboard tubes.

"Yes, we heard," I said.

"Passionflower. Now that's an aphrodisiac," Blaine smiled again. He picked up the tubes and placed them in a metal cabinet and closed the door.

"Actually it's not," Flo said.

TIFFANY BLUES

"Not what?"

"An aphrodisiac. Never mind. Duncan told us about your Venus Fly Traps."

"Venus Fly Traps? Well, I wouldn't go to bed with one. Except for the name, and their obvious resemblance to certain parts of the female anatomy, they're useless as aphrodisiacs. But I've got a few other things I could show you." He moved closer to Flo, "How 'bout we start with Nepenthes and see how far we get. I've got nine greenhouses full."

"Nine?" I asked. Nine freaking greenhouses of carnivorous plants. Florilla would have been in her glory if it hadn't been for our host.

We followed him out and around the trailer, crossed the gravel lot and trudged through the sugar sand to the first greenhouse. Blaine held the door open for us. "You might want to remove a few layers, it's pretty hot in here," he said over his shoulder as he walked ahead of us.

Flo winced. I choked back a laugh and looked around. We were in a jungle of hanging male reproductive organs. I mean the *whole* package.

"Holy tamoly, what are these?" Flo asked.

"You've never seen these before?" Blaine was clearly amused. "Tropical pitcher plants... Nepenthes."

Professor Winship launched into a detailed explanation. "The vines scramble all over the greenhouse. As they develop, the tip of the tendril swells and the tubular pitcher forms, increasing in length and girth as it grows." Blaine paused a second to see if we got his obvious metaphor.

"When it's mature, the so-called "lid" pops open and the peristome curls back. Insects and other small prey like slugs and even frogs are lured to the pitchers by their aromas, their colors and... their secretions. When an insect lands on the lip it falls into the pitcher where it is trapped. It dies by drowning and soon decays. The dead bugs are a source of nutrients. Look at the pitchers at the bottom of the vine." Blaine reached over to fondle one of the bottom plants, obviously enjoying himself. "These are the largest with dark purple veins or flushed with red. Those at the top are slimmer and more funnel shaped."

"Do they come with batteries?" I asked.

Flo smacked me on the arm and said, "Alright...So, is this all ya got?"

Blaine raised his eyebrows, "What else do you need?"

"Well maybe a little yin to go with that yang," Flo said through gritted teeth.

"Follow me, the Dionaea are next. Like I told you, the Venus Fly Trap isn't a medicinal aphrodisiac, but she is the dominatrix of carnivorous plant world." Blaine silently led us to the third greenhouse.

Turns out the Venus Fly Trap lures the same kind of prey as the Nepenthes only Venus plays with hers before she kills. She gives them two shots. Lets them go the first time but if they come back for more, SLAM! Those lips snap closed and they're goners. Blaine had somehow bred them so the ones we were looking at had enormous lips.

"Now I know why Duncan wanted us to see these things. He was raving about them. Did you ever grow any for him?" Flo asked.

"No, it wasn't Venus Fly Traps he wanted." With that Blaine walked out the door to the next greenhouse.

We made our way through the Sundews, Butterworts, and Fibrous, Swollen and Horned Bladderworts. Eight greenhouses later we were horny as hell but still had no idea why Duncan left the carnivorous plant clue.

As we opened the exit door of the eighth greenhouse, Flo and I let out a single scream. Three wild, snarling German shepherds lunged for our throats. It took a second to realize that they were fenced in.

Blaine yelled, "Down!" and the dogs dropped to the ground. "Sorry I forgot to warn you," Blaine apologized, "They're my watch dogs, on duty after hours."

"Geezus! They scared me to death." I heaved a sigh of

relief.

"Why do you need guard dogs? You have a lot of people trying to steal Butterworts?" Flo asked.

"You can't be too careful. Some of these plants are worth quite a bit of money," Blaine answered seriously.

It occurred to me that I hadn't seen anyone else on the property. No workers, no one. "Does anyone else work here besides the dogs?" I asked.

"Staff starts at five and they leave at noon, that way they're not full time and I don't have to give them any benefits," Dr. Slimemold responded.

The sun was starting to set. "Flo it's getting dark. Maybe we should get going," I said.

"There's just one more greenhouse," Flo said heading for it. I noticed the door was chained and locked.

"Clara's right. I'm afraid it's getting late, we'll have to end here," Blaine said.

"But what's in there?" Flo asked.

"Nothing, it's under renovation," Blaine started to walk back towards the trailer.

Flo ignored him and was straining to get a look inside the greenhouse. I could see the wheels turning in her head and grabbed her arm, "Come on, let's just go."

We had to run to catch up with Blaine.

"Are you growing any Ladyslippers?" Flo asked out of breath.

"I've got a few orchids in the back greenhouse." He picked up his pace.

"I didn't know orchids were carnivorous," I blurted.

Blaine and Flo both stopped and looked at me like I just crawled out from under a rock.

"They're not," he shook his head. "Look, sorry, I'm out of time girls." He put his arm around Flo's shoulders. "So, is AstroBotanics interested in doing business today?" He nodded toward the trailer door.

Flo cringed.

"One of those Nepenthes might be fun to have," I

teased. Flo violently shook her head "no" and wriggled away from Blaine.

"We're going to have to think about all this. We'll be in touch. Bye." Flo zipped up her red parka, flung the hood over her head and started walking towards the car.

I turned to Blaine, "Thanks a lot Blaine, thanks for the tour. It was great of you to spend the time with us."

"I'd like to spend more time with you. Let me know if I can be of service," he winked.

"Sure thing," I answered and ran after Flo. As I rounded the trailer I noticed the red truck was gone.

Flo was already in the car when I got there. I climbed in and started it up.

"He didn't show us one pitcher plant," she complained.

"The red truck is gone," I said a little freaked out.

"Not one pitcher plant that grows in New Jersey!"

"I thought all his help left at noon. Who took the truck?"

"The Sarracenias"

"The Sarracenias? What are you talking about? Aren't you even a little curious?"

"Yes I'm curious! We saw three greenhouses of tropical pitcher plants and there were none that grow here in the Pinelands. Sarracenias. He didn't have any of them."

"Well they're not exactly "Exotic Aquatics" if they're from New Jersey, are they?"

"He had Sundews and Bladderworts. They all grow here. This is weird. And he said that last greenhouse was under renovation but then he said he had some orchids in there. Ladyslipper orchids. We need to know what's in that last greenhouse."

"Not tonight we don't. I've got a date with Q. It's four-thirty. How am I supposed to get ready? He'll be waiting for me when we get back."

"I just want to look in that last greenhouse and see what's in there. You go back in and distract Blaine and I'll

TIFFANY BLUES

go look. It'll take like ten minutes."

"Are you nuts? You won't be able to see anything. Besides, how am I going to distract Blaine? He came onto me you know. I'm not going back in there!"

"Tell him you lost your engagement ring while we were going through the greenhouses and get him to help you look for it. That'll buy me some time."

"What engagement ring? I don't have an engagement ring."

"Well I don't have one either."

"Well, you could have one. Oscar would give you one in a heartbeat. You could have a Tiffany's Legacy ring."

"They were nice weren't they?"

"Yeah, I just love that antique look, all the small stones surrounding the big one."

"Maybe a nice two carat center stone with…wait a sec, we're wasting time here. I need you to go distract Blaine. Just make something up." With that Flo jumped out of the car and ran off.

"Flo! The dogs!" I flung open the door and waived my arms but she was already sneaking past the first greenhouse. I left the SUV running and trudged back to the trailer. Blaine was just coming out the door.

"Almost forgot, do you have a price list?" I heard myself call out. He turned around, smiled and waited for me to come to him.

"Sure, inside, come on in." He held the trailer door open for me. Flo had better find something in that greenhouse.

Blaine shuffled papers around on his desk. One flew off and landed at my feet. I bent down to pick it up and saw that it was an invoice to someone in Dubai, for something called a *Cattleya senescence var. Necrophile* for fifty-eight thousand dollars.

"Thank you, I'll take that." Blaine held out his hand and placed the invoice back on the desk. "This is what you asked for." He took my left hand and pressed the price list into it. "We can probably do something for you on this, let's say 15% off." He didn't let go of my hand.

I was trying to think of something to say when a dog started barking. Pyxie! Then more dogs barking frantically. Damn! Flo was going to be dog meat! Blaine dropped my hand and went to the door.

"Must be a deer. Let me walk you to the car and I'll go check on the dogs." He held his breath, listening intently.

"That's OK, you go ahead. Thanks."

"No, I insist. It's on the way."

Blaine took my arm and pushed me out the door. He held onto me as we walked around to the back lot in silence. The SUV was empty. He noticed it immediately and his grip on my arm tightened. "Where's Florilla?" he asked.

"I don't know. She was waiting for me in the car," I lied.

Blaine started walking in the direction of the barking dogs dragging me with him.

"Flo!" I shrieked. "Where are you?"

A bright flood light popped on as we rounded the first greenhouse. Blaine's eyes glowed an eery yellow and his mouth was set into a hard line. The dogs' barking became more frenzied. I tried to twist away from him but he gripped tighter and we began a slow jog towards the far greenhouse. My heart was pounding. If the dogs hadn't eaten her I would kill her myself. What the hell was I doing here in Pineyland anyway? What would Blaine do with us if he caught her in the greenhouse?

"Hey guys. Where you going?" Flo's voice came from behind us back by the first greenhouse. Blaine stopped in his tracks and spun me around. I could make out the outlines of Flo and Pyxie coming towards us. Blaine finally released his hold on my arm.

"WHERE DID YOU GO?" I yelled. I was relieved to see her but the desire to strangle her was overwhelming. In the twilight the fog from her heavy breathing created a halo around her head.

"I had to pee real bad okay? I went into the grove of trees next to the parking lot."

"In this cold? Sorry I missed that," Blaine said, then added "You could have used the bathroom in the trailer you know." He motioned to Pyxie to 'come.' She obeyed.

"I wouldn't have made it that far."

Blaine kept looking back over his shoulder toward the far greenhouse. The dogs were beginning to calm down.

"You girls better get going, it's getting pretty dark." He escorted us back to the SUV and held the door open for Flo. "Be careful going home and don't let the Jersey Devil get you." He winked, slammed the door and took off at a trot around the greenhouses.

I just glared at Flo, my hands gripped the steering wheel and my arms were trembling.

"What?" Flo asked me, her breathing normal again.

"What do you mean, what? You almost got us killed. You should have seen Blaine. He heard those dogs and he went all psycho on me. Grabbed my arm and wouldn't let go. I can't stop shaking. What!"

"Did he hurt you?" Flo asked with genuine concern.

"My arm's sore, that's all. I was more pissed at you and scared that you were dog meat. Was it worth it? Did you see anything in there?"

"I didn't get much of a look before Pyxie and her friends noticed me but that last greenhouse is not under renovation. I had to climb up on some barrel kind of thing to look in. It was packed with pitcher plants and they looked like Sarracenias to me, least what I could see through the tiny screen. All the ones in bloom had little mesh socks over the flowers, like condoms, to make sure the pollen doesn't get in the wrong flowers. He's hybridizing them."

"Why would he keep plants locked up and guarded by four vicious dogs?" I thought for a minute. "Unless they're the fifty-eight thousand dollar Cattleya senesences."

"What are you talking about?"

"I saw an invoice in the office to someone in Dubai for a single plant for fifty-eight thousand dollars, a Cattleya senescense var dot necrophile whatever that is."

"Cattleya is an orchid, but *necrophile*? Like Necrophilia? Like sex with dead people? He's sick!"

"Ewwwww," we said in unison.

"I know for sure the plants in the last greenhouse aren't cattleyas. What I saw were definitely not orchids."

"Well something weird is going on and that red truck disappeared. Someone else was definitely here." I blew out a deep breath and maneuvered out of the parking lot.

"I'll try to find some time to do more research on Sarracenias tomorrow. Right now let's get out of here. I'm starving. Can we stop and get something to eat?"

"No. I have a date, remember?"

"What time is it anyway?" Flo asked pulling her phone out of her pocket. "Ooh, I've got a message. It never rang. Did you hear it ring?"

"The cell service down here sucks. I should probably check mine too. Can you get my purse? It's on the floor in the back." Flo handed me my phone as I started to make my way down the long, rutted lane.

She finished listening to her message and closed her phone. "It was Oz. They're having a memorial service for Duncan on Thursday at the Gardens. He wants me to come. Do you want to go?"

"Sure." I was trying to drive and call my voicemail at the same time. I put the phone on speaker. We heard "You have three new messages." The first message was from Melissa, my sister-in-law from hell.

"Hi Claire, haven't seen you in a while. Chase told us about your brunch at Chez Pareo. How come we didn't get an invitation? Christopher and I want to celebrate your birthday too you know. I'm going to make my famous lasagna just for you on Friday. Dinner's at seven and don't say you can't come."

"A dilemma." I said. "Hate Melissa. Love her lasagna."

TIFFANY BLUES

Second message. *"Hi Clara, it's Quentin. Please call me back as soon as you hear this. Thanks."*

I saved it.

Third message. *"Hi, it's Quentin again. Guess you haven't gotten your messages yet. You aren't going to believe this but I have to postpone our dinner. Sorry. Something came up and I have to be out of town for a couple of days. I should be back by the end of the week. Can we do dinner on Friday? I'll call ya."*

"Yeah, sure you will," I deleted it. "Guess its lasagna."

"How very Leo of him," Flo said.

"Well, it could be true."

"Idiot," Flo said in disgust.

"I need a bacon cheeseburger and french fries."

"Well, if we can't put Mr. Adams on a spit and bar-b-Q him, might as well have a burger."

I hit the gas. It was only ten more miles back to the Vincentown Diner.

ELEVEN

"Hey Sweetie, are you awake?" Flo whispered loudly from the limo seat across from me.

"I am now," I sighed opening one eye. "What?"

"It usually takes about two hours to get to Oz's, right?"

I closed my eye. "Yeah, so?"

"Well, we've already been on the road for over an hour and we're still on I-78 and there's tons of traffic. It'll take another two hours to get to the Gardens. We're going to be late for the memorial service."

"Once we get past the Parkway exit things will open up. Don't worry about it. We can't do anything about it now anyway."

"Talk to me. I can't stop thinking about everything. I'm wide awake. Why do you think someone would want to kill Duncan?"

I opened the other eye and looked at Flo again. She was picking away at her cuticles and chewing the inside of her cheek. "I don't know Sweetie, maybe it was just an accident."

"How do you accidentally get strangled?"

"I mean, maybe he was just in the wrong place at the

wrong time. Maybe he walked in on someone trying to steal the passionflower for their collection. That thing was growing up the wall and across the ceiling and you know how whacked you plant people can get about a specimen like that. Like Dr. Winship and his phallus collection." I closed both eyes again and leaned my head back.

"Speaking of dicks. I never got to tell you yesterday, since we were never in The Diner at the same time. The Sarracenia stuff. Turns out that *Sarracenia purpurea* a.k.a. pitcher plant, was used by Native Americans in an infusion for sore throats, blood clotting and as a febrifuge. And…wait for it…a treatment for smallpox."

I sat upright and opened both eyes this time. She was waving her finger at me like a schoolteacher.

"What the hell is a febrifuge?" I asked.

"I don't know. I think it's a fever reducer or something. But did you hear what I said? Smallpox!"

"What's that got to do with anything?"

"Maybe they were working on a vaccine for smallpox."

"There already is a vaccine for smallpox. That doesn't make any sense and it doesn't explain the cryptogram in the book."

"No, I guess it doesn't." Flo stared out the window. "We're just getting on the Turnpike. This traffic is crazy."

"Does Oscar have any new theories?"

"No, but then he hadn't seen Duncan in months, and he doesn't know any details about what Duncan's really been working on or doing besides his book. Mostly, Oscar's just been emailing to keep in touch."

The neon stardust on the ceiling changed from white to green.

"Phillip really went all out getting us this limo so we didn't have to take the train again. I thought he was just getting us a Town Car," Flo said.

"Me too. I don't think he realized they were giving us a stretch but hey, I'm not complaining."

"You sure you don't want to marry Phillip?"

"Phillip's never getting married."

"You didn't answer the question. Say he got struck by lightning and was desperate to settle down. Would you marry him?"

"It's eight o'clock in the morning, way too early to be having this, conversation. What I need is some tea. With caffeine."

"Maybe we can get the driver to stop at Dunkin' Donuts. There's a Dunkin' Donuts in the Village. Besides, my stomach is growling, I could use a muffin or something."

"We can't ask him to stop, we don't have time. We still have to pick up Oscar."

"Maybe they'll have food at the funeral."

"Doubt it and it's not a funeral," I reminded her. "It's a memorial service. No body, remember? There might be some kind of reception afterwards." I opened my eyes again. "Here, look, there's a dish of Starbursts." I said holding out a crystal dish with a variety of fruit flavored candy.

"If it's not chocolate I don't want to waste the calories. We should have brought the Raisinets."

The limo driver, craned his neck around to look in our direction. "I'm gonna take the Holland. That okay?"

"Sure, not a problem," I answered.

"And where do you think Duncan is now anyway? Who do you think is going to claim his body when the autopsy's done?" Flo shivered.

"Well he's probably in the morgue." I caught a glimpse of the green "Holland Tunnel/ New York City" exit sign. "But you know, that's a good question. I wonder if he has any family here or maybe someone's coming from Scotland to get him."

"Maybe Oz knows." Flo was emptying the contents of her purse into her lap. "Sweetie, did you bring tissues? I forgot tissues."

"Of course I have tissues. I always have tissues. My

mother made me bring tissues everywhere. If I don't have tissues, I'm going to hell."

"My mother never had tissues. She was never much for crying in public."

"What if she had to blow her nose?"

"Hankies."

"Hankies?"

"She had big lacy hankies from my grandmother. She thought tissues were criminal, cutting down trees for tissue paper. She was right, one of the original tree huggers. I've told you how she almost got arrested once when she was in a protest with Ralph Nader, right? That was back when he was an environmentalist, *not* a politician."

"Well you know Delores thought she was Jackie Kennedy. The hat, the gloves, the purse and tissues. She actually told me once that Jackie would hide tissues in her underwear under her ball gowns when she couldn't carry a purse. I know she made that up but she never let me leave home without tissues."

A folded white paper fell off Flo's lap and onto the floor between us. I picked it up and looked at it.

"What's this?" I held the paper out to Flo.

"What?"

"This. The page from Duncan's book."

"It's not the page, it's a copy of the page," she answered.

"And you brought it with you because?"

"Cause you never know who you'll run into at a funeral who might know what it means."

"Memorial service. We're not going to just run into somebody."

"Okay. Well then we'll just go looking for them," Flo answered.

The limo stopped in front of 304 Waverly Street. Oscar lived in a converted Vanderbilt, a third floor walk up in the Village. Cookie and Charles Stern, Oscar's Westport, Connecticut socialite mother and retired financier father, were mortified when their grown son chose to live in such squalor; a building with no elevator. I was out of breath by the end of the second set of stairs.

"This stair stuff is great exercise. Doesn't the night school have a step aerobics class? We should take step aerobics." Flo said gasping for breath.

"These girls don't do step aerobics," I patted my chest. "Neither do these shoes."

We were both dressed in almost matching black coats and pantsuits and high heeled boots we purchased for a steal at The Outlet.

"Finally," Flo said putting the key in the door to Oscar's apartment. She held open the door and let me step in first. "Oscar darling, your ravishing ladies in mourning await you," she yelled out.

Apartment 3C was a tiny one bedroom. Old New York with nine foot high windows, carved molding, parquet floors, and an ancient bathroom with a permanent blue-green stain in the sink and a stopper on a chain. As soon as we stepped in, Flo and I checked ourselves out in the floor to ceiling mirrors which ran the length of the living room. Oscar would be mortified if he knew that I knew that the three inch crack in the second panel was from the time he accidentally knocked over the video camera in a moment of blind passion. I sank into the butter soft chocolate brown leather sofa. Flo sat on the arm of the matching club chair.

Oscar came out of the bedroom dressed in a dark suit, fiddling with his tie. He hugged Flo, who reached up to help him with the tie, and smiled at me. "You both look delicious. Too bad we're going to a funeral. I'm sure Duncan would approve."

"It's a memorial service, not a funeral," Flo corrected him.

"Whatever." He patted his jacket pocket. "I just have to find my keys and I'm ready to go."

"Maybe you left them in the bedroom," Flo picked up

the remote and clicked on the television.

"No, I left them right here somewhere." Oscar rummaged around the built in bookcase. "Damn, not here." Oscar swore and closed the glass doors.

"Maybe they're on your desk. High winds, only thirty-four degrees. Gonna be in the teens tonight. Well at least it's sunny." Flo clicked off the Weather Channel and we followed him into the dining nook-turned office.

The nook was overwhelmed by an early nineteenth century carved oak desk Oscar had inherited from his grandfather. Lion heads guarded the corners and it stood on clawed balled feet. He tipped four big guys a hundred bucks apiece to get it up the stairs. Imagine his surprise when he discovered a secret compartment full of old love letters written to his grandfather by a woman who wasn't his grandmother.

"Poor Duncan," I sighed as Oscar shuffled the piles of papers and books on the massive desk. "Oscar, do you know if Duncan had any family? Will any of them be at the service today?"

"I don't know about today, but he was married a long time ago. She divorced him when he started spending a lot of time doing a medicine woman...I mean research, in Costa Rica."

"Really? A medicine woman?" I had a hard time imagining it.

"A young medicine woman or an old one?" Flo asked.

"She was half his age. In Duncan's words, 'She was young, brilliant and she charmed the pants off of me.'" Oscar's dimples were showing. "Got'em!" he said holding up his keys.

"Was he still seeing her?" I asked.

"No, that ended years ago. He's been a bachelor ever since." Oscar grabbed his coat out of the closet and Flo went over and helped him with the second arm.

Flo was fascinated, "Did he ever have any children?"

"He's got two grown sons from his marriage but they

were estranged. I doubt they'd come."

"That's so sad. Well, you count as family," Flo said patting the perfect knot in Oscar's tie. "We better get going, the limo's waiting."

***

Apparently Duncan knew a lot of people. The rotunda of the Metropolitan Garden's Hall of Botanists was packed. What a shame none of them were family. Tildy, the coat-check lady, was there and so was the Mayor. I scanned the crowd and noticed an unusual number of security people with little earphones talking into their jacket sleeves. Seemed like a lot more security than the Mayor needed. Rows of gun metal gray folding chairs were set in two semi-circles around an octagonal glass case filled with orchids. A small podium was off to the right side.

"There's that woman, Janice Pearl," Flo nudged me.

"Who? Where?" I craned my neck looking all around the room.

"Janice Pearl. Over there," she pointed. "She's in the black suit with the triple strand of pearls. Right there on the end of the front row."

"Over where? I can't see where you're pointing."

"She looks pretty sad. I mean unhappy."

"Okay, I see her now. She looks like she's been crying doesn't she?"

"And like she hasn't slept in days," Flo answered.

"I don't see Blaine anywhere. Wonder if he's coming."

"Hope not".

"Wonder if anyone from Zylanica is here?" I said thinking that Q might materialize.

"Hope not."

Oscar pulled on Flo's sleeve, "Let's get some seats in the back."

As we moved around the rotunda I spotted Duncan's research assistant, Samantha, looking ultra skinny in a long black skirt and turtleneck sweater coming in through the front door. A familiar young man was next to her holding her hand.

"Hey, who's the guy with Ms. Rousseau? Did we meet him? He looks familiar."

"Yes, at Duncan's lecture, remember? Another research assistant, like Samantha. I think Blaine said he was from Sweden or someplace like that."

"They look kind of cute together though, don't they? They're holding hands. Think she was burning the candle at both ends?"

Flo shrugged and turned to Oscar, "That's Samantha Rousseau," she whispered. Oscar just nodded and pulled her into the seat next to him.

I sat down next to them just as the service began. The Director of the Gardens was at the podium.

"Good morning Ladies and Gentlemen. It is with a heavy heart that I welcome you today. We are here not to dwell on the manner in which he left us but to commemorate Dr. Duncan Gavin McPherson's extraordinary life. He hated pomp and circumstance therefore we will be conducting a simple ceremony as he would have wanted. We're honored that the Mayor is with us today. At this time, I ask the Mayor to begin the service."

After the Mayor, a long list of dignitaries took turns outdoing one another with praise for Duncan's life. I glanced sideways at Flo and Oscar. They were holding hands. Sweet Oscar, he looked so sad. I hadn't really thought about how much he would probably miss his old friend. I knew Flo was thinking about her mom's funeral. It was five years ago already, but since then any funeral-like situation made her relive what she went through with her mom's cancer.

I felt a little stab of pain in my solar plexus. Guilt? Fear? Maybe a little of both. I'd call Delores tonight. I would hate to die in a faraway place without anybody around who really cared. Of course Flo would come. Spencer would send a text message. No, he'd be there too. I imagined him and Flo and Oscar flinging my ashes from the top deck of QE10 into the deep blue waters of the Aegean Sea. How dare she outlive me?

Flo poked me back to life. Dr. Pearl was out of her seat, carefully making her way to the podium. She was the last speaker. Her face was expressionless but I noticed her hands were shaking. She was wearing her half-glasses and read from a prepared statement in a monotone without looking up.

"Dr. McPherson was a brilliant scientist and remarkable teacher," she began. "His dedication to uncovering the mysteries of the past have opened the doors to future medical advances. It is this dedication that forged a new cooperative spirit among botanists, pharmacologists and medical professionals. He was determined to bring to light forgotten knowledge which will benefit ours and all future generations. He will be missed." Her voice was shaking. She took her glasses off and left quickly through double doors to her left.

"Boy that was awfully short. She never looked up, not once. Never made eye contact with anyone," I whispered to Flo.

"Her hands shook the entire time. Did you see that?" Flo whispered back.

I started to answer but the same double doors burst open and a solitary bagpiper in full regalia slowly marched into the rotunda. Samantha stood up holding a stunning pink Ladyslipper orchid in full bloom and carried it to the glass case in the center of the rotunda. I wondered if it was the orchid from Duncan's office. The Director unlocked the door of the case as the sound of "Amazing Grace" bagpipe-style filled the room. Samantha was sobbing as she gently placed the orchid inside the case in a prominent empty spot. Okay, so the tissues came in handy.

When the bagpipes ended, the young Swedish guy

jumped up and put his arm around Samantha's waist. She leaned her head on his shoulder as he helped her back to her seat. The Director of the Gardens thanked everyone for coming and closed the service by inviting us to the Koch Education Building next door for refreshments.

We all stood up. Flo was still wiping her eyes. "That's a beautiful paphiopedalum," she said gazing at the orchid case. Oscar put his arm around her.

"Yes it is. Interesting that she was the one to put it in the case," I replied.

"She was sobbing. She must have really loved him."

We looked at each other and said in one voice, "Ladyslipper!"

"Duncan called her Slip!" Florilla said fumbling through her purse. "Where's the paper?" We have to go talk to her."

Oscar took Flo's elbow and pulled her aside. "Can't you just leave this alone? Let's just go have a martini. I could use a drink. Besides, the limo's waiting and Phillip's paying, remember?" He grabbed his coat from the back of the chair.

"Oh Oz, this'll only take five minutes," Flo said, then to me, "She's leaving we have to catch up to her."

Oscar shook his head. "Last time you told me that, it was two hours before we got to the top of the Empire State Building."

"Yeah, but it only took five minutes to get into the building. Besides, wasn't it worth the wait? You never would have done that on your own. This won't take long."

Oscar gave in, "You've got ten minutes Red. I'll be in the Education Center." He pecked her on the cheek and walked past us and out the door.

Samantha had a head start for the ladies room. When we came in she was bent over a sink holding a wet paper towel over her eyes and taking deep breaths trying to calm down.

"It's freezing in here. I'm putting my coat back on," Flo said.

"It's freaking January, it's thirty-four degrees and there's no heat in here?" I put my coat on too.

"I've gotta pee but I'm not sitting on that toilet." Flo put on her gloves.

Samantha was trying to pull herself together and threw the crumpled paper towel into the trashcan. Her red swollen eyes were still brimming. "Funerals are a bitch, don't ya think?" she asked.

"Yeah, they are. We're so sorry about Dr. McPherson." Samantha obviously didn't recognize us.

"Do I know you?" she asked shivering.

"You poor thing. C, give her your coat," Flo said

I looked at Flo. What was wrong with her coat? I took mine off and wrapped it around Samantha's shoulders.

"Oh, Samantha, you don't remember us. I'm Florilla Munrow and this is Clara Martini. We met you last week in Duncan's office. After the lecture on his new book. He gave us the aphrodisiac tour," Flo reminded her.

"Oh yeah, that's right. I remember, sorry. Dr. McPherson told me that you are friends of an old friend of his."

"Yes, that's Dr. Stern," Flo said.

"Her boyfriend," I added.

Flo glared at me and continued, "They met at Cambridge. He's waiting for us at the Education Center."

"Dr. McPherson told me about him. Please, call me Sammy. Everyone else does."

Flo touched Sammy's arm. "I guess you and Duncan were close?"

Tears ran down her cheeks and she just nodded.

"Tissues, C! Tissues!" Flo mouthed urgently pointing to my purse. I dug out the two remaining tissues and handed them to Sammy. She blew them away.

"That was a beautiful Ladyslipper you put in the case," I said, drifting into a stall and yanking off a yard of toilet paper. Sammy buried her face in it. I looked up and shrugged at Flo. This was going to take longer than ten minutes.

"Didn't it look like the Mayor's toupee was on backwards?" Flo blurted out. That worked. Sammy snorted, crying and laughing at the same time.

"Yeah, wasn't it awful? And I didn't think he'd ever shut up." She was just laughing now. I noticed even though they were swollen, her wide set green eyes lit up when she laughed and her skin was flawless, dewy in fact. A wood sprite. That's what she reminded me of. I could see why Duncan was so taken with her.

"I know this is probably a bad time," I said and nodded to Flo.

"But there's something we need to show you," Flo added. Sammy hiccupped and looked at us expectantly.

Flo unfolded the paper and held it up so she could see Duncan's scribble. "He called you Slip didn't he?"

The soggy toilet paper hit the floor along with my coat and she grabbed the paper with both hands. "Where'd you get this?"

TWELVE

The bathroom door squeaked open behind me and Flo's eyes widened. Sammy quickly folded the page in half.

"Here, I think you dropped this," she said handing it to Flo.

I bent down to retrieve my coat. The sleeves were covered with little white specks of God knows what. Now I'd have to leave it at the Bright N' White tomorrow morning before yoga class. I hate the way dry cleaning smells when you get your clothes back. It's got to be toxic. I turned to shake off the gunk and almost took out Janice Pearl. Her face was all puffy and her eyes and nose were red. She didn't say a word, just headed for the closest stall.

Sammy leaned over the sink, turned on both taps full blast and let the water run. She pointed to the paper, put her finger to her lips and shook her head "no".

Flo took off her gloves and stuffed them and the paper into her coat pocket. She caught her reflection in the mirror, made a face and dug a giant purple hairpick out of her purse. She started attacking her spikes but shook her head and gave up.

"It's amazing how crowded the rotunda was." Flo

leaned in close to the mirror. "Sweetie, did you bring any lip gloss? I don't have mine with me."

I dug in my bag and came out with two choices. "You want Hungry Honey or Ravin Raspberrie?"

"Does it taste like raspberries?"

"Geez-o-Pete, it's just a color."

"Give me the Honey." Flo took the honey colored stick out of my hand. "Duncan really knew a lot of people," she said as she painted her lips. I followed suit with the Raspberrie.

"Tons," Sammy said.

"Do you know Dr. Winship? I thought he'd be here." Flo slipped my lip gloss into her pocket.

The toilet flushed and the stall door opened.

"I don't know where he was." Sammy shut off the water, got a paper towel and pretended to dry her hands. She looked at Dr. Pearl. "Do you?"

"Excuse me?" Dr. Pearl focused her attention on the soap dispenser.

"Where was Dr. Winship today? He wasn't at the service," Sammy asked her.

"Dr. Winship? I'm sure I don't know any Dr. Winship." Dr. Pearl dried her hands and checked herself in the mirror. She took a deep breath and fluffed her hair then turned to us. "Ms. Rousseau, I need to have a word with you. Outside." The ice queen nodded towards the door and walked out.

Sammy stared at the bathroom door and bit her lip. "Can you meet me at the education center," she begged. "Please?"

"Sure, okay," Flo said to the back of Sammy's head going out the door.

"Now what's up with that?" I asked unzipping my pants and racing into the nearest stall.

"Dr. Pearl doesn't know Blaine? I don't think so," Flo said, already in the stall next to me.

"Don't sit down you'll freeze to the seat," I said.

"Too late. Call 911. Damn, there's no paper here. C, can you give me some paper?"

"Maybe." I unraveled a bunch of toilet paper and held it out to her under the stall wall.

"Thanks. What time is it?"

I checked the clock on my phone. "Oh shit, we've been in here for twenty minutes. Dr. Stern ain't gonna be happy."

Flo flushed. "Try cheezed off with crap on the side."

***

The education center lobby was packed with people but we found Oscar sulking alone at a table in the back of the room. His coffee cup was empty and he was drumming his fingers on the table.

"Sorry Oz, things got very complicated in the ladies room." Flo sat down next to him. Oscar just stood up and didn't say a word.

We spotted Sammy in the doorway searching the room and I waved. Flo tugged on Oscar's sleeve. "I know you want to go home but can you give us just five more minutes?"

He groaned.

"Pleeeeease?" Flo implored.

He sat back down.

We met Sammy in the hallway and followed her into an empty classroom.

"Sammy, we can't stay very long, we have a limo waiting," I said.

"And an unhappy Dr. Stern," Flo added.

"Very. Do you know if the police figured out anything yet?" I asked.

"I haven't heard anything, but I wouldn't be the first to know either. I'm one of the mushrooms. Can I see that paper again?" she asked.

Flo fished it out of her pocket and handed it to her.

"Where did this come from?"

TIFFANY BLUES

"It's a page from the *New World Apothecary* that Duncan gave Flo last week," I explained.

"Here's the thing," Flo waved her hands impatiently. "All we know is two people are dead, within four days of each other, making the Metropolitan Botanical Gardens the crime capital of New York City and for some reason Duncan gave me a book with all these cryptic... whatever this is. NYPD even trekked all the way to New Jersey to take the book from me," Flo said.

"You gave it to the police?" Sammy asked.

"No, they took a photocopy of the same page. We didn't have much choice," I answered.

"So they think this has something to do with Dun...Dr. McPherson's murder?" Sammy asked focused on the paper in her hand.

"Who knows?" Flo said. "But Duncan must have given this to me for a reason. Sammy, do you have any idea what it means?"

"Let me think." She sat down on a table and stared at the paper. "April 11, 1940. That's like a million years ago. No clue."

"Could it be somebody's birthday?" I asked sitting down next to her.

"I guess it could be but no one I know," Sammy said.

"So it's not Duncan's birthday?" I asked.

"No. I think he was born after that and I know his birthday's in November."

"Could it have anything to do with the girl that drowned? What was her name?"

"Tracy. I have no idea."

"What about this number then? 1200P? Is it a code for something? A pin number?" Flo asked.

"Not that I know of. It could be anything. I really don't know." Sammy was becoming frustrated.

"Duncan wrote 'Slip' on here, so he must have meant it for you. He must have thought you'd understand it."

Sammy shrugged her shoulders.

"Did he call anyone else Slip? Maybe Tracy?" I asked.

Sammy looked like she was going to start crying again and she just shook her head. I felt bad asking her all these questions.

"Okay, what about the 'LA'? Anyone with those initials? Anything special about Los Angeles?" Flo sounded like the D.A. on *Law and Order*.

"I don't think Dr. McPherson was working with anyone in L.A. I'm sorry, I just don't know." Tears were welling up in her eyes.

"Speaking of working with....," Flo put her hands together in front of her mouth like she was praying. "Was Blaine Winship working with Duncan too?"

"Yes, Dr. Winship was providing the pitcher plants. Different varieties. I was doing molecular analysis."

Flo interrupted. "Pitcher plants? Not Venus Fly Traps?"

"Venus Fly Traps? No, we were working with pitcher plants. Dr. Winship was growing them for us."

"Tropical or native pitcher plants?"

"Native. Sarracenias."

"I knew it!" Flo pointed her finger at me.

"And Dr. Pearl didn't know about that?" I asked.

"She doesn't want us to talk about him. I don't know why. Dr. Winship was in her office this morning and I saw them arguing about something. I thought he'd be at the service too. How do you know Dr. Winship?" She looked at us both.

"We went to graduate school together. We both were doing research on some of the cypripediums, orchids, in the Pine Barrens," Flo said.

"What's the molecular analysis for?" I asked.

"I'm not supposed to talk about it. It's a special project for a pharmaceutical company."

My heart jumped and Flo and I exchanged glances. "So what happens to the project now?" Flo asked.

"I'm not sure. Dr. Pearl is probably in charge now. She

had always wanted Dr. McPherson's job," Sammy said in a whisper. "And she was in love with him. They had a thing going but Dr. McPherson had wandering eyes. When Dr. Pearl caught him with um... one of the research assistants, she was out for blood."

"Enough to kill him?" I asked.

"I don't know, maybe. All I do know is she hates me too." Sammy looked down at her feet. That was the first time I noticed her black Mary Janes. I wondered what Duncan thought of those galoshes. "She's made it pretty clear that I won't be here much longer," she added.

A janitor pushed a bucket and mop in through the door. Sammy folded the sheet of paper and asked, "Can I keep this?"

"I guess so. I have the book back at our shop," Flo said.

I stood up and opened my wallet. "Here, take our card. If you have an epiphany about this, let us know." I handed her an AstroBotanics card. "We want to help figure this out. He did give us the book."

"*Me.* He gave *me* the book," Flo interjected.

Sammy looked at the card and smiled. "Chocolate Diner?" She raised her eyebrows.

"It's a long story," I answered as we headed down the hall.

Sammy spotted someone and waved, "There's Andrew. He's probably been looking for me."

Andrew met us halfway. "Hey, Sam, where have you been? I was looking all over for you. I was worried. Are you okay?"

Sammy slipped her arm through his. "That's so sweet. I'm fine. Clara, Florilla, I'm sorry I forgot your last names, this is Andrew Gray."

"I'm Munrow, she's Martini," Flo said. We all shook hands.

"They're friends of D...Dr. McPherson and Dr. Winship. They were just keeping me company."

Andrew smiled warmly and put his arm around Sammy's waist and gave her a squeeze. "Thanks. She's... we've, had a tough week here." Sammy nodded in agreement.

"Now I remember," Flo said. "We saw you before Duncan's lecture last week. We were talking with Blaine."

"You have a good memory. I thought you both looked familiar."

"You're from Sweden aren't you?" Flo asked.

"Sweden? Who told you that?" Andrew asked.

"No, he's not Swedish. He's a mutt," Sammy smiled.

"I was born in France. My mother's French and my father's Scottish. I went to University in Copenhagen and worked in Switzerland before coming here," Andrew explained.

Flo spotted Oscar by the main door. "Uh oh, He's pacing. Not good."

I nodded, "We've got to go. Nice to meet you Andrew."

We said our goodbyes and as we walked away I heard Andrew ask, "What did they want?" but I didn't hear the answer. We met Oscar by the door.

"We're outta here. Now." Oscar stepped out and held open the door. I pushed Flo out first in front of me.

"What were you thinking?" Oscar vented. "You were gone forever. We have a limo waiting and Phillip's paying, remember?"

I darted around Flo to get out of the line of fire and smacked right into a large man coming up the steps.

"Oh, I'm sorry," I said looking up. Detective Mooney was staring down at me. He was wearing a grande cafe au lait.

"Ms. Martini...and Ms. Munrow. How nice to see you again." Detective Carlton was smiling at his partner's dilemma.

Flo answered. "Yes, very nice. Our limo's waiting, gotta go." She grabbed Oscar's arm and kept walking down the stairs.

"Sorry about your coat," I said.

"Not a problem, I'm used to wearing my lunch," Mooney answered. I turned to go.

"Just a minute," Carlton stopped me. "I'm glad we ran into you. So far we're coming up blank on this book thing. Do you ladies have anything else you'd like to share with us?"

Flo yelled up "Come on C, we're late!"

I grinned. "Just follow the pitcher plants," I said and took off down the steps.

When I caught up to Flo and Oscar they were bickering like an old married couple. Oscar opened the limo door. "What'd you tell Batman and Robin?" Flo asked.

"I told them to follow the pitcher plants."

"*What?*"

"You heard me. Follow the pitcher plants. I figure they won't have a clue."

Oscar shook his head. "Red, can't you just leave this alone? Let the cops do their jobs and stay out of it. Duncan was murdered. What makes you think whoever killed him won't come after you if you get involved in this?"

"Oz, you're hallucinating. Why would anyone come after us? That's ludicrous."

"Please, just get in the car," Oscar said.

We climbed in. Flo sat next to Oscar slipping her hand into his. I slid into the seat across from them.

Maybe Oscar was right. Maybe we should just leave it alone. We were definitely diving head first into a bee's nest. Two murders in four days. A pharma project Sammy couldn't talk about. Zylanica? So then was Q involved in all this? And what about Blaine? Where was he and why did Janice lie? Follow the pitcher plants. I closed my eyes and put my head back on the seat. It was going to be a long ride back to Dolly's Ferry.

THIRTEEN

"So you think Sammy was doing Duncan and Andrew at the same time?" Flo's head was between her legs in the Downward Dog.

"We are breathing; we are not talking," our very focused yogi scolded.

I was twisted like a pretzel and couldn't move, much less talk. Whatever possessed us to sign up for advanced yoga? Flo had convinced me it would improve our chi and our sex lives. I was never going be able to get my left heel behind my right ear and all I really needed to improve things was a reliable man.

I whispered to Flo, "I think Andrew's chomping at the bit, but I don't think it's been *consummated* ...not yet anyway." I got on my knees and stretched my back out like a cat.

"Maybe he wanted to get Duncan out of the way so he could have Sammy all to himself."

"I guess it's possible. But wouldn't it be easier to just ask her out?"

Flo flopped to the floor in a very unyoga like manner and whispered back, "True. Oh, you know what he should do? He should take her to that Casa de la Reina on Petronia. It was so romantic and that steak was like butter. Remember that?"

"What are you talking about? La Reina in Key West? You want him to take her to Key West?" I laid flat on my stomach with my arms stretched out behind me. "He could just start with hot dogs at Papaya King. Eighty-sixth and third is a little closer to home." The instructor just glared at us.

"Now I'm hungry."

"We still have ten more minutes of this torture. Don't think about it," I said.

"So we have Andrew, Janice and Blaine. Sammy said Blaine and Janice were arguing. I vote for Blaine."

"Blaine? He's just growing a bunch of plants. Why would he kill Duncan? What's the point of that?" I rolled over and pulled my knees up to my chest as best I could. "I vote for Janice Pearl. Sammy said she was jealous. Remember what Ilyana said, *Death by jealous lover, one hundred percent.*"

"Then why not Sammy?" Flo asked. "Maybe Duncan was seeing Tracy too. Sammy was jealous of Tracy and she killed them both. She was a crying mess at his funeral."

"Oh, I don't know, Sammy doesn't seem capable of murder." I got up on all fours. This wasn't helping my chi. My chi hurt.

Flo mumbled something unintelligible. She was folded in half with her knees up next to her ears suffocating herself with her inner thighs. I couldn't understand a word.

"Your legs are supposed to be straight," I teased.

She unfolded herself. "You know what we need? We need more information about this secret project. I think terrorists killed Duncan for a new smallpox serum." Flo rolled onto her side and gave up on the yoga.

"Terrorists? You thought the little twerpy guy who lived in the apartment over Etoiles was a terrorist."

"Ilyana thought so too. Well, maybe she didn't think he

was a terrorist but she did think he was a spy, and she knows spies. He kept getting those little packages from UPS. Every day for weeks and he'd take the package, look around to see if anyone was watching and scurry inside."

"Yeah, you thought he was making a bomb and you were convinced the FBI planted a video camera in the mailbox on the corner to watch him. Turned out the mailbox was just a mailbox and the bomb making ingredients were fruitcakes he'd ordered from QVC."

"Well, he could've been a terrorist."

A gong signaled the end of the class. I crawled over to the wall, pulled myself up and grabbed my jacket off the hook. We put ourselves through this twice a week and the only part I look forward to is my reward afterwards. A quick stop at Wong's deli for some hot tea and fresh baked daily cinnamon scones.

As we crossed the street to the deli my jacket pocket began to vibrate. I had a voicemail and a deep sexy voice stopped me dead in the middle of the street.

"Clara, Q here. Hoping we can still have dinner tonight. Call me back."

"Q wants me to have dinner with him tonight. I'm supposed to be going to Chris's for lasagna," I caught up with Flo.

"What, are you kidding me? It's Friday morning. You can't go to dinner with him tonight, it's against The Rules. You can't go. End of discussion."

"That's what Delores would say." I yanked open the deli door and let her walk in first.

"Well, Delores would be right. He has to ask you by Wednesday for a Friday date, you know that."

"Rules, shmules. Maybe he just couldn't find my phone number. Maybe his phone wasn't working."

"And maybe he's an idiot. I'm telling you Sweetie, just say you have other plans. If he really wants to ask you out, he'll do it again." I knew Flo was right but this is where I always screwed up.

TIFFANY BLUES

"OK, I'll tell him I can't get together tonight," I said as I hit the call button on the phone again.

Without us ordering, Teresa Wong handed Flo her hazelnut coffee and me some English Breakfast tea. I took a sip and yelped and gave it back to Teresa.

"Hello?" Q answered.

"Hi, it's Clara. Just got your message." Teresa handed the cup back to me, this time with ice in it. I held it up and whispered "Thanks." Teresa pointed to the scones in the display case and I nodded.

"Hey there. Sorry about Tuesday. It couldn't be helped and I was looking forward to seeing you again. Can we do tonight?"

"I..." Flo hit me in the arm. "I have other plans for dinner tonight, I'm sorry. Maybe some other time."

Flo nodded her approval and paid for everything. We started back for The Diner three doors away.

"What about after dinner? Can I meet you for a drink? Where are you going to be?" Q was being persistent. "You promised you'd tell me about Pluto." Flo headed into The Diner and I waited for her to disappear inside.

"Well, I could probably meet you around nine. I'll be in Princeton."

"Perfect! How about Ipanema at nine? I'll be at the bar."

"Great. I'll see you then. Bye." I decided Flo didn't have to know.

Flo and Phillip were unpacking boxes of red and black stilettos and stacking them on a shelf in the back closet. She was bringing him up to date on the events of the day before. Phillip looked up as I came in.

"So, do you have a date?" he asked.

I made a face at Flo. "No, I don't have a date, not tonight anyway," I lied. Phillip looked relieved.

"Well, the joint was jumping yesterday," Phillip changed the subject. "There was some tourist group, a women's club or something, no one under fifty. They packed the store. They all wanted to try on the leopard stilettos. It was like Cinderella's stepsisters trying to stuff their feet into the glass slipper."

"So did we sell any shoes?" I asked.

"No, but they wreaked havoc for at least an hour. A few of them bought herbs and books. Check the sign-up sheet, I think a couple of them registered for the Scorpio Moon workshop next month."

"A tourist group? In January? That's odd," I checked the sign-up sheet by the register. "Yep, three of them signed up. And they were all over fifty? Should be an interesting workshop."

"What does that make? Eight? Ten? We'd better get moving on this," Flo said.

"Speaking of Scorpio Moon," Phillip continued. "Lucille and the kids came in as usual. She was hoping the Scorpio Moon kit was ready. I think she has a new friend. She seemed awfully eager to get her hands on it."

"Really?" we said together.

"That would be so nice for her. She's been lonely since Henri died. All she has are those dogs," I added.

Phillip went on, "Oh, one more thing. Abbs came in looking for you Coco. She said to tell you that Akio is coming to visit for Valentine's weekend and they've decided to put all their decisions on hold 'til then. And she's feeling much better and can work this weekend."

"I'm glad she's waiting. With Mercury retrograde she shouldn't be making any decisions anyway. Besides, I took another look at her locality map. Her Venus is really close to… wait a sec… Flo, is the book here? Go get me the book!"

"What book?"

"Duncan's book. I have an idea."

Flo put down a shoe box and I followed her into the front room.

"Where's the laptop?" I asked. I spotted it on the counter and sat down on a stool. Young Elvis jumped up onto the stool next to me begging for a snack. I gently pushed him off, "Later El, you don't want to look like your brother." He left in a huff.

"Here." Flo handed me the *New World Apothecary*. "What are you doing?" she asked.

"The mapping stuff. It made me think about what Duncan wrote. He was into astrology. Maybe it's a code, like for a place. If I use April 11, 1940 as a birth date, 1200P as a birth time and Los Angeles as a birthplace, we can make an astrology chart. Then we can map it and maybe we'll see something. It's worth a shot."

"Can I see?" Phillip leaned over my shoulder.

I pulled up the astrology program and entered the data. Up popped an astrology pie cut into twelve slices.

"OK now what?" Flo asked.

"Well, all I can tell from this is that Venus, Mars and the Moon are all conjuncting in Gemini in the eleventh house and Leo's rising. The eleventh house rules wishes and dreams, friends and groups. If this is someone's birthday, I'd sure like to meet them."

"Maybe it's his wife's birthday. Oscar said he was married once," Flo said.

"What does his ex-wife have to do with anything?" Phillip asked.

"Good question, let's look at the map of the chart." I clicked on the map icon and a map of North America popped up with lines all over it. "Look at that!" I was excited.

"Look at what?" Flo was peering over my other shoulder at the computer screen. "All I see are sine waves and vertical lines intersecting them. So?"

"Let me 'splain Lucy. These lines," I said pointing to the colored vertical lines, "are the planets at their highest point in the sky that day. Look at Mars, Venus and the Moon lines." I was pointing to three lines right on top of each other. "They all go through the same spot on the map."

"They all go right through New Jersey," Phillip said.

"Exactly! For example, if you drew a straight line from High Point to Cape May and stood on that line, and looked up in the sky on April 11, 1940 you would see Mars, Venus and the Moon in the same spot in the sky," I said.

"What's the actual longitude?" Flo asked.

"74 North 40," I answered.

"That goes right through the Pine Barrens. I mapped it so many times in grad school I know it by heart. I think that's real close to Blaine's place. Look up Exotic Aquatics on one of the web map things and we can look at the satellite photo."

"I need an actual address. What's the address?"

"Where'd I put those directions?" Flo was scattering papers all over the counter. "Here they are. 7 Cedar Mills Road, Pleasant Mills." I entered it on the screen and a satellite photo appeared.

"Look here's the dirt road and here are the blueberry fields." Flo was tracing the road with her finger on the screen. I smacked her hand away.

"Don't touch the screen, you'll get fingerprints all over it."

"No, I won't. Look, these are the woods we drove through with the dark water. Here are his greenhouses. You can actually see them."

"OK, so what do we do with this?" Phillip wanted to know.

"Check the longitude," Flo instructed.

I right clicked and up popped the little green arrow.

"74 degrees North 39, 49 seconds. It's so close. It has to be about Blaine. It's only like a half mile difference," Flo said. "Those pitcher plants locked in the greenhouse were for the secret smallpox serum and he wanted Sammy to know where they were!"

"That's ridiculous. If he wanted her to know he would have just told her. Why would he keep it a secret from her?"

Flo smacked her hand down hard on the table. "To protect her from the terrorists!"

Silence. Phillip and I exchanged glances.

"Well, it doesn't say anything about who killed Duncan does it?" Phillip said quietly. He headed for the kitchen.

"I think Duncan was afraid that Blaine was going to try to kill him so he left this as a clue for Sammy," Flo said.

"Here we go again. What's his motive? Why would Blaine kill Duncan?"

"Maybe he wanted to sell the plants on the black market for smallpox serum. Duncan was trying to stop him so Blaine strangled him."

"Why would he have to kill him? Couldn't he just go behind Duncan's back and sell them if that's what he wanted to do?"

"You don't know Blaine. He had a harem of undergraduate girls doing all his library research for him. As soon as they would finish one part he'd dump them and move on to the next group. Not only that, there was another grad student he hooked up with who did all this field research on orchid pollination for her own thesis and one day, Poof! She's not at Rutgers anymore and all her research ends up in Blaine's thesis. Nobody knows what happened to her or why she left."

"Geez-o-Pete, that doesn't mean he murdered her. I think you should go see Blaine again and ask him if he knows what all this means," I said to Flo.

"Are you out of your mind?"

"Okay, you're right. You don't want to go there, but maybe you could just call him." I got up and handed her the phone.

"I don't have his number," Flo gave me back the phone. "I have to finish putting those shoes away."

I picked up the paper with Blaine's address on it. Yep, there it was right in the left hand corner scribbled in Flo's handwriting. "Flo, wait a sec. It's right here." I followed her, paper and phone in hand, into the back closet.

"Alright already, give me the freaking phone." Flo reluctantly dialed the number.

I opened one of the shoe boxes. "Ooh, these are to die for." I held up one dark blue sequined shoe with a metal spike heel for Flo to see. "Save a pair for us."

"Hi, Blaine?" Flo choked and nodded to me.

There were a few seconds of silence.

"Oh good, wait, it's a message." She listened intently for a minute. Crap." She fumbled with all the buttons on the phone. "How do you turn this thing off?"

I took the phone away from her and clicked it off. "What happened?"

Flo took the shoe from me and ran her finger slowly down the spike. "His voice mail was full. Apparently, Blaine has a carnivorous plant emergency. In Indonesia. Dr. Slimemold has left the country."

FOURTEEN

Friday night I took the back roads to my brother's house. Not that I had a choice, there is no Jersey Turnpike between Dolly's Ferry and Princeton. You can either head east towards Hopewell, winding your way through rolling fields of corn, hay and multi-million dollar McMansions or drive south towards Trenton and cut over later. But if you choose south, you're putting yourself at the mercy of the Delaware and the state designated Scenic Byway that snakes along the river, Route 29. They call it a highway, but for the most part it's nothing more than a narrow two lane ribbon of blacktop with rock cliffs on one side and water on the other. If the river floods, you're doomed. Any way you go takes at least forty-five minutes, even longer at night in the dead of winter. In New Jersey that might as well be eternity.

I took my chances with the river route and headed south towards Washington's Crossing, the very spot where the Father of our Country crossed the icy waters Christmas night in 1776. There's a "Washington's Crossing" on the Pennsylvania side of the river too. It's a huge National Historic Site that used to have a

Revolutionary War museum, battle movies and a gift shop. Every kid in New Jersey, except for my brother Chase, who blew chow all over Wendy Sadowski's backpack right before they got on the bus, remembers taking that grammar school field trip. The school bus crawling over the one and a half lane bridge, the boring moth-eaten movie re-enactment of that fateful night and the requisite tri-corner hat gift shop purchase.

You know how old I was before I figured out that George rowed his boat *from* Pennsylvania *to* New Jersey? Maybe that's because on the Jersey side of the bridge, there's just a bar. Sure, there's a huge State Park somewhere in the general vicinity that also bears the name Washington's Crossing. It's got a museum with hundreds of revolutionary war artifacts in it, not to mention a campground, a nature center, an open air theatre and public restrooms to boot, but I'm telling you, when you cross the bridge into the Garden State, the only thing you see is a bar. Well it's a liquor store and a deli too. It happens to be a great place for a sandwich and a beer, but it's no national monument.

When I got to the bar I turned left, away from the river, and headed towards Princeton. I was still a good half hour from my brother's, but I was too busy obsessing about Q to care about the drive any more. Maybe tonight was a bad idea. It was that time of the month. I was a bloated, beached whale. I'd had to hold my breath just to squeeze into my favorite black pants. He was going to take one look at me and run, I just knew it. What was I thinking?

Okay Clara Mercedes Martini, get hold of yourself. You're beautiful, intelligent and he'd be lucky to have you. If I sucked in my stomach and stayed standing up all night I would be fine. I checked my face in the rearview mirror. I did look good and the plum eyeshadow brought out the gold speckles in my brown eyes.

"If he plays his cards right," I imagined out loud,

TIFFANY BLUES

"We'll go up to Bull's Island this summer. We'll walk along the river, spread a blanket under a tree, sip a little wine, nibble on some cheese, nibble on each other..."

"Sweetie, snap out of it!" I heard Flo's voice in my head. "This is only your first date, and already you're spending the summer with him? First you have to get through lasagna and Melissa, remember?"

The knot in my belly tightened. Geez-o-pete, how the heck was I going to sit there and eat lasagna? "I'll just take a couple bites and leave," I answered myself.

"Flo ees right, one hundred percent." This time it was Ilyana talking. "And dun't you forget, he absolutely ees Leo, one hundred percent."

I took a deep breath and started coughing. "I know, I'll just call Chris and tell him I'm sick."

"Too late, you're already here," Flo and Ilyana snapped me back into the present.

I reluctantly pulled into the circular drive of Christopher's five bedroom contemporary (with separate guest cottage). I shut the car door and was immediately surrounded by three squealing boys under the age of seven. I love my nephews, but these boys are a handful. I'm not sure even Nanny 911 could help. Chris is rarely around and my sister-in-law obviously doesn't have a clue about what to do with them. Her idea of a time-out is to make the boys go shopping with her. I don't quite get how a trip to Bloomingdales is going to keep three little boys from filling the fish tank with Jello again, but hey, what do I know?

I made my way to the front door with Jacob John, the three-year old clinging to my leg.

"Aunt Clara, you see my new truck, you see my new truck," he begged.

I tried to pat his curly head, but couldn't reach it because James Joseph, the almost five year old, was yanking my left pinky finger out of its socket. The "quiet" one, John James who is six and a half, marched beside me humming something that sounded kind of spooky. It'd be easy enough to mistake these adorable brown-eyed devils for triplets, so why they'd been cursed with my mother's "name them all with the same set of initials" gene was beyond me.

My mother chose Christopher Michael for her first born after her two favorite saints. Delores wanted her second son to become a rich New York banker since the first was going to be a doctor. Hence, Chase Manhattan arrived four years after Chris. I was an accident, seven years and one hell of an April Fools' joke later. By then Delores was clamoring for the lead in the local Little Theater productions and was somewhat of a dilettante when it came to prose and poetry. "Clara" came from Lord Tennyson's poem *Lady Clara Vere de Vere:*

Lady Clara Vere de Vere,
There stands a spectre in your hall;
The guilt of blood is at your door;
You changed a wholesome heart to gall.

Tennyson wrote nine stanzas but that's the only one I ever remember. Delores obviously had no plan for me. The "Mercedes" was her maternal grandmother's name not to mention the automobile she'd nag my father into buying for her fiftieth birthday.

Delores had nagged my father about pretty much everything, that is until she decided, at the age of sixty, that they were moving to Rome so she could star in Italian films. For the first time in their forty years together, Dad lit a cigar indoors, pushed back in his recliner, and said, "Tell you what, send me a postcard." Six months later they were divorced. Delores flew off to Italy alone and my father had a heart attack and married his nurse.

Sticking my nephews with their own set of identical initials was Melissa's idea. I suppose she was just trying to impress my mother. That was never going to happen.

TIFFANY BLUES

My sister-in-law was waiting for me at the door.

"Hi, Claire, Happy Birthday." She kissed the air in the general vicinity of my cheekbone. "I can't believe you're forty! I always think you're only a few years older than I am. I forget that it's almost a *decade*."

Nails on a blackboard, I thought to myself. I didn't say anything.

Melissa is Christopher's second wife; two decades younger and pencil thin. You have to picture my sister-in-law. Think Morticia Addams meets Carmella Soprano. The only piece of clothing she owns that isn't black is her wedding gown and even that had a black satin bow on the back above the lace train. Her Diamond Ice jewelry collection weighs more than she does and her hair makes her look more like a groupie for a heavy metal rock band than a doctor's wife; black, down to her waist with bleached out blonde bangs and random highlights for heaven's sake. She must have had some snappin' gyro, why else would Chris have married her?

The boys peeled themselves off of me and started chasing each other up and down the glass and steel staircase that leads to the second floor "gallery". Melissa took my coat, hung it on one of the twenty matching wooden hangers in the otherwise empty hall closet and snapped the door shut.

"Cut it out!" she yelled at the top of her lungs. Her shout echoed off the walls of the two story foyer and the boys immediately evaporated out of sight. Thank goodness Christopher came to the rescue with a tall Jack and Ginger.

Chris looks a lot like me only taller and eleven years older. I think he's handsome even with his salt and pepper hair and those little crinkles near his eyes. The only bling on him is a simple titanium wedding band. He's full of himself but I guess he's earned it; well known and very talented cardiac surgeon that he is. But my big brother is always there for me and I have to say I love him dearly in spite of his dumb-ass domestic choices.

"Hey Sis, happy birthday." He wrapped one arm around me in a half-hug and handed me the drink. "Here, you're gonna need this," he whispered in my ear.

"You got that right." I took a long swallow.

"We've really missed you around here Twinkle Toes," he teased.

"Yeah, I've missed you too." I made a face and stuck out my tongue. He'd called me Twinkle Toes ever since my first ballet recital. There I was only eight years old, adorable in my pink tutu, dancing my heart out. I was so excited I pirouetted right off the stage and landed on Miss Dillman's Steinway piano. I was fine, but the piano lid prop stick broke in two. Delores was mortified and my father and brothers laughed about it for days. I got over it and kept dancing...that is until my girls got too big.

The three of us headed down the long tiled hall that led to the dining room and kitchen. Melissa was a few steps in front of me and Chris, but she stopped short when we reached the arched doorway to the formal living room. I braked before I smacked into her, but my drink wobbled and a little wave sloshed over the rim and dripped down the side of the glass. I was able to catch it with my fingers.

"Missy, what are you doing?" Chris grumbled. I licked my finger and wiped my wet hand on my pants.

"I want to show Claire the living room," she said pointing into the room. "We just had it painted. What do think?" she asked me.

"Her name is Clara. Clara, not Claire," Chris corrected.

"That's what I said, I know her name!"

I took another big sip, leaned over the baby gate that keeps the living room off-limits to everyone except at Christmas and checked out the new paint job. The walls were off-white; just like the forty thousand off-white pillows she piled on top of the nine thousand dollar off-white freeform sofa. Noguchi would die if he saw the pillows. I tried to move one once so I could actually sit down. She had Velcroed them in place.

TIFFANY BLUES

"Well, umm, well... it's a lovely shade of cream," I said, shrugging my shoulders at my brother.

Chris rolled his eyes. "It's off-white Melissa. It's the same color as before. It's the same color it's always been. It'll always be the same color."

Missy started to pout. "No it's not. This is Buttermilk. It used to be Bridal Linen. You don't care about anything I do anymore."

Chris sighed and put his arm around her. "I'm sorry Missy, I care, but you know how busy I am."

Please spare me from this torture. Desperately wishing I could do my nephews' disappearing act, I slipped away from them and headed straight for the overproduced, but perfectly set, dining table. "At least she makes awesome lasagna," I mumbled under my breath.

Dinner was just as I expected, delicious, but interminable. Melissa talked incessantly all the way through the appetizers and salad about how Amanda Baxter was getting a new pool and cabana and how they needed a pool to occupy their boys during the summer; it was ridiculous how the country club was always so crowded and she had just seen on the six o'clock news that someone died from a weird skin infection they got at a health club pool, and of course they would get a curved one with the attached spa just like Amanda's only landscaped with stone walls and a waterfall so it looked natural, like the one she saw in New Jersey Monthly. And oh, yes, the cabana had to have a full operating kitchen with granite countertops and a barbeque and a television and indoor/outdoor furniture and Amanda said they needed to get a contractor now because all the good ones will be too busy if we wait until Spring and was Chris listening?

I was beginning to think the main event was never going to happen when Melissa finally announced it was time for the lasagna. Wearing oversized oven mitts up to her elbows, she carried in the hot, bubbling casserole and set it down in front of my brother. Now this was aromatherapy!

Christopher picked up a gigundo sterling serving spoon and carefully loaded molten lasagna onto all our plates. He set the casserole dish on the buffet and launched into an excruciatingly detailed account of our mother's latest escapade.

"She said she was actually "this close" to Brad Pitt as an extra in a movie he's filming near Positano." Chris held his thumb and forefinger about an inch apart. "The woman's out of her mind. Traipsing all over Europe at her age, staying up 'til all hours."

"Seventy's the new sixty," I said as I scooped up some of the steaming pasta and twirled the melted mozzarella around my fork. "She's following her bliss."

"That's bullshit," Melissa hissed.

John Jacob giggled, slid off his chair and disappeared under the table. Before I knew it, there were three empty seats and a whole lot of whispering and loud giggling going on under there.

Melissa poked her head under the tablecloth, "JJ, get up off the floor, all of you or I'll have to take you to the mall tomorrow." She looked directly at me. "Your mother should be here with her grandchildren, they don't even know her. Besides, I could use the help."

She needed help alright I thought.

"She raised three kids of her own. She's entitled to live the rest of her life whatever way she wants to," I said feeling just a little guilty that when Spencer was born Delores and Dad were there to help me. I was only nineteen, a junior at Douglass and a year older than Delores was when Chris was born. My idiot fiancé, who promised he'd "pull out," pulled out of the relationship as soon as he heard I was pregnant. Amazingly, my parents didn't freak. I realized later why not when I counted backwards nine months from Chris' birthday and went a month and a half past their wedding date. Delores of course told her social circle that we had run off and gotten married but never bothered to explain my MIA husband. While I finished school and began my career, my father paid for a wonderful woman to care for Spence. My mother spoiled my son but never changed his diaper or lifted a finger to actually help. I tried to imagine Delores here helping Melissa with the JJ's. It would be a disaster.

I wanted to chug my wine but I reached for my water goblet instead. I'd probably have a drink at Ipanema and still had that long ride home. I didn't need to have my senses impaired any more than they already were.

Chris pulled the three squirming boys out from under the table one by one and sat them back in their chairs. "Stay put," he commanded. Then to me he asked, "Did you hear from Dad on your birthday?" He sat back down, picked the last piece of garlic bread out of the basket and dipped it in the red cheesy sauce on his plate.

"Spoke to him and Ginny. They were in a golf cart on the eighth hole. Sounds like they're doing great. Golfing almost every day."

"How was brunch with Chase?" Melissa asked.

"Well I was a little distracted. Someone I know was murdered."

Silence.

"You think you could strangle a person with a plant vine?" I asked Chris.

Dead silence.

Melissa held up the bread basket. "Does anybody want more garlic bread?"

"No thanks," Chris and I said together. Melissa reluctantly put down the basket and poured herself her third glass of Merlot.

"Geez, I'm, sorry to hear that. I take it this someone was strangled then?" Chris asked.

"Yep, in the conservatory with a passionflower vine."

"You're joking right?" Chris asked.

"No joke. A passionflower vine."

"It'd have to be a pretty strong vine, but it's doable. Who died?"

"This botany professor, a friend of Oscar's. Flo and I just met with him last week at Metro Gardens and two days later he's dead. So, technically, how do you die from strangulation?"

"It depends on exactly what happens. Could be asphyxiation if the air supply is cut off, or the blood supply to the brain could be cut off. Of course if they snapped his neck, the spinal cord could be severed resulting in instantaneous death. Have they gotten the autopsy results?"

"Well, isn't this sparkling dinner conversation." Melissa slammed her full glass of Merlot on the table sending a burgundy shower over the sea of white linen. I flew back away from the table and Chris jumped out of his seat. All three boys scrambled back under the table and stayed there.

"Get the Oxy! Get the Oxy! Get the Oxy!" Melissa vibrated in a high pitched squeal then vaulted into the kitchen. Chris pushed the kid's plates out of the way and grabbed all their linen napkins and proceeded to fling them on top of the red puddle in middle of the table.

Melissa reappeared, took aim and pulled the trigger of the cleaning spray bottle, shooting her husband right in the chest.

"Have you lost your mind? How about shooting the table instead of me?"

"Those are my Italian handmade linen napkins, ruined. Everything's ruined," Melissa sobbed. The bottle slipped out of her hand and fell with a thud on the hardwood floor.

"Okay everybody, calm down. Let's just take the tablecloth off, throw everything in the wash, and try to salvage the rest of this dinner," I said. I wanted to finish my lasagna.

Melissa sank into her chair and held her head in her

hands. Chris and I cleared the mess giving us a clear view of the three curly heads huddled under the glass tabletop.

"Boys, come out of there and give your mother a hug." Chris poked his foot at the closest rear end. They crawled over to their mother and entwined themselves around her ankles.

"That's not a hug. Come give me a real hug."

"See, everything's all better now, let's just eat already," Chris said.

"Okay." I pulled my chair in and dove back into my pasta.

"Where's Spencer?" Melissa handed the bottle of Oxy to John James. "JJ put this back under the sink for Mommy. We wanted him to come tonight. He never answered our email."

"You should have texted him. He's in San Diego with Cicada," I told her.

"Cicada? Isn't that a bug?" Melissa picked at her mound of lasagna like she expected to find one hidden in there. I realized she hadn't actually taken one bite of her dinner.

"No, it's his band Miss," Chris corrected her.

I continued, "He's touring all over the country with the band. After California they're headed up to British Columbia." Melissa stared at me blankly.

Chris shook his head. "Canada. I swear Dad and I are the only sane ones in this family."

He was right.

The antique Seikosha clock on the far wall bonged nine bongs. "I hate to say this, but I gotta go."

Melissa shook her head and frantically waved her tenticles. "Oh no. No, you can't go yet. It's time for birthday cake." She got up and disappeared into the kitchen. The kids followed her singing. "Birthday cake! Birthday cake!"

A blazing vanilla ice cream cake the size of the Empire State Building came rolling into the room on a tea cart.

Thank God the three boys got to the candles before I did or the house would have burned down. Melissa handed me a Nordstrom's box wrapped with an elaborate gossamer bow and started cutting the cake. Hidden under reams of sparkly tissue paper was a beautiful deep v-neck, black, Donna Karan sweater. Size six.

"I hope it fits," Melissa blew me a kiss.

I took one itsy bitsy slurp of cake, stuffed the sweater back in the box and stood up. "Thank you so much, Melissa. It's perfect. I'm sorry you guys, but I really have to get going."

Jacob attached himself to my leg again. "Aunt Clara, sleep over. Sleep over."

I picked him up and hugged him. "I'm sorry honey. I can't tonight. But you can help me get my coat."

We headed for the hall closet. As Christopher pulled my coat off the hanger my pocket beeped an ominous warning.

"Damn, my battery's going dead."

"Going on a first date without a phone. Not a good idea." My brother helped Jacob help me into my coat.

"I'll charge it in the car. And who said I have a date?" I mumbled taking the phone out of the pocket. It was dead alright.

"I know you Twinkle Toes. Just make sure he's not packing a passionflower." He grinned and gave me a squeeze.

"That's not even funny." I gave him a peck on the cheek and flew out the door before Melissa could say a word.

FIFTEEN

I drove the mile and a half to Palmer Square in fifth gear and only had to circle the block once before I found a parking space in front of Ipanema at exactly nine-twenty. *Please let him still be there.* I checked my face, slathered on some lip gloss, tossed my hair back, popped a papaya tab, and breathed into my hand to make sure I didn't smell like garlic. Leo or not, here I come.

Ipanema was crowded. Even at this hour the intimate dining room was still full and about four couples were standing by the door waiting for tables. I scanned the dimly lit lounge next to the dining room. Very metro, sparse furnishings. No chairs to speak of, just ottomans really, red velour, with tiny round black lacquer tables in front of them. Miniature steel pendant lights were suspended above each table. The bar was a sleek "L" and every seat was taken except for one on the far end. Q was perched on the high back metal stool next to it grinning at me. I weaved my way through the tables holding my breath.

"Ah, finally, the Divine Miss M. Definitely worth the wait," he said handing me a glass of Pinot. His eyes were smiling.

"I'm sorry I'm late. I tried to call but my battery died." I took a gulp of my wine.

"Oh, good. I called you and it went straight to voice mail. I thought you were trying to avoid me." He was drinking a scotch on the rocks. The empty glass on the bar told me it was his second. "You look stunning." His eyes traveled the length of me and stopped at my feet. "Love the shoes."

I was wearing the black patent leather pumps from Stilettos that he had admired so much. My pants were long and hid most of them. How the heck did he even notice? I slipped out of my coat and placed it on the empty bar chair.

"You don't look so bad yourself," I answered. Black leather jacket, light blue cashmere sweater, black jeans, black loafers. Yummy.

"Did you have a nice dinner with your family?" he asked.

I groaned and took another sip. "Disaster. Yep, that pretty much sums it up. Great lasagna though."

Q's index finger reached out, headed straight for my left boob. His fingertip brushed my white silk sweater about an inch above my nipple. "Merlot or Chianti?" he asked.

I looked down at my chest in horror. Sure enough, there was a bright pink wine stain about the size of a dime. Thank you Melissa.

"Merlot. The girls get in the way sometimes." I giggled like an idiot and chugged the rest of my Pinot.

"I doubt they ever get in the way."

Our eyes locked. The girls jumped to attention and an involuntary kegel took me by surprise. I reached for my glass forgetting it was empty. Good thing too, because I was starting to feel pretty tipsy.

"So your bother lives here in Princeton. Are you a Jersey girl by birth or choice?"

TIFFANY BLUES

I moved my coat and tight pants be damned, hopped up on the empty bar stool facing him. "Both really, I was born and raised in North Jersey. After college, I chose to stay down here.

"Did you go to Princeton?"

"No, Rutgers. Douglass, actually, the women's college at Rutgers...well it used to be. Now it's been eaten up by the University. A shame really." I drifted off remembering parts of my college life that one should really forget. How I survived in one piece, I'll never know.

"So, is your degree in Astrology?" Q asked trying to keep a straight face.

"No, that's my advanced degree," I smiled. "Social Psychology came first. The astrology just seemed so much more practical. You can learn a lot about a person pretty quickly."

"Well you really had me pegged. Especially about the moving around as a kid and all. How'd you meet Florilla?"

"We met at work. We both used to work for the same government agency."

"Which government?" Q looked surprised and took a sip of his scotch.

"The U.S. government."

"FBI, CIA or IRS?" Q asked as if those were the only three choices. He squirmed a little on his stool.

"If I told you I'd have to kill you."

Q didn't laugh.

"Just kidding silly. None of the above, it was an environmental agency. Flo and I both had this idea that we could somehow help to save the world. Big mistake. Anyway, I think the universe just put us there so we could become friends."

"So how did you make the leap from the U.S. government to astrophysics?"

"AstroBotanics. We realized right away that we had lots in common; chocolate, shoes, herbs, metaphysics, Key West. It was a no brainer that AstroBotanics Chocolate

Diner and Metaphysical Emporium just had to be."

"Yeah, that's a no brainer alright," he laughed. He downed the rest of his scotch and put the empty glass on the bar next to the first.

"So do you want know about your Pluto?" I asked.

The bar was getting really packed and people were closing in around us. Q leaned over and whispered in my ear, "It's too crowded in here. I know a quiet little place on the Square. I hear they make a delicious cappuccino."

I couldn't imagine where he meant. Princeton's got a little bit of everything; hip college hangouts, gourmet restaurants, coffee shops, and Albert Einstein's house (but not his brain, they lost that). As far as I know there is no "quiet little place" on the Square. I guess we could get a cappuccino from Tiger Coffee and go sit on a bench by the Christmas tree. Maybe that's what he was thinking. But they already took the lights down and damn, it was brutal out tonight.

"Okay, sure, that sounds good to me. You lead the way."

Q jumped off his stool and threw a twenty on the bar as a tip. He helped me back into my coat, took my elbow and guided me out of Ipanema into the bitter night.

I shivered and Q pulled me closer to him as we stepped out into the frigid air. "Don't worry it's not far."

We had only walked half a block when he stopped in front of the Puffy Muffin bakery. He dropped my arm, fished around in his jacket pocket, and pulled out a key.

"What are you doing?" I asked, a little more than concerned.

"I'm taking you for cappuccino."

"But the bakery's closed."

"I know, I live here."

"In the Puffy Muffin?"

"Wouldn't that be delicious? No, I'm in the condo upstairs. And I make a serious cappuccino." He unlocked a red door and held it open for me with his left arm.

TIFFANY BLUES

I bit my lip and hesitated.

"Don't worry, you're perfectly safe. I won't do anything but make you good cup of coffee, I promise."

The chocolate chip muffin over my head exploded sending sparks and shards of the bakery sign spotlight in every direction. My survival instincts took over and I buried my face in Q's chest. Next thing I knew, I was inside, wrapped in his arms.

"Whoa, you okay?" He took my face in his hands and did a quick inspection. "No blood," he said and picked something out of my hair. He held up a sliver of glass.

"Perfectly safe, huh?" I laughed.

"Did I say that?" He took my hand and led me up a narrow staircase to his apartment. The condo was warm and toasty.

"Smells like cinnamon buns. I'd weigh a thousand pounds if I lived here. How do you stand it?"

"Lifetime membership at Giga Gym."

"Do you own this place?" I asked taking off my coat. I didn't know where to put it so I just held it.

Q was already in the kitchen area playing with the cappuccino machine. "No, the company pays for it. Make yourself at home." He looked up. "Just throw your coat on the chair."

"The company? So you're just here temporarily?" My heart sank. I took a good look around and was astounded. It had clearly been decorated by an expert. Deep greens and burgundies, warm mission style furniture. Frank Lloyd Wright style tiffany lamps flanked the velour sofa and a leather recliner sat in the corner next to the window. A chenille throw in a soft sage was draped over the arm. I put my coat on top of it.

"Well, it's a temporary assignment. Could last six months could be a couple of years. It all depends."

Some hope.

"So it comes furnished and everything?" I settled down on one of the oak stools at the breakfast bar.

"Well, the little things are mine. The big stuff was here already, sofa, chairs, bed. The home theater and the TV are mine too. It's not bad."

"It's fantastic."

"It's also..." The woosh of the cappuccino machine drowned out the end of his sentence.

It was hard to keep from drooling. He looked delicious fussing with the chocolate shavings and whipped cream. There were significant biceps bulging under that sweater. His black jeans were just tight enough to notice his other equally significant bulges. He turned his back to me and opened the refrigerator. Nice view there too! When he turned around again, I noticed a photo, a black and white studio head shot, of a stunning blonde on the refrigerator behind him. Written in one corner with a blue Sharpie was: "XOX 2 you 007". He saw me staring at it.

"That's my sister. She's a model. Hard to believe we're related, huh?" He handed me a steaming demitasse cup. "Here try this."

I took a sip while he waited expectantly. I couldn't get the woman's picture out of my mind. I was sure I'd seen her somewhere before.

"Well?" Q asked.

I took another sip. It was the best cappuccino I'd ever had. "Yum. What did you put in it? There's a flavor I can't identify."

"Sorry, if I told you I'd have to kill you," he smiled. "Glad you like it." He came around the counter and took me by the hand. "Let's move to the sofa. It's more comfortable."

Uh oh, not the sofa. I was perfectly fine on the stool. The sofa was big and soft and comfortable and dangerous as hell. I sat down nervously on the middle cushion and put my cup on the coffee table in front of it. Q motioned to the spot next to me and said. "May I?"

He sat down and rested his arm across the back of the sofa behind me. His armpit smelled like chocolate. I hoped he wasn't using that new chocolate deodorant for men.

Chocolate and sweat, who came up with that? Maybe I was imagining it. Maybe it was just the bakery. The aroma permeated everything up here.

"So was your week as busy as mine?" he asked.

"It was crazy between clients and everything else, and we spent yesterday at Duncan McPherson's memorial service."

"Really? You went to the memorial service?"

"Remember I told you that Flo's boyfriend was a good friend of his? Oscar was going so Flo had to go. Since Flo had to go, she wanted me to go with them. Besides, we both really liked him when we met him. The man was adorable."

"I think you're adorable." Q's finger brushed my neck behind my ear. I flinched. "I've thought so ever since Flo tripped me with the Tiffany box."

"She didn't...that tickles," I said reaching for my cappuccino.

"Not the reaction I was looking for. Was it a nice service?"

"It was very nice, simple. In the rotunda of the Hall of Botanists. I think Duncan would have approved, well except for all the long-winded politicos. A bagpiper played *Amazing Grace* while Samantha Rousseau placed a beautiful ladyslipper into the orchid display in his memory. Do you know her?"

Q leaned forward and picked up his cup. "I don't think so. Who else was there?" He sipped it slowly.

"The Mayor, the director of the Gardens and the whole Board. And other Garden people. Janice Pearl, gave a half-assed eulogy. I thought maybe you'd be there to represent Zylanica."

"I was working. They probably sent a VP to something that high profile." He leaned back again and put his arm around my shoulder.

The heat from his body was causing a not altogether unpleasant tingling you know where. I absentmindedly intertwined my fingers with his. "I was surprised that Blaine Winship wasn't there."

"Who?"

"Oh, I thought maybe you knew him. He's supplying the plants they were using for research. You do know Janice Pearl, don't you?" I asked.

"Not really, I've met her once or twice. She seemed pretty cold, scary almost. I wouldn't want to have to work with her." Q tightened his squeeze on my fingers and kissed the nape of my neck softly.

A rush of warmth poured down my back, spiraled around my belly and flowed right to the spot between my thighs. I squeezed my legs together and realized it wasn't just happy sensations that were threatening to flood the sofa.

I pulled away from Q. "I hate to say this, but I really have to use your bathroom. Can we continue this conversation when I get back?" I asked standing up.

"Of course, sorry. I should have asked. The bathroom's right down the hall on the left."

After I flushed, I couldn't resist checking out his medicine cabinet. Shaving cream, razor, deodorant (not chocolate thank goodness), dental floss, toothpaste, condoms. Normal guy stuff, clean teeth and safe sex too. No girl stuff in sight. When I came out into the hall I heard Q talking on the phone. Good, more time to explore. I sneaked down the hallway.

There was an office on the right side done in the same tasteful style as the living room. Next to the office were the draped French doors that I supposed led into the bedroom. I couldn't resist. I turned the brass handle and gasped. A massive king size bed overpowered the room. It looked like a throne with its carved headboard and sumptuous bedding.

I closed my eyes and sensed Q behind me. He wound

his arms around my waist and pulled me to him. His lips brushed the back of my hair, my shoulders, my neck. He unwrapped his strong arms, turned me around and took my face in both of his hands. His blue eyes penetrated me. They melted into pools and his lips gently brushed mine. Teasing me. My knees caved. He held me up. His tongue was in my mouth, exploring. I could feel his hardness pressing against me. I was fast approaching the point of no return and...

"If you wanted to see my bedroom all you had to do was ask."

Oh My God. I slowly turned around and peeked out of one eye. Q was in the doorway, arms folded. "It's OK, I have to admit I was hoping we would end up here, eventually." His eyes locked onto mine.

"I...I...uh, I'm really sorry. I wasn't snooping, I was just curious about these condoms... I mean condos. Never been in one."

"Not a problem." He filled in the gap between us.

Something blue on the dresser behind him caught my eye. Robin's egg blue. Unmistakably Tiffany's. Unmistakably a ring box. Sister, my ass! I needed to go.

"You know it's getting really late. I have to get home, early client tomorrow." I slipped away from him and hurried down the hall.

He followed me. "It's okay Clara, you don't need to go, really. At least let's finish our cappuccino."

I could feel myself relenting when his hip buzzed. He cursed softly and took out the Smartphone. "Sorry, I have to take this. Hang on just one second, please."

I put on my coat. He held up his finger and mouthed "wait" before he disappeared into the bedroom. I was sure I heard a woman's voice on the other end. He was back in less than five seconds.

"It's almost midnight and I really do have a long day tomorrow. The cappuccino was fabulous. Thanks." I headed for the stairs.

I felt his hand on my arm, stopping me. "Let me at least walk you to your car." He casually brushed the hair away from my eyes like he had done it a thousand times before. "You still haven't told me about Pluto," he smiled. "I really want to see you again."

Bad idea. Bad, bad idea.

"I'd like to see you again too," I answered weakly.

The wind whipped at us as we stepped onto the Square and Q put his arm around me as we walked. The weather had turned even more frigid, if that was possible. I remote started my car halfway there.

"How about tomorrow night?" Q asked. Damn. I was hoping for at least a day or two breather, to try and get my head on straight about this man.

"How can that guy stand out in this cold just to smoke a cigarette?" I digressed. There was a man pacing in front of Ipanema smoking a cigarette. "It's amazing to me ever since the ban what people will do just to get a smoke. It's nuts." Q didn't answer me. I thought I felt him squeeze my shoulder a little tighter.

"Here you are," Q said. He walked all the way around my car, then opened my door and looked all over the front and back seats. "Honda Hybrid," he moved so I could get in. "Do you like it? "

"How did you know this was my car?"

"Uh, because you started it half a block away?"

Well, he might as well know the real me right off the bat. I got in and closed the door. Q tapped on the window and motioned to me to put it down.

"Tomorrow night, eight o'clock. I'm cooking you a meal you'll never forget."

"Let me think about it. Call me tomorrow," I answered.

"Okay." He leaned in and kissed me softly. Our first kiss. Nice. He glanced up at the cigarette man again. "Be careful on those back roads."

"Not a problem."

SIXTEEN

I was just a few miles out of Princeton and some idiot was on my tail. Had to be a guy. Only a male of the species could be such a jabronie at twelve-fifteen in the morning. Why didn't he just pass me already? I turned onto Cold Soil Road and the car behind me followed suit. Somebody else was going where I was going.

Oh no, maybe it was Ed from across the street. He was an aide at Princeton Hospital and I was pretty sure he was on the twelve to twelve shift on Fridays. It was dark as all get out when I reached the river. I couldn't make out what kind of car it was behind me, only that it looked like a sedan. Ed drove an old Mercury Cougar, had to be him. I really didn't want to get home the same time he did and have to change our relationship to one that required actual conversation. I sped up a little. So did he. Just for the hell of it, I made a couple of turns I didn't need to make. The car stayed right on my butt. OCD Ed wouldn't have done that. If it wasn't Ed, I was being followed, but by who? I pushed the hands-free link on the steering wheel.

"What name or number would you like to call?" a disembodied voice asked.

"Call Flo's cell," I answered.

"Do you want to call Flo's cell?"

"Yes, that's what I said."

"I didn't understand your response."

"Call Flo's cell."

"Main Menu. What number do you want to call?"

It would be faster if I just dialed the damn phone myself.

"Flo's cell," I yelled.

Flo's phone finally rang and kept ringing until her voice mail took over. Where was she at this hour?

"Flo it's me. Call me back. I think someone's following me. I'm kind of freaked. Call me NOW!"

I tried Phillip; voicemail again.

I checked the mirror; they were way too close for comfort. I floored it and was doing fifty-five until I hit the curve coming into Stockton. Any second now my heart was going to rupture. I slowed down but was still going way too fast for the twenty-five mile an hour speed limit through town. I burned past the school and church praying I'd get pulled over for speeding. No such luck. Where's a cop when you need one?

I sailed right past Bridge Street. Out of nowhere, a cop passed me going the other way. He immediately did a u turn, lights flashing. I hit the brakes in a panic, but it wasn't me that was getting pulled over. *Yes!* My stalker was toast. I did twenty-five the rest of the way through town and didn't breathe again until I saw the sign welcoming me to Dolly's Ferry.

Even then I didn't go straight home. I cruised past my street and made a left on Ferry instead, just in case the maniac was somehow still following me. But there was no one behind me and the streets were deserted.

Dolly's Ferry is a ghost town this time of night. All the businesses close up at six and the restaurants at eleven. The Pub would still be open, but even that would be getting ready to close soon. That's one of the attractions of living in this town. It's small, friendly, and quiet when the tourists leave. On the other hand, once the clock strikes midnight, if you're still out and about, you'll find yourself completely alone on a dark, empty street that leads right into the black hole of the Delaware River. It can be downright creepy and the last thing I needed was creepy.

Out of nowhere a small dark figure darted out in front of me. I let out a scream and slammed on the brakes. What the hell? It ran back across the street. It wasn't alone.

Lucille was spinning in circles on the front walk of The Diner and Bobo and Bosco were going berserk in the snow. Inside, the lights were on and the front door was wide open. I did a one-eighty, screeched to a halt and jumped out. The dogs almost knocked me down as they galloped around me.

"Blanche! My baby!" Lucille called out hysterically. "Where is my little baby?"

I made a grab for Bobo's leash, but missed and almost stepped on a quivering little mound of snow. I rescued the shivering snowball and Lucille scooped her out of my hands and smothered the wet fur with kisses.

"What's going on?" I had to yell to Lucille over Bosco's barking.

"I don't know," she yelled back. "I couldn't sleep. We came out for some air. When I turned the corner at the pub, two... I think two, men came running across your lawn and almost knocked us to the ground. Bobo! Bosco! Come. Come here." She stomped her foot. "Asseyez Vous!"

I noticed two sets of deep footprints that began at the bottom of the porch and crossed the front lawn to the street. "Oh God!" I pulled out my cell phone and pressed "three." Answer me Phillip, I prayed.

Phillip didn't answer so I left another panicked voice mail. I started to text him when he called back.

"It's one o'clock in the morning. Are you okay? What's

up?" Phillip sounded like I just woke him up.

"Why don't you ever pick up your phone?" I complained and then, in one run on sentence, I told him everything that had happened in the last forty-five minutes.

"Where are you now?" he asked. This time his voice was wide awake and shaking a little.

"Standing out here freezing my ass off in front of The Diner."

"Okay I'll be right there. Do not go in alone." He hung up.

"I'm not alone," I said as Bobo and Bosco finally collapsed on my feet. Lucille stooped down and picked up their leashes. The dogs were panting hard, tongues on the ground.

"Lucille did you recognize them?" I asked pulling my collar up around my chin. "Geez-o-pete it's freezing out here." I could see my breath like smoke hanging in the air.

"No I'm not completely sure if they were even men. I think so. No. It all happened so fast." Lucille shivered and pulled her poncho tight around her and Blanche.

Phillip came flying around the corner armed with a fireplace shovel. He slid to halt just short of Bobo's nose. I looked at the shovel then up at him.

"I was at the Pub," he shrugged. "It was all I could grab. Are you girls okay?" he asked.

The dogs were up again wrapping themselves around Phillips legs. He absently patted them and said, "Well, let's go take a look."

He led the parade up the walk and porch steps aiming the shovel like it was a sawed off shotgun. I was sandwiched between the two dripping and drooling dogs. Lucille brought up the rear, her little baby safely stuffed inside her poncho. At the front door Phillip stopped short. I bumped into his back, Lucille bounced off of me. Larry, Moe and Curly. Larry poked his head in and pulled it back out quickly.

"Damn." Phillip wheeled around and pulled me close.

TIFFANY BLUES

The shovel smacked me in the butt.

"Ow!" I yelped, exaggerating the impact.

"It's not good, Coco. Maybe we should wait a little, and call the cops," he said sniffing my hair. "Is that men's cologne?" he asked.

"No, cinnamon buns."

The dogs ripped away from Lucille and bulldozed past Phillip.

I wriggled out of Phillip's arms and stumbled in the door. "Oh my God," I fought back tears. The place was a disaster; a real tornado couldn't have been worse. Broken apothecary jars, herbs everywhere. Bookcases and chairs overturned. The chocolate case was miraculously untouched. "Who would do this to us?"

"Well, Kelly was pretty ticked last night when I broke up with her," Phillip said.

"Then why didn't she wreck your place?"

"She may have, I haven't been home yet."

"Geez-o-pete. Is anything missing? I can't tell."

"All is not lost, the black velvet stilettos are still here," Phillip waved the shovel in the direction of the shoe display.

"Halleluiah, we're saved. Stilletos and chocolates, what else do we need," I said.

"Bobo! Spit that out!" Lucille commanded. She grabbed Bobo in a headlock, squeezed his jaw open and shoved her fingers down his throat.

"*Bleh,*" Bobo said, heaving a big wad of green gook. So much for the lemon balm.

Crash! My adrenaline kicked into overdrive and I hit the floor. Lucille threw her body over as many dogs as she could and Phillip just stood there swinging the shovel every which way over his head. The dogs squeezed out from under Lucille and bounded straight to the storage closet. *Crash!* Uncontrollable barking and clawing at the closet door. Phillip silently signaled to me and Lucille to stay put. Screw that. I crouched next to him and we tiptoed our way to the closet. Phillip held the shovel over his head like a baseball bat and nodded to me. I flung the door open.

Nothing could have prepared me for the sight in front of me. There was Flo plopped on the floor of the closet, the fur-edged hood of her winter parka tightly zipped around her face, wrapped from head to toe in duct tape and buried under a mound of high heels. Cheeks squished together, green eyes bugged out and angry. She was trying to talk.

"Sweetie! Geez-o-pete, What happened? Are you okay?" I asked as I ripped the tape off her face.

Flo screamed in pain. "What the F took you so long? How many pounds of lasagna did you eat?"

"Sorry, I didn't get the Bat Signal." I stifled a laugh.

"Get me outta here. I gotta pee!"

Phillip shot to the potting room and came back with a pair of pruning shears.

"Cut me out of this! Hurry up."

Bosco muscled his way past us and climbed onto the mountain of shoes. He contorted his head and shimmied a wet dog shake right in Flo's face.

"*Ugghhhh,*" Flo spit.

"Bosco! Stop!" Lucille tried in vain to pull him away. "Mon Dieu!" she cried.

The last of the stilettos fell off the shelf and hit Flo right on the head. Bosco scampered to his mama. "Forget the pruning shears!" Flo screamed. "Just get me to the bathroom. NOW!"

Phillip and I picked her up by the arms and dragged the mummy to the bathroom. He ran back to get the shears while I tried to pull down her jeans. Phillip handed me the shears through the door, covering his eyes. I managed to cut through the tape on her legs.

"I'm gonna die. I'm gonna die," Flo moaned as her legs were freed. "Too late, I'm dead." She started to wet her pants.

TIFFANY BLUES

"Oh, man, gross! Couldn't you hold it for just one more second?" I said as I cut her arms free.

"Obviously not. I've got an extra pair of yoga pants back in the potting room."

"I'll go get them Sweetie. You clean yourself up." And I left her to do her thing.

I knocked on the bathroom door and handed off the yoga pants and a plastic bag for the wet ones. Next time it opened, Flo was holding her taped up parka in one arm, the full plastic bag in the other, tears streaming down her face. Her red spikes were matted down on her head. The tears stopped when she saw the shop. "Holy shit! They trashed the place."

***

"I didn't see anything. I came back to grab those black shoes." Flo looked at me, "You know the ones with the metal spikes." Then to Lieutenant Saunders of Dolly's Ferry's finest, who was writing down everything she said in his little notebook, "I was going to take them with me to Oscar's for the weekend, as a surprise."

The young lieutenant looked confused. "Were they here when you got here? The perpetrators?"

Flo was curled up with a blanket around her in the now upright comfy chair. "You really call them perpetrators?"

Saunders nodded and tried again, "Were they here when you got here?"

"They must have been. I didn't hear anyone come in. I was reaching up into the closet for the box and next thing I knew a giant flabby cold hand was slapped over my mouth. I couldn't breathe. I thought I was going to die. He told me not to scream so I kicked him hard in the shin."

"You go girl!" Phillip crouched down next to her and pretended to punch her in the arm. He handed her a mug of steaming tea, the good witch mug.

"Did he let go?" I asked.

"Hardly, that's when he threw me face down on the closet floor and sat on me." Flo sipped her tea. "He must have weighed four hundred pounds. His partner came over and told him to tie me up. Once he was done duct taping me they shut the door and told me if I tried to get out they'd kill me. If C hadn't come I would have peed my pants in the closet."

"Did you recognize either of them? Can you describe them?" Saunders asked.

"Big, dark, scary, ski masks... no I didn't recognize them. I kept my eyes shut tight. I told them I was keeping my eyes shut so they didn't have to kill me because I couldn't identify them. That's when they taped my mouth."

"No kidding," I said. Phillip and I were checking the cash register and the rest of the inventory. Lucille had taken the puppies home after she gave the Lieutenant her story about the two men running across the lawn. "Looks like all the cash is still here. I can't find anything else missing," I informed anyone who was listening.

"Where's the computer?" Phillip asked.

"I left it right here," I said pointing to the empty shelf behind the cash register counter. "Damn, they took the computer."

"Crap," Flo said.

"My astrology program. How are we going to function without the astrology software? I have charts to do," I lamented.

"Don't worry, I'll lend you my laptop," Phillip offered.

"Thanks, that'll help a little but I still don't have the astrology programs, they cost a couple hundred dollars."

"Maybe we can claim a loss of income on the insurance," Flo said.

"Maybe you..." Phillip was interrupted as Jason and Louis, burst onto the scene all done up in their Friday night best. They had been on their way home from a show in New Hope and saw the flashing lights outside.

TIFFANY BLUES

"OMG! What is this town coming to?" Jason cried when he saw the mess.

We fell over each other explaining what had happened.

"Florilla darling, are you alright? How utterly terrifying! Somebody get the poor woman a drink!" Jason scurried over and sat on the edge of the chair and hugged Flo with both arms. "Louis, run next door and get the girl a vodka gimlet. Never mind, get her an entire bottle of Grey Goose."

"No, Louis, don't bother I'm fine, really," Flo said but her protests went unheard.

"Why me? Why can't you go? I did all the driving tonight. I'm tired." Louis was getting defiant in his old age. "I can stay here and comfort Florilla just as well as you can." He folded his arms across his chest.

Jason glared at Louis and huffed off to the pub. "He's not the boss of me," Louis said as he took Jason's place on the arm of Flo's chair. "He's been bossing me around all night. He even made me change my clothes, twice, before we went out. Honestly."

"Well, I'll let you ladies be for now. If you think of anything else, call me." Lieutenant Saunders handed me a card. Phillip started to pick up some of the broken glass but the Lieutenant stopped him. "We'll be back in the morning to do a formal investigation so please don't touch anything else. I'm going to put up some crime scene tape. You should all go home and get some rest."

"Crime scene tape?" Flo moaned. "That'll be great for business."

I thought of telling him about the car following me, but decided against it. Whoever did this was after something and I was pretty sure it was more than the Dolly's Ferry Police Department was prepared to handle. Besides, I didn't know if the two things were even related.

"Flo, after Jason comes back, I'll take you home. Want me to stay with you tonight?" I didn't really want to be alone either even though that meant I was going to have to sleep on Flo's awful pull out chair. The one with the metal bar that went right through my spine.

"Thank you Sweetie, it's been a terrible night."

"For you and me both. Wait'll you hear what I went through."

"Did you pee in your pants too?"

"I'll tell you about it later."

Jason was already back, out of breath, arms loaded with a liter bottle of Grey Goose, a liter bottle of Roses Lime Juice, three green olives on a stick and even a chilled martini glass.

Louis came over and took the glass from Jason. "Well at least you thought enough to bring a glass, you still have a little class." They were not having a good night either.

"Make that a lot of class, way more than some people I know." Jason grabbed the glass out of Louis's hand and ambled back to the kitchen to make Flo a martini.

Three martinis later, Phillip said, "Okay Flo, time to go home." He helped her out of her chair.

"Good idea or I won't be able to walk." She plopped right back down.

"She'll sleep like a baby now," Jason whispered in my ear.

"Yes she will," Louis agreed. He gave Flo a big hug, but she was pretty oblivious.

On their way out, Jason turned back around. "Girls make sure you lock your doors tight. We'll check on you in the morning...'night 'night," he said.

Phillip and I gathered up Flo and her ruined parka and rolled her into my car.

"I'll lock up. Get her home and try to get some sleep, okay?" Phillip kissed the top of my head.

"Fat chance."

***

We drove the ten minutes south along the river to Flo's house in silence. She had her eyes closed, but I knew she wasn't sleeping. I kept scanning the rearview mirror, but there was nothing to see. As soon as I turned left off Rt. 29 and headed uphill, Flo mumbled "I think I drank too much."

"You're not going to throw up, are you?" I started to drive faster. "This isn't another calamari incident, is it?"

"No, I'm not going to be sick. I'm just a little dizzy."

"It's okay, we're almost home." I pulled into her driveway, helped her out, tucked her dead jacket under her arm, and steadied her as she made her way up the path to the house.

I waited, shivering while Flo fished around in her purse for her keys.

"I give up. I can't find my keys. Maybe they fell out in the closet," Flo said still rummaging through her purse. I bent down and took the spare key out from under the *"Quiet, the Garden is Sleeping"* rock and slipped it into the lock of the front door to Raspberry Cottage.

Originally built in the late 1700's as the caretaker's quarters, Flo's little house reminds me of a hobbit hole; tiny but adorable. It's painted moss green, has an old fieldstone foundation and leaded glass windows that can turn sunlight into rainbows. The cottage sits up on a bluff overlooking the Delaware, tucked in a grove of mature white oaks that rain down acorns by the thousands every fall. From the bedroom you can watch the sunset over the ridge on the Pennsylvania side of the river. From the living room you can watch the sunrise over Flo's garden and the fields of raspberry brambles that grow wild around it.

Charming as the fairytale setting is, I sure wouldn't want to live there. It may be romantic, but it's got almost zero closet space, ancient plumbing that is in constant need of repair, uneven, random width pine floors that generally list to port and a crack in the kitchen wall that reappears every winter no matter how many times she has Oscar fix it. Flo doesn't care. It suits her earth spirit perfectly and she loves it just the way it is.

I pushed open the creaky kitchen door and the Elvi came running to greet us. I'd forgotten all about them. Glad they weren't in The Diner tonight. I picked up Old Elvis and kissed his nose.

"I want to call Cody," Flo announced letting her ruined parka fall to the floor. She dropped her purse on the blue painted drop-leaf table and dug around in the bottom until she found her phone.

"It's almost three in the morning. You're going to wake him up," I said bolting the door and turning the handle to make sure it was locked. I glanced up at the old barn beams across the ceiling, hoping Flo still had her bunches of dried sage hanging overhead for protection. Good, she had dried mint up there too.

"He must know there's something wrong. He's probably lying in bed just waiting for me to call."

"Go ahead, call him. I can't wait to be lying in bed asleep."

"Want some jammies?"

"I guess so." I set Elvis back down on the slanted pine floor. He ran off downhill towards the living room.

While she was waiting for Cody to answer, Flo picked her parka up off the floor, walked over to the sink and opened the cabinet underneath. She stuffed the jacket into the trash as she held the phone to her ear with her shoulder. "They're in the bottom drawer of my dresser. Pick any pair you want," she said pointing to her bedroom.

I crossed the twelve feet of rustic kitchen to the little hallway with three doors. The one to the right was the bathroom/laundry room, straight ahead was the bedroom, and the one to the left, was Flo's shoe closet. This whole half of the house is practically new; it was added on sometime around 1940. I slowly opened door number two knowing that there was just about a quarter inch of clearance between the corner of the bed and the edge of the door.

Although it's so Flo, the art deco bedroom furniture is

way too big for the room; the set was her grandmother's, then her mother's. The dresser is the kind with a huge round mirror with an etched glass border and curved drawers with crystal pulls that look like cut jewels. I squeezed my way over to it, bent down and pulled at the knobs on the bottom drawer. The drawer stuck, the dresser quivered and a silver marcasite framed photograph fell to the floor.

It was a picture from a Halloween past. Flo was her usual Glinda, the Good Witch, in her pink toile gown complete with mylar crown and sparkling butterfly wand. She had her arms wrapped around a beaming Oscar, the Scarecrow. They had stuck a broom through the sleeves of his shirt to give him fake arms that pointed straight out and stuffed real hay in his sleeves and collar. That was some party. He almost set the room on fire when one of the fake arms took out the jack-o-lantern on the kitchen counter.

One of the few Halloweens that Flo wasn't Glinda was the year I wanted to be Cruella DeVil. Flo and Oscar really got into the idea and conjured up punkified versions of Pongo and Purdie complete with spiked collars, leather leashes and safety pins through their sock ears. Pongo's spots even spelled out "Bite Me" across his butt. That party was a blast and got even better when I hooked up with the Green Hornet in his Black Beauty. But that was a long time ago. I put the photo back in its place next to the shadow box of dried red roses and the card that read *My love for you will last longer than the Universe*. Why didn't she just marry the man?

I finally got the bottom drawer open and rifled through Flo's collection of flannel pajamas. I knew the leopard pair was off limits. Instead I chose the blue striped cows jumping over yellow Moons. They were better than the pink ones with bacon and eggs and frying pans all over them or the lime green ones with pink flamingos in santa caps. Flannel pjs are like comfort food for Flo. For me, well, it's been a long time since I've slept in anything but my own skin.

I listened as I slipped out of my clothes. Flo wasn't talking. Not good. I hoped she'd get hold of Cody or we weren't going to get any sleep. Must be a twin thing, she always wants Cody in a real crisis. They were best friends growing up and watched each other's back all through the angst of high school. Flo felt lost when Cody went off to the University of Miami to study marine biology instead of going with her to Rutgers. Their father wasn't happy about it either since being a professor at Rutgers, Doctor Munrow could have gotten them both free tuition. After graduation Cody went for a job interview in Key West, discovered chocolate covered frozen key lime pie on a stick and never came back. I buttoned the last cow button and heard Flo curse.

"Any luck?" I came back into the kitchen. Flo was holding onto the slate mantle, swaying slightly as she peered into the darkness of the cold stone hearth. The hearth gave the house so much character. It was such a shame, instead of a warm crackling fire the unusable walk-in fireplace was filled with a copper tub of dried hydrangeas. From the looks of things, it wouldn't be long before Flo was in the tub too.

"He didn't answer. I need to talk to him!" Flo's voice cracked.

"Could be he's out on the boat in the Dry Tortugas with no cell service. Why don't you call Oscar?"

"I'll do that when I get into bed," she said, turning around and walking ever so carefully past me to the bedroom. "Those jammies look cute on you."

"Adorable." I followed her. Flo dropped her phone on the nightstand, then got on her knees to wrestle with the sticky dresser drawer. I curled up on the bed while she took out the leopard pajamas and started to undress. "So what happened with you tonight?" she asked me.

"I had a date with Q," I blurted.

TIFFANY BLUES

"I was taped up in a dark closet while you were out dancing and doing the Q man? No lasagna?" Flo said from underneath her pajama top.

"We didn't dance or do. I met him after dinner with Chris and company. I just had a drink, well, and a cappucino with him," I yawned. "I'll tell you all about it tomorrow."

"So you didn't sleep with him?"

"Give me a little credit. No, I didn't sleep with him. Nothing happened...until my ride home. Somebody followed me all the way from Princeton. Scared the bejeezus out of me. I tried to call you, but you, now I know why, didn't answer. I finally lost him in Stockton, then I got to The Diner and, well, you know the rest."

"Do you think there's a connection? This wasn't just a random break-in and robbery. They were methodical and prepared. With duct tape," Flo said as she stumbled back out to the bathroom.

"Sweetie, I think they used *our* duct tape." I yelled so she could hear me.

"Damn."

"Why do you think anyone would want our computer? There's nothing on it but emails, invoices, and our AB stuff. I guess there were some really good love spells..."

I heard the toilet flush. "Or, maybe they wanted to know our source for peony roots," Flo laughed.

"I can't think about this now. I'll go crazy. I rolled off the bed. "Let's think about this tomorrow. I'm fried," I said.

"Me too," Flo climbed into her bed. She grabbed her cell phone off the nightstand and pulled the thick pink floral comforter over her. Young Elvis was already curled up near her feet. "I'm going to call Oscar then I'm going to sleep. Do you want help with the chair? The pillows and blankets are in the coffee table chest. You know where."

"I'm good. Try to sleep Sweetie. We'll talk in the morning. G'night." I blew a kiss in the air. Flo blew one

189

back and unlocked her phone.

The last thing I heard as I closed the bedroom door was "Oh Oz, it was *terrrrrrible*! My bladder almost burst. I could have died like Tycho Brahe!"

SEVENTEEN

I woke up with a start, beads of sweat rolling down my face. The room was pitch black and stifling. Something was wrong with my right leg, as if my ankle was being squeezed in a vice. Pins and needles up my thigh. I turned on the lamp and yanked back the covers.

"What the f...?"

A hideous diamond-backed mother of a reptile was coiled around my leg, slithering over the blue striped cows and yellow Moons. The snake's tail was hanging off the end of the bed and its head, the size of a grapefruit, was about to delve into my crotch. The grapefruit slipped between my legs and paused, forked tongue darting in and out. Another taste and the snake slid across my stomach, up between my breasts, over my shoulder. *Around my neck.* Was it going to cut off my airway or snap my neck? Either way, if I was going down, I was going down fighting. I grabbed the snake with both hands and tried to pry it off my neck. It curled tighter. I heard a hiss and its jaws opened wide. Fangs sunk into my cheek and hot toxin oozed up into my eyes. Oh God, I was going to die in flannel pajamas.

I bolted upright, eyes popping, sucking air. I slapped the covers. No snakes. Only a petrified cat crying by the side of the pull-out chair. Shafts of sunlight streamed in through the arched window casting a rectangular pattern of shadow and light over the entire living room. It was morning and I wasn't dead; I only felt like I was.

I rolled over the cold metal frame and reached out to comfort poor Old Elvis. "Sorry babycakes, Mama had a nasty dream." I scratched his head and crawled out of bed.

My legs felt like rubber as I put on the tea kettle. The fat one was at my heels, meowing pitifully until he heard the magic tinkle of the crunchies in his dish. Young Elvis heard it too and started scratching wildly at Flo's bedroom door, whining to get out. I opened the door for him and caught a glimpse of the third cat sprawled across the bed like a dead leopard. "Shush," I whispered as Elvis slipped by me, but it was too late.

"It's okay, I'm awake," Flo groaned.

"Morning Sweetie, I'm making you coffee," I yawned.

"Thanks, I need it. Make it a double."

I padded back to the kitchen and dug around the cabinets for some kind of tea with caffeine and the stash of instant coffee bags Flo keeps in case of emergency. I stood on tiptoe to feel around the top shelf and an unopened package of Dunkin' Donuts ground hazelnut jumped out, bounced off my forehead and landed on the floor. I rubbed my head and just stared at it.

Universe you've got to be kidding. I bent down to pick up the foil pouch and a little stab of pain shot through my lower back. Instant karma courtesy of the night-from-hell in a sleeper chair? I frowned at Flo's bedroom door. Too bad, it was the instant coffee bags or nothin'.

Flo was sitting up in bed staring out at the river when I returned with the caffeine. "Look at those ice flows. It'll be May before the snow is gone," she lamented.

I handed her the hot mug. "Want to go to Key West for a few days?"

TIFFANY BLUES

"I wish. Never did get hold of Cody."

"Well, we should try to get down there. We could use a vacation, even if it's just for a long weekend."

"Maybe we could get away in March, but it'd have to be before Spring Break hits and gardening season kicks in. We could go with Cody to the Dry Tortugas, it'd be fun."

Cody Munrow fulfills his nature loving genetic imperative by spending a lot of time in the Dry Tortugas studying sea creatures. He rents a small one bedroom apartment, on Southard, in a converted Bahamian that's been owned by the Castellanos family since the late 1800's. Flo and I stay in the cozy little guest cottage in the back whenever we visit. Comes complete with live rooster wake-up calls.

"Fun? The only thing other than marine life in the Dry Tortugas is the prison where they sent Dr. Mudd because he helped John Wilkes Booth escape. But you two can go to the Tortugas and I'll wait for you back at the Green Parrot."

"Whatever. Maybe we don't have to wait until March either. Soon as Valentine's Day is over we're good to go."

"Okay, when you do talk to Cody tell him to have old Mrs. Castellanos get the guest cottage ready for us."

Florilla gave me a thumbs up and took a sip and looked up at me over the brim. "Coffee bags?"

"Sorry, I left my coffee grinder at home."

"But I have a new package of Dunkin' Donuts hazelnut in the cabinet."

"Yeah, I know." I shook my head and went back to the living room.

Flo staggered in after me and flopped down on the loveseat. Her spotted leopard pajamas made a striking contrast to the cabbage roses on the small chintz sofa. Leopard and roses, a perfect combination for this high maintenance redhead I thought.

Flo yawned. "Sorry Sweetie, don't be mad at me. I'm still not myself. I know Jason and Louis meant well but I downed almost a whole bottle of Goose. My head hurts something wicked."

"My head hurts too," I said.

"Did you make yourself some tea? Do you want something to eat?" she offered.

"Like what?"

"I think there are some cranberry muffins in the breadbox and cantaloupe in the fridge." Flo went to look in the refrigerator. She stood there gazing at its contents for a few seconds then started juggling juice cartons and Tupperware containers. Flo's fridge is always bursting at the seams, even though she lives alone. Well unless you count Oscar or me on weekends. A gallon of Mud Fudge Brownie, a dozen chocolate éclaires, a pound of canolis. I guess it's a Taurus thing. With Venus as her ruling planet, Flo feels compelled to have mass quantities of yummies on hand at all times. "You never know when one might have to whip up dessert for all forty five members of the Delaware Valley Garden Brigade on a moment's notice," she says.

I came and peeked over her shoulder. "Oh, and I also have cinnamon buns and a chocolate pecan pie." She reached way in the back and pulled out the pie. I got out two forks and we headed back to the loveseat.

Bright sunshine now filled the pink and cream living room of Raspberry Cottage and I was struck once again at how beautiful the light and the views were in this house in spite of its miniscule size. We took turns at forkfuls of chocolate pecan pie and gazed out the floor to ceiling window that overlooks Flo's garden and her little stone potting shed. We silently chewed and watched the chickadees and titmice come and go at the bird feeder, eagerly filling their beaks with sunflower seeds. The blanket of ice must be making it almost impossible for them to find their own food now. It was hard to believe that in just a few months the frozen beds would be filled with irises and roses and daylilies in full bloom; a patchwork quilt of purple, red, and gold. Flo liked to call her garden "The Ladies Room" in honor of all her female relatives that bore flower first names, the same as the old fashioned perennials she had planted out there. The antique roses were her favorite; they were for her mother.

Flo broke the silence first. "Doesn't this make you think of my Nana Iris's house?" she asked wistfully, still staring out the window.

I knew this was coming. She always does this when she's really upset; reminisces about her grandmother's house and her childhood. Hallucinating is more like it.

"Always does." I agreed in spite of the fact that Raspberry Cottage is a far cry from Nana Iris's rambling Greek Revival mansion in the Finger Lakes where Flo and Cody spent their summers as kids. Flo's mother, Rose, and Rose's only sister, Aunt Violet, grew up in that 16 room maze. When Flo's grandfather Raoul died, Flo's crazy-as-a-loon Great Aunt Lily moved in so Iris wouldn't be alone in that big house.

Great Aunt Lily, Iris's schizophrenic older sister, is ninety-two now. She claims that ever since she was little she's been able to communicate with dead ancestors through the family crystal; a talent she puts to good use every October thirty-first.

Flo's got some wild stories about Halloweens at her Nana's house, probably the reason she's got such thing about the holiday. Iris would don her witch hat and set out the candles and jack-o-lanterns while Lily prepared the dining room for elaborate séances with the dearly departed. Flo's great aunt would cover the massive ebony table with every piece of stemware from the china closet then arrange them in ways that were "harmonically compatible with the spirits of the dead." Iris always played along, pretending that she did indeed feel the presence of Aunt Lily's beloved poodle, Chauncy Charles, under the table. But come the end of the evening, Iris would fill two of the largest goblets with a bottle of Raoul's favorite red wine and she and Lily would drink to his continued good health. It was easy to see how much Flo had inherited from Nana Iris, but sometimes I wondered if the universe had slipped her one too many of Aunt Lily's genes in the process.

I looked over at Flo and decided to change the subject. "Wanna hear about my nightmare?" I asked through a mouthful of pie.

"Your date or the car chase?" Flo answered.

"Neither, I had a god-awful nightmare last night. I woke up screaming and sweating. Scared the bejeezus out of Elvis."

"I didn't hear you scream."

"I was paralyzed. It was a silent scream. There was this giant snake in my bed crawling up between my legs, up my body and it wrapped itself around my neck and strangled me then sunk its fangs into my cheek. I really thought I was dead."

"That's horrible Sweetie. Why didn't you come wake me up?"

"I did. I had the nightmare right before I came into your room. What do you think it means?"

"What kind of snake was it?"

"I don't know. An enormous brown snake with these beige-diamondy sort of patches all over it. Why does it matter?"

Flo got up and went over to the built-in book shelves that flanked the floor to ceiling window. You can tell a lot about people by their book shelves and it's amazing how different Flo's are from mine. My shelves are filled with things like healing crystals and angels and several hundred books on Reiki, astrology, psychology, spiritual self help, tantric sex, dating do's and don'ts, chakra therapy and a collection of biographies of both famous and infamous women, including way too many books on Jacqueline Kennedy Onassis and the Queens of England. Flo's bookshelves are filled with plant presses and horse chestnuts and several hundred books on gardening, herbal lore, the lives of trees, antique maps, spellcrafts, faeries, and wildlife of every kind, including way too many books on reptiles and amphibians.

She ran her finger along the rows until found what she was looking for; *Field Guide to Common Reptiles of New Jersey*. Who even has a book like that? She flipped through it, and came over to show me a color plate.

"Did it look like this?"

I peered at the book, "I guess so."

"Well then it's a Copperhead." She started reading aloud from the book, "They are poisonous pit vipers that can grow to be about 5 feet long. A copperhead can inflict a bite that is extremely painful and may cause extensive scarring and loss of use of a limb. Their bites do not usually result in death unless medical attention is ignored."

"Oh that's comforting. So what does it mean?"

She stuffed the book back in its place. "What does it mean? It means we're both completely traumatized, that's what. I was wrapped in duct tape from head to toe last night. You were followed by a maniac. The snakes are after us! Of course, then again, the snake totem is supposed to be a symbol of sexual desire, the hidden force moving through you, trying to snake its way out."

"Get your dream book," I told her.

She put the snake book back on the shelf and grabbed a thick, well-worn paperback.

"Okay, here it is. *Snakes*," Flo read aloud. "*If you see a snake or are bitten by one in your dream, you are being threatened by hidden fears. The dream is a signal that there is something in your life, conscious or unconscious, that you are not paying attention to but should. The snake is also a phallic symbol and a sign of dangerous or forbidden temptation. If you are afraid of the snake in your dream, it could signal a fear of sex or commitment. The snake may also symbolize a person who can't be trusted.*"

"Well, I think that sums things up pretty well," Flo snapped the book shut and jammed it back onto the shelf.

"Okay, never mind. Let's talk about something else. Want me to tell you about my date?"

Flo sat back down and lifted another forkful of chocolate pecan pie. "Mmm-hmmm," she mumbled.

I gave her a blow by blow starting with Melissa's living room paint job, the wine spill of the century and the size six sweater. I worked my way up to the bar and cappuccino. I just got to the description of Q's bedroom when she interrupted me.

"What were you doing in his bedroom?" she asked licking her fork.

"Having an incredibly hot fantasy, which, he walked in on. I was so embarrassed I had to get out of there. End of date."

"Any signs of other women?"

I picked at the pie trying to decide if I should tell her. "I'm pretty sure he got a call from a woman right before I left. And there was this signed head shot of his, quote unquote, sister, on the refrigerator who is supposedly a model and who by the way, had an uncanny resemblance to the woman at the Plaza."

"Sister my ass. Sounds like Q's the snake in your bed."

I decided not to even mention the Tiffany box.

"So he walked me to my car and someone started following me almost from the minute I left the square. I took all the back roads and I thought for a minute it might be Ed, from across the street, leaving the hospital."

"That makes sense. Maybe it *was* just Ed."

"Nope. Couldn't have been. I made a couple turns I didn't need to make and the car stayed right with me."

"You're right, Ed wouldn't have done that. He'd have had heart failure if he had to alter his routine. Remember the time he didn't come out of his house for a week and I went to check on him because Lyla his next door neighbor came over and said she was sure she smelled something bad coming from his place and she was afraid to go over. And since you refused to talk to him I finally went over.

TIFFANY BLUES

Remember that? He'd called in sick to work the whole time they had the road detour in Lambertville."

"Like I said, it wasn't Ed. Anyway, the car followed me all the way up the river. It was a chase just like in the movies."

"What did you do? I would have been hysterical from the minute I noticed the car behind me."

"I sped up and by the time I hit Stockton I was praying the cops would stop me, but the cops stopped the guy who was chasing me instead. I hauled my butt out of there and then I got up here and all hell broke loose."

"C, this is really scaring me. Duncan's dead. Blaine hightails it out of the country. I get bound and gagged in a closet and almost die from a burst bladder and some luneball's chasing you. What the hell's going on?" Flo stabbed her fork into her last piece of pie.

"You know it could all just be a coincidence and maybe none of these things are related."

"I guess. That'd be an awfully big coincidence don't you think?"

"Yeah, but Mercury is retrograde so who knows. I mean what are the odds that I'd see a gorgeous guy at a lecture, then run into him hours later, meet him, give him my card and actually get a date with him?"

"And lose the Tiffany box, all in one day."

"Okay, just for shits and giggles, let's say everything really is related. Obviously, somebody thinks we know something about something. But why take the computer?" I asked.

Flo leaned back and thought for a few seconds waving her fork in the air. "Okay, so Sammy's having an affair with Duncan..."

"Or Tracy."

"Or Tracy, and Janice is jealous. Janice pushes Tracy off the waterfall and strangles Duncan. They're dead. She gets his job and fires Sammy. She wants our computer to get our love spells so she can get a new guy."

"Gee, why didn't I think of that?"

"Hey, it's possible."

"Look, Janice doesn't know us from a hole in the wall. And what about Blaine? Why did he skip the country?" I stuffed my last big chunk of pie into my mouth. Flo leaned forward, fork still in hand.

"Okay, so Sammy's having an affair with Duncan. Andrew and Blaine are both in love with Sammy. Blaine strangles Duncan. Duncan's dead. Andrew kills Blaine. Blaine's dead. He's not in Indonesia. Tracy committed suicide because she was in love with Andrew and he loved Sammy. Janice needs a new guy so she steals our computer to get the love spells."

"You're on crack."

"No, seriously, you and I both know that this has to be about Blaine. If he didn't kill Duncan himself, he had to be working for somebody who wanted Duncan dead."

"I still don't get it. If it is Blaine, why would he want Duncan dead?"

"I don't know. But it can't be a coincidence that the message in Duncan's book would lead us directly to Exotic Aquatics and the pitcher plants," Flo dropped the fork into the empty pan. "Duncan was trying to tell us that Blaine was his killer. He knew he was going to die!"

"That's got to be it. Whoever robbed us thought that since Duncan gave us the book we must have had more information. They didn't really want the computer, they must have been after the book. Where is it?"

"It's here. I brought it home last night when I closed up The Diner. It's safe in the nightstand in my bedroom." Flo jumped up and ran into the bedroom. She was back in a second leafing through the *New World Apothecary*.

"But Blaine didn't know about the book. Besides, he's dead or out of the country. Who else knows about the book?" I asked.

"Sammy. She may have told Andrew about it too. Maybe they are all in this together. It's a conspiracy," Flo said.

It suddenly occurred to me that I had told Q all about the book but I wasn't about to share that with Flo. Not yet anyway. I needed to talk to him again first.

"Or maybe it was NYPD," She offered as an afterthought.

"You think Carlton and Mooney are going to come all the way back to Dolly's Ferry to trash our place looking for a book that they've already seen? I don't think so." I picked up the little rumpled pile of sheets next to the pull-out chair.

"Well, Duncan said that he knew a little bit about Astrology. I think he knew a lot about Astrology," I said rolling the sheets into a ball. "And if he was really leaving that message for Sammy, then maybe she knows a lot about astrology too, maybe more than she's saying."

"But we gave her a copy of the page, so she doesn't need the book."

"Unless there's more secret information in that book that we haven't uncovered yet."

Flo opened the book to page one and began examining it closely. "We need to talk to Sammy again."

"I can't think about this anymore right now, The Diner's trashed and we've got insurance agents to deal with. Let's talk about this later, okay?"

Flo shrugged her shoulders and put the book down on the coffee table. She gathered up the empty pie pan and forks and headed for the sink. I went to the bathroom, stuffed the sheets in the washer and poured in the liquid detergent that smelled like fresh limes. Just as I closed the lid, I heard the front door creak open, then bang shut. Flo squealed and I flipped the knob to "start." Not even the churning water of the washing machine could drown out the sounds of the blissful reunion in the other room.

I came out of the bathroom and whizzed past them to grab my clothes from the living room.

"Oh OZ, thank God!" She hugged him tightly. He was

kissing the top of her hair. Geez-o-Pete.

"Hi Oscar," I said as I zipped back into the bathroom to change. I took my time getting dressed and threw the flannel pajamas into the washer with the sheets. I even considered changing the cat litter. Oscar and Flo were still embracing when I finally came out.

"I'm going home to take a shower and put on clean clothes. I'll meet you at The Diner in about an hour," I said as I closed the door behind me. I don't think they even heard me.

EIGHTTEEN

Flo, Oscar and Abby were already there when I rounded the corner by the Pub. They were all pacing and bouncing on the porch of trying to keep warm. Two police cars were parked out front and the whole place was surrounded by yards of yellow crime scene tape. The Lieutenant had gone a little cop happy. As soon as she spotted me, Abby jumped off the porch and ran to give me a bear hug. She almost knocked me to the ground with her arm tackle.

"Oh Clara this is awful. How could anyone do this to us? I'm so so so so sorry."

"Thanks Abbs, don't worry, it'll be okay," I said hugging her back. "Nothing that can't be fixed. We'll just clean up, get more herbs, and we can always get another computer. It will be a bitch to duplicate the contact files though."

"I'll help you. I have a kick-ass memory," she volunteered. "And I know all of our customers."

"They're almost done," Oscar said as I joined them on the porch. I could see Lieutenant Saunders and the one and only detective in Dolly's Ferry, Sergeant Roberta Figarino, Figgy to her friends, inside dusting the cash register for fingerprints. Lieutenant Saunders was working overtime on this.

I opened the door a crack. "They didn't take any money, we checked," I yelled.

Oscar nodded. "They still have to check everything, C."

"Look, here comes Ilyana," Abby announced. "Word spreads like wildfire around here."

"Yep, all this yellow tape has nothing to do with it." Flo cracked.

Ilyana was bustling up our front walk clutching a brown overstuffed deli bag in her arms. She was wearing tight black leggings and low cut top with a gold lame sweater wrapped around her shoulders. Elegant gold pointy-toed slides finished the outfit. It didn't matter that it was noon and freezing, Ilyana always dressed to the nines no matter what the time of day or weather.

Little puffs of her breath hung in the air as she hurried up to the porch. Oscar met her at the bottom of the stairs, took the bag from her and reached out his hand to steady her on the slippery steps.

Ilyana grabbed my hand, "I heard about last night. The police are here, yes?" I nodded. "It ees terrible." She shook her head and clucked her tongue. "Oy, I brought you all sandwiches. Meat. You need your strength. And..." she smiled pointing to the bag in Oscar's arms, "Keglevich. Medicine." Flo cringed.

"Thanks for the sandwiches Ilyana, we weren't even thinking about lunch yet, this'll be great," I said.

Ilyana shivered. Oscar offered her his jacket but she shooed him away and wrapped her sparkly sweater tightly around her ample chest. "Do zey know anyzing yet? Did zey catch the basturds?"

"They still have no idea who did this," Flo said shivering. "And I'm beyond freezing in this flimsy excuse for a coat because of them. Flo moved close to Oscar and hid her face in his ski jacket.

"She had to throw away her new red parka. The duct

tape ruined it, you know... when they tied her up," Abby explained.

"Basturds." Ilyana chafed Flo's arms like she was rubbing sticks to start a campfire. "Vy dun't you all come to Etoiles and stay varm until you can go in. I just made a fresh pot of café."

"Thanks Ilyana, but Saunders and Figgy'll be done soon and we need to talk to them right away. Why don't you go back before you catch your death," I suggested.

"Besides, NYPD will probably be here soon too." Oscar announced putting the bag down on the steps by the rail. Flo lifted her head up and pushed Oscar away clearly annoyed.

"What's NYPD got to do with this?" Figgy asked, standing in the doorway.

Oscar explained. "A friend of ours was murdered in New York a week ago. Clara and Flo were among the last to see him alive. NYPD has been here once already to question them. It's all very suspicious."

"Okay, but who called them in on *this*?" she asked.

Oscar confessed, "I did. I called them last night after Flo told me what happened. I think there might be a connection. It's complicated." He looked at us. "This is out of control. You both have got to let the police handle this."

Lieutenant Saunders joined us on the porch. "The professor here is right. You need to let us handle this. When those New York hot shots get here you tell 'em to talk to us. This happened in Dolly's Ferry, it's our baby."

Figgy looked down at her feet trying to stifle a laugh.

Saunders continued, "We've got all the evidence and, if they're nice, we'll be happy to share it with them." Lieutenant Saunders was puffing out his chest as he talked.

"Did you find anything, Figgy?" I asked.

Figgy shook her head. "The place is pretty clean. Seems like they were professionals. There are fingerprints all over the place, most of them are probably yours. We'll get the State Police to run them for us. It's a mess in there but it smells minty fresh, all those herbs all over."

Roberta Figarino was single, in her mid-thirties, athletic build, zero percent body fat. Figgy grew up in Cinnaminson and quickly worked her way up to detective on the local force. Dolly's Ferry hired her about three years ago. She was a frequent candy customer and once bought a pair of red patent leather stilettos for a hot date she had in Philly. Flo and I have shared a lot of Toll House cookie pie with her at the Pub. Detective Figarino was not as tough as she looked, or wanted her male co-workers to believe.

"Oh, but we did find this." She held out a zippered baggie with a small metal object in it.

"What's that?" Abby asked.

"A bug," Saunders stated matter-of-factly. Ilyana's eyes bulged.

"A bug? Where'd you find that?" Phillip appeared bleary-eyed as he took the porch steps two at a time.

I leaned in to get a closer look.

"Under the counter near the register. Know why anyone would be bugging you?" Saunders asked.

Flo and I looked at each other. "For the same reason they wrapped me in duct tape. For the same reason they followed C home all the way from Princeton. Who knows? This is nutso." Flo flung her arms in the air and marched into the shop. Abby followed her.

"This makes no sense. Bugging us. Taking the computer. Leaving the money. What happens next?" I asked.

"We'll need to get a statement from you Clara," Figgy said. "And I'll need more from Flo too. I want the whole story about the New York thing and about your trip home last night. After that, you can start cleaning things up. We're done here."

"What do you mean done? You have to catch these guys. What if they come back?" I asked.

TIFFANY BLUES

"Don't think they'll be back but we'll step up patrols on Ferry Street just in case. We'll let you know if we come up with anything. Doubt you'll see your computer again though. Hope your insurance covers it," Lieutenant Saunders said.

Ilanya frowned at me. "See I told you. Play with bee comb, you get stung. Be careful." With that she inched her way down the steps and headed back towards Etoiles. When she reached the curb she turned around and yelled, "Dun't forget your medicine!" I waved and watched her tiptoe across the icy street. I thanked the universe for neighbors like her.

Oscar retrieved Ilyana's survival kit and the three of us followed Figgy inside. As Flo and I rehashed the last week with her, Oscar and Phillip ate fresh roast beef sandwiches and Abby started the impossible task of putting *AstroBotanics Chocolate Diner and Metaphysical Emporium* back together.

***

I finished with my story and walked Figgy to the door. Her next stop was going to be Lucille Carlisle's house.

Flo was at the candy counter inspecting a tray of caramel turtles, "Hope they didn't bug the chocolate." She reached into the case for a dark chocolate raspberry jelly ring and took a nibble. "No bugs. The diet is officially *over*."

"What are we going to do with the two cases of Sno-Caps in the back?" Phillip was on the floor cleaning up shards of glass from the broken apothecary jars.

"Don't worry, we'll eat them." Flo knelt down next to him. "Phillip, Sweetie, don't throw out the herbs. We can still use them for something."

"Easier said than done. There's glass everywhere."

"Well, we can't just throw them out…I'll help you," Flo said trying to pick the glass out of the peppermint.

Abby joined them on the floor. "Know what? We

should do a clearing and make protection charms out of what's left. To get rid of all the negative energy and keep it away."

"Excellent idea Abby, that's exactly what we'll do," Flo agreed pouring a handful of glass shards into the trash can on her right.

Phillip looked up from his glass picking on the floor.

"Not to change the subject, but NYPD is going to making an appearance any minute now. What *are* you going to tell them?" Phillip asked.

"Nothing," I said. "We'll tell them to go down to Dolly's Ferry PD and talk to them."

Oscar wasn't happy. "You have to give them the details on Flo's attack and they have to know about you being followed. We have no idea what's going on here." He was slamming books back into place on the bookcases.

"We don't know that the two things are even related." Flo said. "The person who followed C home may have just been a private investigator that Q's blonde bimbo, *NOT* his sister, hired to keep tabs on him for all we know."

The front door chimes rang. "What do you think you're doing?" Detective Mooney bellowed as he banged his fist on the wall.

Detective Carlton came in behind him. "This is a crime scene. Who told you that you could be in here?"

Flo and I exchanged exasperated glances, negative energy alright. She spoke up first. "Dolly's Ferry's finest gave us their blessing. They just left. They told us to tell you to go talk to them."

"Did you bug our store?" I asked Carlton. He looked at me and frowned.

"I don't know what you're talking about. What do you mean bug?" asked Carlton.

"Lt. Saunders found a bug under our counter. Who else would have put it there?" Flo asked. Oscar shook his head and scowled at her.

TIFFANY BLUES

"Ladies, I'm sure your conversations are very enlightening but we would need a court order to bug this... 'metaphysical emporium' and I doubt any judge would be convinced that either of you had anything to say worth bugging. Is there something we should be listening in on?" Mooney asked swiping two caramel turtles from the tray Flo had left on top of the candy case.

"Not unless you want to overhear astrology readings and the weather report," Phillip laughed.

"Have you figured out who murdered Duncan yet?" Flo asked.

"No, but it is curious to us that your shop would be trashed, and now we find out, bugged. A little more than a coincidence. Do you know why anyone would want to break into your shop?" Carlton answered.

"Isn't it your job to tell us why? You already know everything we know," I lied.

Oscar tried to calm things down. "Look, we're all stressed, we're all tired. The Detectives are just trying to do their job." He turned to Mooney. "Once Flo and C fill you in on the details can they continue to clean up here?"

Mooney took another turtle and swallowed it whole. "Yeah, this place is already contaminated. We'll just take your statements then we'll go talk to the local PD and hope they haven't screwed this up."

An hour later, after we answered their questions and went over everything in detail for the umpteenth time, Oscar escorted Carlton and Mooney out to the porch, directed them to the police station and we went back to work.

I was reorganizing the books on the astrology shelf when I heard the musical sound of gurgling water. I turned in circles trying to remember where I put my bag. I found the phone under Phillip's jacket. It was Q.

"Hello?" I answered.

"Hi, I've been thinking about you all day," Q said.

"Me too," I added. Flo looked up from salvaging the

herbs and shot me a warning. I headed to the kitchen to get the broom.

"Are we on for dinner?" he asked.

"I don't know. I've had a hellatious night. I mean after I left your place." I took a deep breath remembering my ride home the night before. "The first part wasn't hellatious, that was pretty good. The cappuccino was great by the way. But I don't think I'm up for going out tonight."

"Then we'll stay in. Can you be here around seven?"

"There? No, you don't understand. I had a terrifying ride home from Princeton last night. Someone followed me all the way to Stockton 'til the cops pulled them over for speeding. Then I got home and found Flo duct taped like a mummy locked in a closet in the store…"

Q interrupted me. "Whoa! Slow down. Flo duct taped in the closet? Is she alright? What happened?"

"She's fine, sort of. We don't know. They trashed the store, took the computer and threw her in the closet and apparently planted a bug. The cops have been here all morning and I'm freaked."

"Bugged your shop? That's insane. Why on earth would anyone want to bug you? I'm sorry Clara. Tell you what, how 'bout if I come to you tonight, we can have a quiet dinner and you can tell me all about this from the beginning. I'll bring Chinese take-out, that okay?"

It was tempting. I knew it was probably a bad idea but since when has that ever stopped me?

"Clara? Are you there?"

"How about you just bring dessert. We'll be here cleaning up for a while and I'll probably eat here."

"How's eight then?" Q asked.

"Okay." I gave him directions to my house, hung up and turned back around to face the music.

***

Phillip, Abby and I carried the last bags of garbage out

TIFFANY BLUES

to the Pub's large dumpster. Phillip opened the lid and Abby threw hers in making a face. "Whew! Nothing as rank as aroma of rotten burgers and stale beer. Yuk." She brushed her hands together. "You guys want to go to the Pub and drown our sorrows in some potato skins and cookie pie?"

Phillip looked at me expectantly, waiting for me to answer first.

"No thanks Abbs, It's almost seven already. I need to get home and boil my body in the shower. I've got to wash these creepies out of my hair," I scrubbed my fingers on my scalp.

"You're sure? Abby asked.

I nodded.

"Okay. I'll come in early tomorrow. Just sleep in and call me when you get up. Doubt it's going to be too busy. You probably don't even have to come in at all."

"But what about the candy case? The glass still needs to be cleaned and the herbs..."

"Abbs, you want some help? I can stop in for a few hours in the morning," Phillip offered.

"Don't worry. I got it covered. I'll wipe down the candy case and put the trashed herbs out in the sunshine with some amethysts to clear them all. That'll make them happy, then we can still use them to wash the creepies out of this Diner. Then I'll take an inventory of what else we're going to need to order and we're back in business."

"But..."

"No buts." She put her arm around me to hug me, then hesitated. "Well, maybe one but. What do I do about all the crime scene tape? Will I get arrested if I take it down?"

"I'll come by and take it down," Phillip offered. I don't care if I go to jail. I got nothing going on tomorrow." He added his bag of trash to the stinking pile.

"Good. Then I'll see you in the morning Phillip," Abby turned and bear hugged me for real this time. "Clara, you get some sleep. After you enjoy your dessert of course."

She gave Phillip a little wave and danced off down the driveway.

"Are you sure you want to have dessert with the Q man tonight? You could come crash at my house if you want. Anytime," Phillip said.

"I know I can, maybe one of these days I'll take you up on it."

Phillip took my bag of garbage from me and threw it in. "Well, the offer's open. If you change your mind I'll be next door." He put an arm around my shoulder as we walked back inside.

Oscar was standing in front of the shelves of aromatherapy products reading aloud to Flo from the labels on two different jars of massage cream. "Neroli for stress relief or Pink Grapefruit for uplifting?"

"I think we could use both of them. Neroli for me and the Grapefruit for you."

Phillip and I just looked at each other. Oscar put the creams in one of our small purple *Chocolate Diner* shopping bags and put his arm around Flo's waist.

"I'm taking Flo back to the city with me. C, are you going to be okay? You could scratch the date and come with us if you want."

"Yeah, like I'm going to give up a date while you two are slathering each other in fruit salad. No, thanks. I'll be fine. If I need anything I can always call Phillip."

Phillip nodded in agreement.

"Sweetie, we're stopping back at the cottage so I can get my stuff. We'll drop the Elvi off at your house on the way back up. Is that OK?"

"Sure." If Q didn't work out at least I'd have some company in bed tonight.

I grabbed a Scorpio Moon prototype on my way out. Might as well test it out. Couldn't hurt. We all left through the back door. Oscar pointed the Beemer south. Phillip walked west to the Pub and I flew home.

NINETEEN

The sensuous aroma of lavender and vanilla from the Scorpio Moon ritual followed me into the shower. I bathed all of my chakras with rose petal soap, paying special attention to my second chakra, the center for passion and pleasure just below my navel. After tonight the only picture on Q's refrigerator was going to be mine.

I stepped out of the bathroom fog and into the bedroom with exactly five minutes to get dressed. I went for the third drawer of my lingerie chest, the special date drawer filled with all black lace. A thong with a tiny pink rose at the "T" and a demi-bra, was just the ticket. I covered it all with a black V-neck long sleeved tee and black jeans. Sexy but not over the top. I waived the hairdryer at my head just long enough to make it damp instead of wet, applied my standard war paint and flew, barefoot, down the two flights of stairs to the living room.

The fireplace came on with the flip of a switch. I dimmed the lights, lit a couple of red candles, and set the IPod to Rod Stewart's, *American Classics*. I was just pouring myself a glass of Pinot when the doorbell rang. The Elvi scattered upstairs.

"Who's the nut job across the street with the glow in the dark dumb bells?" Q asked when I opened the door.

I didn't even have to look. "Oh that's just Ed, the neighborhood wacko. He's training for Rocky fifteen."

Q gave me the once over and smiled. "Great color," he said staring at my newly manicured toes.

"I hate shoes in the house. Never wear them inside."

"Should I take mine off?"

"Only if you want to."

"Maybe later."

"What's in there?" I asked pointing my wine glass at the grocery bag in Q's arm.

"Let me in and I'll show you," Q smiled.

He put the bag down on the half wall between the foyer and the living room and took off his jacket. I motioned to the ottoman and he laid it there carefully. I couldn't believe it, we were dressed like twins. Wondered for a second if he was wearing a black lace thong too.

"I brought dessert, as promised."

"Is it chocolate?"

Q reached in the bag and pulled out a red velvet box tied with a black satin ribbon. "This is for you." He set it down on the ottoman next to his jacket.

"And this is for me." He reached back into the bag and came out with package of homemade linguini and a crusty loaf of Italian bread. "I'm hungry and I know you said no dinner but I thought you might have forgotten to eat."

"You thought correctly." He hadn't known me long enough to know me this well, I thought.

"Good, I'll cook."

"The kitchen is that-a-way." I said, pointing to the stairs.

"First things first. Do you have champagne glasses?"

"Kitchen, first cabinet on the right."

Q started for the kitchen, tripped on the third step and the grocery bag went flying. He did a pirouette and made a diving catch, landing on his feet right in front of me.

"Good save," I said.

"Wide receiver in college." He headed back upstairs, grocery bag tucked under his arm like a football.

Damn. Mercury was still causing mischief, I had forgotten all about that. I had a sinking feeling that Mercury retrograde might trump Scorpio Moon.

He reappeared with two flutes and a chilled bottle of Veuve Cliquot. Q wrapped the towel carefully around the bottle and easily popped the cork.

"That's impressive. I usually need to hold the bottle between my knees and pop with both hands," I said.

"The key is slowly twisting it." He poured two glasses, handed me one. "Let's sit for a minute, I want to show you something."

We got comfortable on the sofa and he untied the ribbon from the box of candy and let it slide across his hands.

"Close your eyes. Tight," he said.

"Close my eyes?"

"You're perfectly safe, I assure you."

"Yeah, that's what you said just before I was attacked by a giant chocolate chip muffin."

"That was an act of God and I saved you, remember?" he laughed. "Come on, close your eyes. You'll love this. Just relax."

Relax? Was he joking? I felt him slip the ribbon over my eyes and tie it behind my head. I lifted it up from one eye and squinted at him.

"No peeking." He pushed my hand away. "Now, take a sip of champagne," he said.

The bubbles danced on my tongue. Exquisite.

"Open up."

I hesitantly parted my lips. Bittersweet chocolate followed by a burst of raspberry.

"Another one," Q ordered. It wasn't a question.

I took another sip of the bubbly then opened my mouth, wider this time. I tasted rich dark hazelnut chocolate and the tip of his warm tongue at the same time. If this was going to be death by chocolate, I was ready to meet my maker.

"Dessert's always been my favorite meal," Q whispered and pulled me closer.

I pushed the blindfold up onto my forehead. "Mine too, but I'm just not ready for this yet. I'm sorry." Geez-o-pete, I thought, we're going to have to put a disclaimer on *Scorpio Moon*: *When used as directed, this product may cause instant arousal and impair your ability to make rational decisions.*

Q sat back and looked at me intently. "Nothing to be sorry for." He gently undid the ribbon and began kneading my traps. "Is this okay?"

"This is more than okay. Thanks." I closed my eyes and the tension in my shoulders released.

"So the car that followed you home? Are you sure it was really following you?"

"What?" I mumbled.

"The car that followed you last night. Are you sure it was following you? Did you see the driver?"

I took another sip of champagne. "I'm sure. It followed me even when I changed my route. At first I thought it was crazy Ed since he works late in Princeton on Fridays but after a while, I knew it couldn't be. I think whoever it was had been parked a few cars behind me on the square last night. They must have pulled out right after I did."

Q maneuvered me so my back was to him. His thumbs made circular motions as they traveled down my spine. He'd done this before. "If I'd have known, I would never have let you leave. Why would someone follow you?"

"I have no freaking idea. Scared the bejeezus out of me."

He stopped massaging and just held me close to him, my back against his chest. I could feel his heart beat. Slow and strong.

"So what happened with Flo?"

"Flo had gone back to The Diner around nine to get a

pair of shoes and two guys were either in there already or they came in after she did. They wrapped her in duct tape and threw her in the closet, then trashed the place."

"She must have been scared to death."

"Once she realized they weren't going to kill her she just ended up pissed…literally and figuratively."

"Huh?"

"By the time we found her, she had to pee desperately. She didn't quite make it to the bathroom, with us trying to cut her out of the tape and everything."

"Man, talk about adding insult to injury. She okay now?"

"I think so. Her coat was ruined with the tape but she's alive and safe so she's good. She's mostly upset about The Diner. Me too. It was a hell of a mess to clean up. We have to replace some things, like the herbs that ended up all over the floor."

"Did they take anything? You don't keep much money around do you?"

"No, in fact the money was all there. Only thing they took was the laptop. Scary."

"What would anyone want with your laptop?" Q was gently stroking my hair.

"Who knows? Flo thinks they wanted our love spells."

"Well I could understand that." He nuzzled my ear.

"We think they really were looking for the book," I said.

Q stopped stroking. "Book?"

"You know, remember I told you about the book Duncan gave Flo? The one that had stuff written in the middle of it?"

"Vaguely," he said.

"Well, turns out it was a secret message from Duncan to Samantha Rousseau."

"Secret message? You're kidding, right?"

"Well, it's really just a date, a time and the letters L and A. We haven't figured out what it means."

"So who is this Samantha Rousseau anyway? You asked me about her last night."

"She was one of Duncan's research assistants. We think they were... um, hooking up. She's working on some drug project at the Gardens for a pharmaceutical company. I just assumed it was for Zylanica." I sat up and turned to face him.

"She wasn't working with us. We're not the only pharma in bed with the Gardens you know."

I studied his face, he looked like he was telling the truth. "So, how do you make a drug from a plant anyway?"

He raised an eyebrow, "Do you really want to know? This isn't exactly scintillating conversation."

"Yes, I really do want to know. Tell me. I can take it," I laughed.

"Okay, here goes. First, probably about twenty five percent of medicines contain at least some compounds from plants. Only about ten percent of major drugs have plant extracts as an active ingredient."

"Compounds?"

"The chemicals in plants that have a medicinal use. Sometimes the compounds can be created in a lab. In some cases we don't know how to synthesize them so they have to come from their natural source."

"Why not just use the plant all the time?"

Q leaned his head back on the sofa and rested his hand on my thigh. "You're really interested in this?"

I nodded.

"Well, it's a matter of cost and being able to get enough plants to make significant amounts of the drug. Take quinine for example. Quinine comes from the bark of a tree. In South America it was used as a cure for Malaria; natives who drank tea made from the bark didn't get the disease. Eventually Europeans caught on. Ever wonder why gin and tonic is such a popular drink in the tropics?"

"Gin comes from the bark?"

"Nope, the tonic water. It's easier and cheaper to make

quinine synthetically, so now they don't need the tree anymore."

"So Samantha told us they were analyzing pitcher plants. What would they be making from pitcher plants?"

"I don't know anything about that." He stood up and clapped his hands together. "I'm hungry. How about I get dinner started? You stay here and relax, I'll bring it down. It'll only take about ten minutes."

He took the steps to the kitchen two at a time.

If Zylanica was involved in any of this, Q wasn't letting on. I put my feet up on edge of the ottoman and stared into the fire. I don't have a clue how they did it, but the gas fireplace crackled just like a real wood fire. Q was sneaking his way into my heart the way the fire was warming my core.

The ottoman suddenly vibrated under my feet. I glanced at the stairs and almost called out to Q but decided against it. They'd leave a message if it was important. Q's jacket buzzed again. I gingerly lifted up the lapel and eased the smartphone out of the inside pocket. A slender billfold slid out with it.

The mental argument for respecting his stuff lost out to my insatiable curiosity.

Inside the billfold was a passport and an e-ticket. The passport picture was the typical mug shot, but in Q's case typical is pretty damn good. My passport picture looks like I just inhaled helium and hadn't let it out. Flo's is hysterical. Her hair is everywhere, green eyes bugged out and her mouth is open since she was giving detailed instructions to the photographer. She made them retake it five times.

The problem with Q's passport wasn't his picture, it was his name. *Jack Carrigan*, middle initial *D*. And his date of birth wasn't July twenty-third, it was January eighteenth. *A Capricorn?* I checked the tickets. Round trip tickets to London leaving at six in the morning with an open return under the name Jack Carrigan. The champagne bubbles were making their way back up my throat. Who the hell was making me dinner?

"How you doing down there?" Q suddenly called from the kitchen. I spazzed out and the passport and ticket ended up under the chair across the room.

I kept my eyes on the staircase as I crawled on my hands and knees to retrieve everything and stuffed the billfold back into his pocket. "I'm good. Just chillin' by the fire." I answered.

"Good. Almost done up here, be down in a minute."

The smartphone was still on the ottoman. I could hear Q, or whatever his name was, still fussing upstairs. He had a voicemail. No way I would be able to listen to that. The phone wasn't asking for a password so I started tapping away trying find his text messages. I found a wine list, a play list, and directions to someplace in D.C. before I figured out how the message thing worked. The last two text messages were from someone named *Candy*. Her name is *Candy?* Isn't that special. I scrolled down. The next one was from *BWShip*. Blaine Winship? My hands shook as I tapped it open.

BWShip at 11:38pm Friday: *It's raining in Paddington. Need umbrellas pronto.*

I could see the replied icon and found QJack's reply at 12:27 am Saturday: *It's sunny at Q. Tours begin at 11:00. Enjoy!*

Blaine had texted Q while I was at his apartment last night. So Q *is* working with him! Damn. Paddington? Was Blaine really in London? What happened to Indonesia? Was QJack going to meet him? It's a five hour time difference. This was written last night and QJack's not leaving until tomorrow morning. I heard footsteps on the stairs and quickly slipped the smartphone back where it belonged. I tried to look relaxed while fighting back the overwhelming urge to vomit.

"Okay beautiful. Dinner is served." I searched QJack's eyes and saw nothing but affection. He put the full tray of linguini with clam sauce, garlic bread and salad with black olives on the end of the ottoman. The vibrator went off again.

He fished out the smartphone, and checked it. QJack wasn't happy.

"Love, I don't believe this. I am so sorry. I have to go again. This, unfortunately is my life. I should have just been a doctor. I hope it's not a game breaker. I have an unexpected meeting."

"At nine-thirty on a Saturday night?"

"I'm always on call. The pharmaceutical business is cutthroat; you never know when an experiment will hit a wall. I hate leaving you like this. But at least you have some linguine a la Quentin. Eat, please. Any chance you'll give me another rain check?"

Not a chance in hell. "Fine," I said as I bit off a hunk of garlic bread. I just wanted him out of my house.

"Clara, I'm sorry, I wish I didn't have to go...it's complicated. We'll see each other again soon, I promise."

He put on his coat and leaned down to kiss me. I gave him my cheek instead. He grabbed a hunk of bread, "Enjoy our dinner, I'll talk to you soon."

The door closed behind him and I ran to set the burglar alarm. My mind was racing. Jack Carrigan. Why did Q have a passport in another name? I didn't even have a computer to do an online search for him.

I curled up on the sofa and pressed "2" on my cell. Answer this time for Pete's sake. I reached for another piece of garlic bread, but stopped myself.

"Hi Sweetie. What's up? You okay?" Flo answered.

"Flo! Geez-o-pete. Thank God you're there." Old Elvis emerged from his hiding place in the closet and pulled himself up on the sofa.

"Why? What's the matter?" Flo asked.

"You're never going to believe this."

"Are you being followed again?"

"No!"

"You slept with Q."

"Well, I wanted to but I didn't. He's gone and he's not Q, or maybe he is but that's not what his passport says." I sniffed some linguine. Lots of garlic.

"What are you talking about, passport?"

"Wait a sec." I swallowed. "He had his passport in his jacket pocket and the name on it wasn't Quentin or Adams,"

"You were snooping in his jacket?"

"No, while he was making me dinner his phone vibrated and I just went to get it for him and the passport fell out."

"He made you dinner?"

"Oh Flo, he made me linguine and clam sauce and garlic bread and a salad with black olives even. It's an oral orgasm. And you wouldn't believe what he can do with chocolate covered raspberries and champagne."

"Raspberries and champagne? Now, that's what I call an o-o. But wait a minute. Let me get this straight. His passport has someone else's name on it? What about the picture?"

"It was him alright. He's got this little half smile on his face and looks like he's the poster boy for the State Department. Who looks that good in their passport picture?"

"C, there's something fishy in the state of Denmark."

"And that's not all. The garlic bread is awesome. He used roasted garlic."

"Look, forget about the food for a second."

"He has an open ended round trip plane ticket to London for six in the morning."

"And he's not taking you with him? Maybe he has a wife and six kids in London and he's going to keep you here...like that book...what was it...about a pilot?"

"*The Pilot's Wife*. And there weren't six kids in that book." I popped a black olive. "And, his birthday is January eighteenth."

TIFFANY BLUES

"There's no way he's a Capricorn," Flo said.

"Depends on whether the passport is real or not and whether Q is Quentin Adams or Jack Carrigan. But it gets even worse. Are you sitting down?"

"I'm prostrate on the sofa."

"I got a look at his text messages."

"What? How the heck did you do that?"

"Carefully. There was a message from B W Ship."

"Blaine Winship."

"It just said B W Ship but I'll bet my life it's him."

"Q and Blaine? Yeowza."

"Yep, B W Ship said it was *raining in Paddington*, whatever that means, and *need umbrellas pronto*. Then QJack wrote back. *It's sunny at Q, tours begin at eleven*."

"Say the first part again."

"It's raining in Paddington," I repeated.

"Paddington is in London. QJack is going to London tomorrow. What did the message say about a Q tour?"

"It said *it's sunny at Q* and that tours start at eleven and to enjoy but they couldn't have met at eleven, Q's still here."

"He means tomorrow, when he gets there. So, Blaine and Q are in cahoots and not in Indonesia."

"Flo, I told him about the book."

"Are you out of your mind?"

"I wanted to see his reaction when I told him about the stuff Duncan wrote." Old Elvis curled himself up in my lap and I stroked him absentmindedly.

"Okay, so?"

"He didn't even flinch. Last night I mentioned Blaine and he acted like he didn't know who I was talking about. Tonight, he claims not to know Sammy or anything about the project she's been working on."

"Well, there's one way to find out. Let's just…"

"Ask Sammy."

TWENTY

"Want another piece?" Flo poked around in the red and white striped bag for more of the giant chocolate chip pretzel. "These Penelope Pretzels are to die for."

I nodded and Flo handed me a big chunk of the sugary fried dough as we passed through the North gate of the Gardens. "How many calories you think are in one of these?" I asked.

"Too many. Just eat it. Don't think about it." Flo brushed the pretzel crumbs off her new lime green parka.

The sun felt strangely warm on my face as we chewed and trudged up Lilac Lane for the third time in a week and a half. The icicles that dangled from the tips of the silver branches were dripping and puncturing holes in the snow just like the metal spikes on those shoes Flo wears to aerate the lawn. The winter wonderland of the Metropolitan Botanical Gardens was defrosting.

I unbuttoned my coat. "Aren't you hot?"

"I suppose. I probably shouldn't have worn this, but isn't it chic with this fake fur edging? I can use the cuffs like a muff. End of season sale. Seventy percent off."

"Sweet deal, but geez-o-pete, I'm melting. I thought I

was going to freeze my ass off today so I wore three layers under here. Big mistake."

"*Local on the 8's* said it might even get up to fifty-two by noon."

"So why didn't you call me this morning?"

"Because the last time I called you at five in the morning to give you the weather forecast you hung up on me."

"You could have texted me."

We turned left at the corner. Little rivulets of melting snow were flowing down the road from the top of the hill and most of the sidewalk was submerged under several inches of slush and murky water. We opted for a detour that wound past the Visitor's Center and the Garden Shoppe.

"You know, how many times have we been here already and not once have we stopped in the gift shop?" Flo remarked as we gingerly sidestepped slush puddles on the slate walk. "Maybe we should try to get them to carry our AstroBotanics line. Scorpio Moon would probably sell like hotcakes."

"Forget about it. Any more aphrodisiacs around here and the whole place would spontaneously combust."

We kept walking, winding our way back to Oak Alley and the long wet trek uphill. By the time we got to the research building, we were both carrying our coats. I held the door open for Flo praying this wasn't going to be a wasted trip.

"Yuck, my feet are soaked; these boots are supposed to be waterproof. I hope they're not ruined." Flo stopped in the entryway and looked down, stomping and inspecting her boots. I eyed the little bubbles squishing out of the leopard microfiber. For once I had the sense to wear my waterproof trekkers. Not real sexy but my feet were dry.

"They'll be okay. You won't be able to tell if they're stained with that print anyway. I just hope Sammy got the message we were coming today."

"We have no clue where her office is, we'll have to ask at the security desk," Flo said.

"Only there's nobody at the security desk." I nodded to the empty reception area. We checked up and down the hall, there was no one around. "Is there a directory anywhere?" I asked.

"Here it is." Flo turned to the wall behind us. "Applied Botanical Research, second floor."

"We know that already. Are there any names?" I pushed the elevator button. The fluorescent lighting gave my hand a slightly greenish tint and I imagined alien invaders turning the blood cells of innocent Metro Garden employees into chlorophyll. Maybe that's what was really going on here. I could see the headlines now, "*Aliens Turn Botanists Into Plants.*" Applied botanical research alright.

"No, no names. Let's just go up and try to find her," Flo said. "Somebody's got to know where she is."

The second floor hallway was empty too. "Where is everybody? This place is deserted," Flo said turning right, the click of her heels echoing on the speckled tile as we headed down the corridor.

"Duncan's office was this way," I said nodding to my left.

"No, I remember turning right off the elevator," Flo answered over her shoulder. She took two more steps and stopped. "Whoa! C, this is Janice Pearl's office."

She peeked in the open door in front of her, pulled her head back out and whispered, "No one's in here." Before I could stop her, she disappeared inside.

The office was no bigger than Duncan's but much neater, obsessively so. A floor to ceiling bookcase full of alphabetically arranged scientific texts and journals took up the entire left wall. On the right, three diplomas were identically matted and framed; burgundy mats with white frames. Doctorate and Masters from Cornell, in cellular biophysics; B.S. from Barnard, magna cum laude. An immaculate wooden schoolteacher's desk occupied the middle of the room. One burgundy upholstered guest chair faced it squarely and a laptop was sitting open on top.

"Come here, look at this!" Flo said pointing to the computer screen.

"What are you doing? We're going to get caught," I whispered and slid around the desk to look. "Zylanica's home page."

"She's got a couple of windows open here." Flo clicked on another window and a map came up. "Holy shit!"

"What?"

"This map. It's the topo map of Pleasant Mills. Look, here's Exotic Aquatics." Flo touched a spot on the screen. "This is the same map as the paper topo on the wall in Blaine's office. And it's just like the one we looked at when we did the astrology mapping with the stuff in the book."

"So is everybody in cahoots with Blaine?"

"Damn straight, it's a conspiracy," Flo said and started clicking away at the other open windows.

"Flo, stop. We have to get out of here. Wait, what's that? Go back one." I said. "It's a letter but not addressed to anyone."

We both read at warp speed.

"...in regard to your last correspondence with Dr. McPherson, the results of our research to date indicate that only one of the hybrid crosses of the Sarracenia purpurea, D43, has shown any promise as a antidote for Variola XL5. However, as we discussed, the inadvertent discovery of its potent analgesic properties may warrant a revision of our research plan. We wish to assure you that Dr. McPherson's death, although unfortunate, will not in any way impede our further investigation into the efficacy of D43. Our only issue at this time is the availability of enough genetic material to perform the necessary tests. I expect that issue to be resolved in the very near future."

'Looks like a draft; she hasn't finished it yet. Who do you think she's writing to?" I said.

"Who knows. Zylanica's website is up here, it's probably them," Flo whispered.

"Wait, look. There's a note at the end to *copy Rangivonjy Janhairy at Kew Gardens.*

Kew Gardens. Q tour starts at eleven!

"Why would Blaine be going to Kew Gardens?"

"To kill Janhairy!" she exclaimed a little too loudly.

"Shhhhh. Someone's going to hear us."

"What's Variola XL5?" Flo asked quietly this time.

"No clue. You know I didn't tell you, but I made a point of asking Q, before I found the passport, what they were making from pitcher plants."

Flo looked at me.

"He said 'I don't know anything about that'"

"He lied, he lied a lot."

"What's D43?" I asked.

"A new version of WD 40?"

"Would you *stop*."

"Well what do you think it is?" Flo asked. "Look, she says *antidote for Variola XL5*. I bet you XL5 is smallpox… What else do you need an antidote for?"

"How about HIV? The common cold? Ebola virus? Doesn't have to be smallpox. She says it could be an analgesic. That's just pain killer."

"Or deadly toxin. And there's plenty of genetic material. He's got a whole greenhouse full of Sarracenias under lock and key."

"Can I help you ladies?" A deep male voice startled us. We both jumped away from the desk. Andrew Gray was standing in the doorway.

"Hi Andrew," we squeaked like two frightened mice.

"What are you doing in here?" he asked, more concerned than angry. He came in towards our left. We shuffled together to the right around the desk.

"Looking for Sammy?" Flo said.

TIFFANY BLUES

"Sammy? This is Dr. Pearl's office and you're going to be in the toaster if she finds you in here," Andrew warned as he maneuvered around the desk to check out the computer screen.

"Okay, well, we were just leaving. Can you tell us where we can find Sammy?" Flo asked. We both started to inch backwards towards the door.

"She is not here today," he said.

"Oh. We need to talk to her. We called her yesterday and left a message," I said.

Andrew took off his glasses and was reading the computer screen intently. "She's taking a few personal days. She's totally shattered over her father." He stopped reading and shook his head. "So awful, the autopsy results indicated that strangulation was not the cause of death. He was actually poisoned first."

Flo tripped and fell backwards into the chair. It popped a wheelie and her legs went up over her head, little heels pointing at the ceiling, arms flailing. Florilla Munrow, the upside down flying chicken. I lunged for one of her leopard boots. Too late! The chicken did a backflip and landed with a belly flop on the floor. I fell right on top of her.

"Did you say father?" Flo moaned from somewhere underneath me.

"Father?" I repeated pulling myself up using the seat of the chair.

Andrew leaned over the desk stifling his laughter. "You didn't know Duncan was Sammy's father?"

"Oh my God, no. We thought they were…an item." I reached out my hand to help Flo up off the floor. "Sweetie, are you okay? You landed pretty hard."

"I think I threw my back out." Flo got up slowly and rubbed the base of her spine with both hands. "The way he treated her, we just assumed they …"

"Were shagging?" Andrew chuckled. "No, there was no incest involved. Are you ladies all right?"

I nodded and looked at Flo. She flinched, "Nothing six months in traction won't fix."

"So Duncan was poisoned? Not strangled?" I asked.

"Well, maybe poisoned isn't technically accurate. There was a toxin in his body in sufficient quantities to stop his heart," Andrew explained.

"Poor Sammy, she must be devastated," Flo said.

"Is there any way we can get in touch with her?" I asked.

"I check on her every day. I can give her a message for you," Andrew offered.

Flo twirled her finger at him "So, then you two are...?" I swatted at her hand, but she pulled it away.

"She is totty, isn't she?" he winked. "But it is very complicated and it is hard with our careers and now with all that's happened," his voice trailed off. He thought for a second and shifted his attention back to the computer screen.

"Look, could you just tell her we need to talk to her? It's pretty important," I asked, as Flo and I set the chair upright.

"What, may I ask, are you doing in my office?" Dr. Pearl's nasal pitch pierced the room as she glared at all of us. Andrew slid around the desk and stood next to me. Dr. Pearl went directly to the desk and slammed the top of the computer shut. Flo and I backed out the door.

"Sorry, wrong office." I grabbed Flo by the sleeve and pulled her out into the hallway. A few steps down the hall she stopped me.

"Wait a minute," Flo whispered. She tiptoed back and flattened herself against the wall within earshot of the door.

"Flo, come on," I hissed. I high tailed it to the elevator and pressed the down arrow. Tapping my foot I focused on the crack between the doors. Hurry, open please.

"Listen to this," Flo squeezed into the elevator just as the doors were closing. "Janice was reaming Andrew out the wazu about us being in her office. He kept trying to tell her that he accidentally walked in on us. The last thing I heard him say was. 'Look, I just want to know if we are going to continue with the project?' She told him that since she's in charge now things would be taking a new turn and she'd be cleaning house. Then she said, and I quote, 'Don't worry, you're too valuable to let go now'."

"She's going to fire Sammy."

"Or kill her too."

I shivered. "Sammy, Duncan's daughter. Who woulda thunk?"

"C, your dream!" Flo grabbed my arm. "It was about Duncan. The snake strangled you and then bit you and killed you with toxin! The Universe was trying to tell you."

"Why do they always have to tell *me*?" The elevator doors opened. "Usually my dreams are symbolic, but they're not that literal. Eewww."

There was a guard at the security desk now. Several other people were milling around. We smiled and waved like we belonged there and calmly walked out the door.

It was still bizarrely warm as we made our way back to the gate. "Maybe the dream is about Sammy. It could be a warning," I said.

"That's a definite possibility. Andrew said something weird to Janice I didn't understand. He said something about hypocrites not perceiving their deception and lying with sincerity. Wonder what…"

The sudden blast of a tornado scared the shit out of me. Flo frantically dug through her purse but the music stopped. The phone was in her hand when it wailed again.

"Hi Oz. We're heading back to your apartment right now. Could you do us a huge favor?"

Pause.

"I know that, but is there any way you can meet us and bring us some lunch?"

Long pause.

"I know you're working but we're starving. Please?"

Longer pause.

Finally she nodded her head "yes" at me. "And Oz, before you leave your office, could you look up what 'variola' means? Oh, and one more thing, look up the word 'totty'. T-o-t-t-y."

***

"Nothing like a couple of hot tottys on a cold afternoon," Oscar called from the kitchen.

"So define totty," Flo yelled back to him, slipping off her drenched boots and laying them on the radiator to dry.

I shed my clodhoppers and threw several layers of clothing on the club chair. It was hot in here too. Once the heat came on, it stayed on until May. Oscar had all the windows cracked open but it didn't help much.

Oz came into the room with something behind his back and a huge smile on his face. "Totty, T-O-T-T-Y, an attractive or beautiful woman or group of women," Oscar said in a perfect British accent.

"Could you use it in a sentence?" Flo joked.

"Lord take me downtown, I'm just looking for some Totty," smirked Oscar.

Flo and I looked at each other. "Allrighty then," I said. "That explains it."

Oscar held out a bright yellow bag that we recognized instantly. "Surprise!"

Oscar surprised us with three foot long turkey subs on whole grain bread from The Yellow Submarine over on Bleeker Street, which currently held the number ten spot on *Clara and Florilla's List of All Time Good Eats*. They saturate the bread with extra oil and vinegar, garlic and Cuban oregano. I like extra onions on mine, but Flo and Oscar go for heaps of spicy banana peppers. The subs were perfect; Oscar knows what we like.

Maybe if Q was really Q, he would actually turn out to be something like Oz after all. He certainly liked things spicy. I gazed into my ever-present mental crystal ball.

TIFFANY BLUES

There was Q, a year from now, coming up the steps of my townhouse with a perfect 12 inch juicy sub just for me. Well it certainly seemed like 12 inches. Maybe there was a perfectly reasonable explanation for the tickets and the passport and the Blaine connection. I sighed. Who was I kidding? Zylanica, XL5, analgesic, poison, Jack Carrigan. It wasn't looking good.

We all sat on the floor around the coffee table using the yellow paper sandwich wrappers as plates. The old steam radiator banged away as the heat blasted the apartment and we munched silently in time with the rhythm of the ancient plumbing. Once we had completely devoured the subs, along with every last shred of lettuce, onions and peppers that had fallen off the rolls onto the oily yellow wrappers, Flo launched into a more than slightly fictionalized version of the morning's events. I leaned back against the leather sofa and closed my eyes.

She conveniently left out the parts about sneaking into Janice's office, snooping in her laptop and doing the flying chicken. She made it sound like Andrew volunteered all the new information, so I just let her do most of the talking. I didn't want to get the story wrong.

Oscar didn't say much either. After Flo told him about the autopsy results he silently got up and turned on his 1976 *Marantz Stereophonic Receiver Model 2230 with Gyro-Touch Tuning*. Oscar was the only other person I knew, besides my idiot boyfriend in college, who owned a vintage Marantz stereo with an aquamarine backlight. Oscar's still worked, but it was the IPod on top of the stereo that he usually used to listen to everything from Mozart to Pink Martini. He shuffled through some vinyl LP's while Flo talked. He picked an old Rickie Lee Jones album and put it on the turntable.

He had his back to us when Flo finally asked, "So, Oz, why didn't you tell us Duncan was Sammy's father?"

"I didn't know."

Rickie Lee sang softly in the background and Oscar

turned to face us, hands on hips. "All I knew was that he had the thing with the medicine woman. He never once said anything about having a child with her."

"You probably just weren't listening. That's not something a good friend would keep secret from you," Flo said.

"Well he did. I doubt anyone knew."

"Andrew knew," I said. Oscar looked surprised and a little hurt.

"That's only because Sammy told him." Flo got up off the floor and sat down on the sofa, curling her legs up under her. "How did we get the Duncan-Sammy relationship so wrong C? I can understand how I would have missed it, but you're usually all over this sort of thing."

"They had me fooled. I just assumed it was Sammy too," I said. "But hey, we get points for figuring that Andrew had the hots for Sammy though. You know I wonder if Janice knew Sammy was Duncan's daughter. You think that could've had anything to do with how much Janice hated Duncan, enough to want him dead?"

"Sammy told us Duncan dumped Janice for a research assistant. Tracy Bennett?"

"Makes sense. Wonder what her autopsy results said."

"Know what? This could really just be death by jealous lover."

Oscar stood by the coffee table towering over us, arms folded. "Red, stop. You don't know what any of this is about and you're not going to know. By the way, I looked up 'variola' and you're right, it's smallpox virus…"

"I knew it!" Flo slapped her thigh.

Oscar continued, "But. Whatever was in that book wasn't meant for you. I don't know how you got twisted up in this, but it has to end now. You've both been in danger. The Diner's been trashed, robbed, and bugged. Who knows what's next. None of this is about you; either of you." He pointed an accusing finger at Flo, then at me.

TIFFANY BLUES

"Yeah, but..." Flo tried to interrupt.

"And furthermore, it's about time you let the police do their job and you both get back to doing yours. Don't you have a business to run? Phillip is actually thinking about giving up his career as a travel writer to sell chocolate and shoes." Oscar leaned down and started gathering up the garbage from the table. I had never seen him so upset.

Flo and I exchanged glances. I felt kind of sick. I had to admit, Oscar had a point. And he didn't even know about QJack. Where were we going with all this anyway? I certainly didn't want to end up as carnivorous plant food.

"He's right Flo. We need to let this go. It's the third week of January and we aren't even close to ready for Valentine's Day."

"We've got Scorpio Moon done."

"Scorpio Moon isn't packaged yet. We need more dark chocolate and we need to restock Stilettos. Not to mention that we need to order new apothecary jars and a whole new shipment of herbs. And to top it all off Mercury's going to be retrograde for two more weeks," I said.

"It is? Oh great, just what we need," Flo sighed. "Okay. Fine. But if we all start dying from smallpox you'll both be sorry."

Oscar shook his head, leaned over the couch and kissed the top of Flo's head. He took the rest of the remains of lunch and headed for the kitchen.

Water gurgled from the sofa behind my head. It was Phillip.

"Hi Hon," I said.

"Hey Coco. I guess you didn't get to see Sammy at the Gardens?" Phillip asked.

"How'd you know that?"

Flo scooted over behind me on the sofa and leaned her ear next to the phone so she could eavesdrop.

"Because she just called looking for you. Thought you'd want to know."

"What'd she say?" Flo yelled into the phone.

"Hi Flo. She said she got your message and she wants to talk to you but not on the phone and not at the Gardens. She's coming here with an Andrew tomorrow at nine. Who's Andrew again?"

"Her um... friend. He works with her at the Gardens."

"So anyway, when are you guys coming back? Things are getting crazy here and the Valentine's Day window is done. Want me to put the *Moon* stuff out? Abby finished them up yesterday."

"Oh, good. No, just leave them out, we'll do it. We're leaving now, we'll see you in a couple hours."

"Good. I've been with the insurance claims adjuster all morning. You need to fill out a bunch of forms, he's coming back tomorrow. I think you're in luck, the computer's covered. I brought over my spare laptop for you to use until you get a new one."

"Phillip, you get the employee of the year award. Thanks."

"Hey, that's why you pay me the big bucks."

"See you soon. Bye." I clicked the phone off.

"Oz, we have to get going," Flo yelled, uncurling herself from the sofa. She bounced up and went over to the radiator. "They're almost dry," she said as she zipped her feet back into the boots.

Oscar came out of the kitchen wiping his hands on a towel. "Who called?"

"It was just Phillip begging us to come home. You're right. He misses us," I said. My right knee cracked when I pushed myself up off the floor and I felt a tiny stab of horror at the thought that I might be developing old lady knees. Better pay more attention in yoga class.

"I told you so," Oscar said.

Flo scrunched her nose at him and wrapped her arms around his waist. "Can you come back to Jersey with us? I don't want to sleep alone tonight."

"No, Red. I just can't. I'm teaching again this week. Plus I have a deadline for an article. Why don't you stay with Clara again tonight?" Oscar grinned at me. "Of course the thought of the two of you in the same bed together is tempting…"

Flo tried to push him away, but he pulled her back to him smiling broadly. "I love you Red," he said teasingly. "But you know as well as I do that Clara's always going to be the other woman in my life."

How true. I gathered up my layers and walked over to the door. I turned the knob and held it open for Flo. "Bye Oscar, thanks for lunch. She'll call you when we get home," I said.

"Oh, wait. My bag!" Flo ran back to the bedroom and came back with a giant black tote bag. "I almost left the book here."

Oscar gave Flo a sweet kiss on the mouth and pecked me on the cheek. Then he got serious. "Look you two, I just lost a great old friend and I miss him dearly. I can't imagine what I'd do if the Martini Munrow show got cancelled. Go back to Dolly's Ferry and stay out of trouble!"

"We will," we said together.

We flew down the stairs and didn't speak until we reached the corner.

"Good thing we didn't tell Oz about sneaking into Janice's office today. He would have gone completely berserk," Flo said.

"That's an understatement."

"But at least now we know for sure that they were using the pitcher plants for smallpox research."

"What would make the analgesic thing worthwhile enough to stop researching smallpox and switch? What would make Zylanica the most money?" I wondered out loud.

"It would have to be some kind of toxin. Something no one's ever heard of before. Shoot, they just discovered a pitcher plant that can dissolve a rat for crying out loud. Of course it's one of those tropical pitcher plants like the gonads in Blaine's first greenhouse."

"Toxins are not just for killing people, right? I mean in small quantities they could actually be a medical breakthrough for some kind of treatment, right?"

"I suppose. But, Blaine and Q are both in London. Why? See, this is where the terrorists come in. Because of the new toxin. Metro Gardens is working with Kew Gardens and there's a mole at Kew, probably that Janhairy guy, who's arranging for Blaine and Q, who's ripping off Zylanica, to hook up with the terrorists so they can make millions."

"Flo, get serious."

"I am serious. Why couldn't they be jumping on this 'inadvertent discovery' and try to sell to the highest bidder? It's right up Blaine's alley."

I scanned the street for a taxi. A group of NYU students in shorts and tee shirts, one of them in a tank top, came around the corner. They seemed to be heading towards Union Square Park to enjoy this winter thaw. The only taxis around were already occupied.

"Don't you think it was weird the way Andrew just showed up like that? I mean the building seemed deserted when we got there. I think he was snooping too," I said.

"Then Janice tells him he's too valuable to let go now. He's probably the one who discovered the 'analgesic properties'."

"Him or Tracy Bennett. Maybe he's not as cute and innocent as he looks. Maybe he's trying to get a piece of the pie."

"There are way too many fingers in this pie."

"True, but what I don't get is the whole issue about the genetic material, not having enough plants for the research."

"It's a problem if the greenhouse pitcher plants aren't the research plants," Flo announced.

"Or, Janice was just using that as an excuse to Zylanica. Why would Blaine have three rabid dogs guarding that greenhouse if those weren't the right plants?"

"They may just be valuable rare hybrids. Like Blaine said, there are crazy plant collectors out there who would pay a lot of money to get their hands on a rare hybrid. You know what I think?"

"Yes I do," I said.

"No you don't. I think the plants that Janice was talking about in the letter are not in the greenhouse at all. Blaine's hiding them somewhere else."

I checked down Waverly again for a cab. They all seemed to have their "Off Duty" lights on. If I didn't know better, I'd swear they went off duty as soon as they saw us.

"You know, the line on the map didn't go right through Exotic Aquatics. It was just close, right?" I asked.

"We need to look at that map again," Flo said deep in thought. "If I was wrong about the map pointing to Blaine's greenhouse, then it's got to be close. Only problem is all we have is a longitude line that goes from the North Pole to the South Pole and just happens to run right by Exotic Aquatics."

"So the plants could really be in South America?"

"Not exactly. They mostly grow on the East Coast of the U.S., so it's got to be close to Blaine's, probably out in a bog nearby. But without a latitude we can't get an exact location. If the map is, in fact, pointing to the location of the secret hybrids, then Duncan knew that location and wanted Samantha to know too, in case anything happened to him."

"And he knew that they could make a nerve toxin. And the location of plants that can make nerve toxin is worth a lot of money."

"Well Blaine has connections and I wouldn't put it past him to use people for money," Flo said.

"But do you really believe he'd kill? Or work with terrorists?"

"He's working with Janice. You realize how much

money they could make?"

"Yeah, but would they really kill two people over this?"

"Perfect guinea pigs for testing the toxin."

"And how were they going to get the information to the so-called terrorists?" I asked.

"Who do we know who is using a fake name, has international connections and just happens to have access to all the research for Zylanica? C, you're going to have to face this, Quentin Adams, or Jack Whatever-His-Name-Is may be way more than an idiot. He lied about who he is. He lied about his sister, NOT. He lied about knowing Blaine and about the pitcher plants..."

"We're not sure he lied about that." I waived my hand wildly at a passing cab.

"Don't start defending him. He lied about everything."

"My brain hurts. I could use an analgesic right now." I stepped out into the middle of the street and forced a cab to stop.

"Penn Station," Flo said to the driver as we climbed in.

I stared out the window. "Look, all I know is that whoever Q is, he can do things with dark chocolate that should be illegal. Did I tell you he blindfolded me?"

TWENTY-ONE

We finally made it back to Dolly's Ferry by early evening. The sky was layered with the dark blue and bright pink clouds that linger right after the sun disappears from sight. There was a glow over the river as we headed west on Main.

Phillip already had his jacket on and was antsy to leave as we greeted him with the tales of our adventure at the Gardens.

"Here's the insurance claim form," he said handing me a piece of paper. "I did what I could but you're going have to fill in the blanks."

"No problemo. Are you meeting Kelly for dinner?" I asked.

"Not Kelly. That's over, remember? Tonight's a first date. Alana. Met her last week in Philly."

"Damn. Flo, I owe you five bucks," I said.

"Double or nothing, eight weeks tops," Flo said.

"You're on."

"What?" Phillip asked.

"Never mind. Have a nice time with *Alana*," I said.

Once Phillip was gone, Flo and I worked into the wee

hours trying to get our business lives back in order. Well actually, I worked while Flo mostly sat in the kitchen with Phillip's laptop, obsessing over the maps of Exotic Aquatics and its surrounding area.

Phillip had filled out almost the whole insurance form and he had done a beautiful job with the Valentine theme for the front display window; all pink toile, dried roses, and black velvet hearts full of passion and romance. That was the last task on my list for the night, getting the passion charm kits on the shelves for the pre-Valentine's Day sale.

Supposedly Abby had finished putting them together, but where had she left them? I checked the backroom and found a big cardboard box sitting under the farmhouse table with the words "*Sex, Sex, Sex, Sex!*" scrawled in red Magic Marker on all four sides. "Nice work Abbs," I laughed, as I dragged it out from under the table. But when I opened the cardboard flaps, and breathed in the intoxicating perfume of lavender and vanilla coming from the neatly stacked velvet charm boxes, my face flushed and my insides got all warm and tingly. Sex, sex, sex, alright!

I carried the big box into the front room and started to stock the shelves. The TV in my brain kept switching back to the "Q channel." Reruns of our erotic champagne tasting with annoying commercial interruptions from Duncan's ghost, or Flo, or my mother scolding, "Clara Martini, who is this masked man anyway?" Enough already. I yelled to Flo, "Sweetie, I'm exhausted. Let's go."

Flo was still afraid to go home alone so I took her home with me but neither one of us got much sleep. Five hours, two cups of caffeine and two and a half cinnamon buns later we were both in the car heading back to The Diner.

***

The roads were slick from the icy mist that had rolled in from the river overnight, and in spite of my driving only twenty-five miles per hour, my car still skidded as we made the turn by the bank. For a second I thought I was going to take out the old Franklin Thermometer on the corner. Actually, it would have taken us out. The thermometer was a cast iron and bronze contraption and a cherished historic landmark. It had been commissioned over a century ago in Paris by the town's wealthiest citizen, Joshua Franklin (no relation to Ben) to commemorate the dedication of the steel bridge that connects Dolly's Ferry with the rest of America. The original wooden covered bridge had been swept away in the Great October Flood of 1903. They say the river crested at twenty-eight feet and the roar of the collapsing bridge could be heard all the way to Fenwick Street, almost a mile away.

Thanks to Franklin's money, Dolly's Ferry got a brand spanking new modern steel suspension bridge. The christening was celebrated to the max with a parade across the Delaware, fireworks and the unveiling of what would forever be known as the Franklin Thermometer. More than a hundred years later, the thing can still tell the temperature with one degree accuracy!

Flo and I both got a too-close-for-comfort view of the filigree dial. Thirty-one degrees. I righted the wheel and drove like a turtle for the next block and a half. I couldn't wait to get to work; I needed a nice hot chai latte.

"Damn, it's only eight fifty-five in the morning and we already have company," Flo said as we pulled up to The Diner. Sure enough, there was an old white Honda Del Sol parked right at our curb and Sammy and Andrew were waiting for us on the front porch.

"I forgot they were coming today."

"Me too."

Kiss that chai goodbye, I thought.

"Boy you're here early," I greeted them as I unlocked the metal door and led us all inside. They were dressed in similar outfits. Jeans, sneakers, pea coats, scarves wrapped around their necks. Sammy was hatless, her long curly hair blowing in the cold wind. Andrew's head was covered with a wool duffer's cap.

"We left at six and made really good time. We weren't sure how long it would take us to get all the way out here with rush hour traffic and all," Andrew said taking off his hat. "It is not as far as it looked on the map."

"We even stopped in that odd little coffee shop on the way into town to get this." Sammy held up a Bow-Wow Café cup with shaky hands.

"Yum, they make great coffee. Did Mr. Chubbs sniff your crotch?" Flo asked with a straight face.

"Excuse me?" Sammy replied.

"I hope Mr. Chubbs is a dog and not the owner," Andrew said.

"He's a sweet fat, old mutt who just l-u-v-s women," I laughed. "He must have been sleeping in the back. Marley's the owner. He's just like his dog, loves women too but he's a hugger, not a sniffer."

"I wasn't sniffed or hugged but I did like the abstract doggy wallpaper. You know, and I mean this in a good way, this whole town's kind of funky," Sammy said. "It's old, but you've got all these wicked cool shops. Who knew New Jersey had places like this?"

"All the river towns have their own personalities. Some are artsy, some new age-y and some are just... old. Dolly's Ferry has it all. 'Funky' is a good word for us," I said.

"I need more coffee. Do you guys need a refill?" Flo asked, heading to the kitchen.

"Oh, sorry. If we'd known we would have brought you some. I'm good. Thanks," Andrew said.

"I'm fine too. Thanks," Sammy slipped off her jacket and handed it to me.

"I'll take a chai latte," I yelled.

"Fat chance. But I'll make you some green-plum," Flo yelled back.

Andrew wandered around until he got to Stilettos. "Andrew, let me take your coat."

"Is this part of Astro or Botanics?" he smiled.

TIFFANY BLUES

"Neither," I answered. "It's part of The Chocolate Diner. Another Dolly's Ferry landmark."

"So was Dolly a real person?" Andrew wasn't looking at me. He was checking out the shoe display. Hmm, so the scientist appreciates nice high heels. Too bad Sammy only wears flats, at least in public. I took all the coats and hung them up in the vestibule.

"Yep, in the early 1700's a guy named John Barnes bought a tract of land along the Delaware from the Indians. He started a ferry service and called the town Barnes Ferry. His son, John, married Dolly Hart. She was pregnant when she was swept away by the flood of 1758. They renamed the town Dolly's Ferry for her."

"Poor Dolly," Sammy said sadly. She was browsing around the shop taking everything in. Andrew didn't say anything. He plopped himself down in one of the comfy chairs and sipped his coffee.

Sammy put her cup down on the counter and picked up a black velvet box from the pile on the floor. "Magical Intentions Scorpio Moon? What are these?"

"Oh, those shouldn't be on the floor. I haven't had a chance to put them out yet."

"But what is it?" She opened the velvet heart.

"Well, it's a passion charm. You know, to help spice up your love life. Trust me, it works." I smiled and added, "Your father called vanilla 'the ultimate aphrodisiac.' Take a whiff."

Sammy inhaled the heady aroma of the herbal sachet. Her green eyes met mine. "That smells so delicious. My father…" Her voice broke.

"The heart boxes are special for Valentine's Day," I said quickly, changing the subject. "We usually use baskets." I pointed to the baskets stacked on the top shelf. "Our charms are all handmade. We wouldn't trust anyone else to put enough love in each one. Good fortune, wishes, dreams, healing, love, astrological signs. You need it we can help you get it." I was babbling.

It didn't matter. I don't think Sammy heard a word I said. She closed the box and started over again. "My father was a Scorpio, he would have loved this. He was a very passionate man and so into astrology."

"I know, he told us that he dabbled in it."

"Oh, way more than dabbled. Astrology was critical to his understanding of ancient herbals." She handed me the heart and I put it back on the pile on the floor. "But," she continued, "He took a real personal interest in it too. He was always looking at what Saturn was doing to his sun and telling me about retrogrades. Now I wish I had paid more attention."

"How much are they? The passion kits." Andrew set his cup on the floor, got up and went to inspect some of the other baskets we had on display. He pulled down a basket labeled *Good Fortune for Cancer* and looked it over.

"Thirty-five. But most of the others, like the one in your hand, are around twenty-five. It depends on what it is and what you want to do with it."

"Scorpio Moon would make an excellent gift. Will it work on Geminis?" He winked at Sammy. Embarrassed, she turned her back and focused her attention on the dark chocolate truffles in the candy case.

Flo came out of the kitchen holding two steaming mugs. Hazelnut coffee and green tea. I was surprised when she handed me the "Good Witch" mug.

Flo noticed the basket Andrew was holding. "Are you a Cancer?" she asked him.

"Yes, I am. June twenty-eigth."

A Cancer and a Gemini, I thought. That could be a challenge.

"We need to do one of those for Protection," Flo pointed to more charm kits up on the right. "Did Clara tell you that the place was trashed a few days ago? We're still putting it back together."

I flashed a warning glare her way. I still wasn't sure we should trust either of them.

"Trashed? Everything looks fine to me. What happened?" He put the basket back up on the top shelf.

"Probably a high school prank. Someone got in and smashed our herb jars." Flo glared back at me. "It took forever to clean up, herbs everywhere."

Andrew sank back down onto the same seat he had before and patted the chair next to him. "Samantha, maybe you should explain why we came out here."

Sammy's eyes welled up with tears as she sat. I looked at Flo. She shrugged her shoulders. We parked ourselves in the other two chairs.

Sammy took a deep breath before she finally spoke. "Andrew told me you were looking for me yesterday. I don't know what you wanted to see me about, but I need to talk to you too."

"Okay, you first," Flo said.

"Dr. Pearl came to see me yesterday. She was livid. She had just gotten word that Blaine Winship died in London of an apparent drug overdose."

"This was after you both left her office," Andrew interrupted.

"Blaine's dead? In London?" I cut my eyes to Flo.

"You mean like not breathing, dead as a doornail kind of dead? Like *dead*?" Flo asked.

"Apparently," Andrew answered. "Obviously, we're a bit shocked. We didn't even know Blaine was out of the country. He was due to bring another delivery of plants to the Garden today."

"Janice is acting crazy. She keeps asking me where the plants are," Sammy said. "She thinks my father..." Sammy broke down in tears. Andrew patted her thigh to calm her. She continued, "She thinks I'm hiding information about our research from her. She accused me of interfering with national security and threatened to have me arrested." She looked down and hugged her knees.

We waited for her go on. Nothing.

Andrew spoke for her. "Look what happened to Tracy.

Janice was insanely jealous of her relationship with Duncan and now she thinks Samantha was involved with him too."

Guess we weren't the only ones.

"No one knew he was my father."

"Why the big secret?" I asked.

"My father was a very private person. Let's just say it's a long story but it would have been very difficult to work there as his daughter... and he wanted to protect me."

"Protect you from what?" Flo asked.

"That's what we're trying to figure out. Two days before he died he told me that he was going to give me something to keep in case anything happened to him." She took another breath, then went on, "He said, 'Slip, If anything happens to me look between Mars and the Moon', and that he would explain it all later, but he never got a chance." A tear slid down her cheek and she wiped it away. "I'm sure the book Poppy gave you was meant for me."

"Isn't it too strange that Blaine's voicemail said he was away in Indonesia. Then he shows up dead in London?" Flo said.

"It's stranger than that. They found his passport in his office. There's no record of him leaving the country. I don't know if he's really dead or what's going on." Sammy broke down and she started to cry softly.

"This all gets weirder by the minute," Flo said.

I bent down and pulled a tissue box from the bottom shelf of the bookcase. I handed it to Sammy.

"Thanks." She blew her nose loudly several times and made a little pile of the wet tissues on her lap. Andrew held out his empty cup to her and she stuffed the wad of tissues inside it. He put her cup of grief back on the table.

Sammy finally calmed herself enough to continue. "Janice wanted my father out of the way. She was furious when she wasn't put in charge of the project and it got much worse when my father ended their personal relationship."

"Now that Duncan and Blaine are gone and Janice is in charge, she's putting everything on hold," Andrew explained. "She's firing people and talking about a new direction for the project. We think she may be selling the research data but we can't prove it."

"So what are you saying? You think Janice is behind all this?" I asked.

"If she's not behind it all she's definitely involved," Andrew answered.

I was dying to ask "What's Q got to do with all this?" but what came out of my mouth was a quiet, "So what is this project about anyway?"

"We really shouldn't even be talking about it," Sammy answered. "We all had to get top secret security clearances from the government. If we get caught talking we could be arrested."

"Well we're not going to tell anyone. What's so secret anyway? You mean there's something else going on besides the fact that you're using Sarracenias for smallpox research?" Flo asked smugly.

"How do you know about that?" Andrew asked.

"I know a lot about *Sarracenias*. I was mapping them in the Pinelands when I did my graduate research with Blaine. I also know that Native Americans used *Sarracenias* to treat smallpox. What I want to know is what's Variola XL5?"

Andrew hesitated and looked to Sammy. She shrugged her shoulders and nodded for him to answer.

"XL5 is a new deadly strain of smallpox. There's no vaccine for it yet."

"What do you mean, a *new deadly strain*? Where'd that come from?" I asked not sure I really wanted to know the answer.

"Apparently, there was a mutation of the virus during a government genetic engineering experiment and some of it is missing. No one has come down with the disease yet. Our project is to develop an antiviral just in case."

"Just in case what?" Flo was picking at her cuticles on both hands.

"Just in case. That's all," Sammy answered.

"Then, what's D43?" I asked.

They both looked perplexed. "I have no idea. All I know is that Poppy was responsible for researching plants that had promise as an antidote. Once we zeroed in on the pitcher plants, Dr. Winship was our supplier."

"What does all this have to do with your father's book?" asked Flo.

"I'm getting to that. The *Sarracenia* hybrid we found to have the most promise as the antidote grows in the wild. It's very rare. I assumed both my father and Dr. Pearl knew the location of the plants but apparently Dr. Pearl wasn't in the loop. I don't think he trusted her. She thinks I know and that I'm keeping it from her."

"But Blaine had a locked greenhouse full of them surrounded by rabid guard dogs," Flo said.

Andrew stood up and started pacing. "Those weren't the right hybrid."

"Really?" Flo cut her eyes to me. Her little smile was hidden behind the rim of the bad witch mug.

"The pitcher plants in the greenhouse were being used for research but they weren't the hybrid we needed. The new hybrid Blaine discovered a few months ago is a miniature variety about the size of my index finger." He wiggled his finger. "I have never seen it in its natural habitat. It's growing in the wild and Blaine didn't want to collect them until he knew for sure he could grow them in the greenhouses."

"And to keep them for himself. They would have been insanely valuable to him on the plant collector's black market. I don't think he's dead," Flo said.

"I don't know, some of those rare species collectors would absolutely kill to get their hands on these plants." Andrew blurted and immediately bit his lip.

The blood drained from Sammy's face. When she

spoke it was in a whisper. "Right now, those plants are the only hope for an antidote. This strain is resistant to everything. It would be devastating."

"But Sammy, we saw an email letter on Janice's computer yesterday, Andrew you read it. She said that the hybrid you're talking about was probably useless as an antidote for Variola XL5. Why would she care where the hybrid is if it's useless?"

"It's not completely useless. It showed some promise," Andrew said.

"It doesn't matter anyway. She's lying. She's trying to sabotage the project," Sammy cried. "I really think my father wanted me to know where these damn plants are. And for some insane reason he thought you could help me find them. Do you still have my father's book?"

"I haven't let it out of my sight," Flo got up. "And, relax. I think we may already have figured this out. That's why we came to see you yesterday."

"You know where the plants are?" Sammy and Andrew sat up in their seats.

"We have a good idea. We think they have to be somewhere near Blaine's operation," I stood up too. "Do you know anything about locality mapping with astrology?"

"Are you joking? You're telling us you found the plants using astrology?" Andrew turned to Sammy, "Your father was a scientist. This is lunacy."

"It's possible. When Poppy told me to look between the Moon and Mars I knew it had something to do with astrology but didn't know what he meant."

I tried to explain. "We took what your father wrote in the book, *4/11/1940, LA, 12 pm,* and pretended it was someone's time, date and place of birth then made an astrology map out of it. The Venus, Mars and the Moon lines go right through New Jersey."

"I have no idea what you are talking about," Andrew interrupted.

"Look, I know this sounds like Greek to you, but the planet lines are the same as longitude lines. The Venus line is about 74 degrees, give or take a few minutes. It goes through the Pine Barrens very close to Blaine's greenhouses. *Right between the Moon and Mars lines.*" I did my best to simplify things.

"We don't have an exact location because we don't know the latitude. You need latitude and longitude to find an exact location." Flo held up her arms like plus sign. "X marks the spot, but it's more like a "t" really."

"Can I see the book?" Sammy asked.

Flo and I exchanged glances. "It's locked in your trunk. Give me your keys." I tossed them to her and she disappeared out the back door.

Flo was out of breath when we all gathered around the table in the studio. "Go through it page by page... slowly," Sammy instructed. Flo flipped open the cover and started turning the pages one by one.

"When I was little, Poppy would bring me books and we'd play word scrambles. He would have me try to guess a word or, as I got older, a phrase hidden in the book. He would leave clues by circling or underlining letters or words throughout the book and after I found them I had to put them in the right order. There! Stop!" Sammy pointed to page thirty-seven. You had to look real close to see it, but the page number in the bottom right corner was very lightly underlined three times.

"Holy tamoly, I never noticed that before. Did you C?" Flo asked.

"Nope. You can barely see it."

"Turn the page." Andrew reached over and turned it himself.

The page number thirty-eight was underlined twice. Number thirty-nine was underlined once.

"The latitude! It's thirty-nine degrees, thirty-eight minutes and thirty-seven seconds!" Flo announced triumphantly.

TIFFANY BLUES

"You're right! That's exactly how we used to play the game," Sammy exclaimed.

"C, where'd I put Phillip's computer? Is it still in the kitchen?" Flo asked.

I retrieved the laptop from behind the counter and set it on the table next to the book. This time everyone gathered around me.

"Go to the map," Flo instructed. Sammy and Andrew were looking over my shoulder, practically foaming at the mouth.

When I plugged in all the numbers we had, we were looking at a satellite image of a wooded area just a stone's throw from Exotic Aquatics. Right between Mars and the Moon.

Andrew pointed to the screen. "But where is that?"

"It looks like it's part of Wharton State Forest about a half mile northeast of Blaine's greenhouses." Flo studied the road map image on the screen.

"How do we get there?" Sammy asked.

"It's easy. You just drive south for two hours and turn left onto 542." Flo laughed and took the last sip of her morning caffeine.

Andrew sat down. "Look Florilla, you're familiar with the area. Is there any chance you could help us find it? Today?"

Flo choked and almost spit out her coffee. "Are you on drugs? No way I'm going to Blaine's. What if he's there...dead? Or worse, what if he's there alive?"

"I really doubt he's going to be there dead or alive. Janice said he was found in London. He's been missing a week, I'm sure his place has already been thoroughly searched," Andrew reasoned.

"Besides, it's January," Flo added. "We'd have to slog through a swamp or a bog in the middle of nowhere. That means cold and wet."

"Sorry, I don't do cold and wet and definitely not in the Pine Barrens," I said. "And there's no way I'm taking my car down there."

Sammy sank into a chair, deflated. Andrew took one look at her and pleaded with us. "Look, Duncan obviously wanted you to help us and we're running out of time. If Janice gets her hands on these plants we don't know what will happen."

"I would really like to see this wild hybrid. It'll be a hell of a thing to find it though in this weather. The pitchers will be all shriveled up," Flo said.

"You mean shrinkage?" I giggled.

"Exactly. But, no one is dressed for slogging through bogs."

"Please?" Sammy pleaded.

"Alrighty then!" Flo said in her best brogue. "But you're going to need galoshes."

One of these days I'm going to take my own advice and listen to that voice in my head. Cold, wet and barren is never a good idea. Going on a wild plant chase and closing up shop again, another bad idea. Abby was nursing a sick mini dog and couldn't come and Phillip was still with his Alana and wouldn't come. I was willing to make the sacrifice and stay behind to ward off probable bankruptcy but no, they all argued, they wouldn't dream of it.

Within half an hour, we were all wearing hats gloves and "galoshes" from the boot box that Flo kept in the store room with all the other stuff she can't fit in her house. Of course, the three of them ended up with the basic black insulated, waterproof mid-calf model boot and I got the pair of camo-green, only comes up to your ankle, duckboots. They were a little big for me and looked ridiculous with my favorite grey Ponti jeans with the embroidered "P"'s on the back pockets. I had to turn up the cuffs of the jeans but it was either camo or the bright yellow rubbers with the dancing vegetables all over them and I don't do vegetables.

***

TIFFANY BLUES

We all piled into Flo's red Mini Cooper. Flo took the wheel and Andrew rode shotgun leaving Sammy and me cozy in the back seat.

"Hope Minnie starts. She's been sitting out in the cold for days now."

I prayed for failure to launch, but no, Minnie started right up. "Can you put the heat on? I'm freezing back here."

"I'll die with the heat on. I'm wearing two sweatshirts and a down vest. I'm sweating up here."

"Take your vest off"

"I can't even move, how am I going to take the vest off?"

Andrew tried to change the subject. "There's a lot more room in this car than I imagined there'd be. Maybe I'll go for one of these if I ever buy a car."

"That's not your Honda?" I asked.

"Rent-a-Clunker. Twenty-one ninety-five a day, unlimited mileage. It costs too much to keep an auto in the city." Andrew pointed to the myriad of switches and buttons on the center console. He reached for one. "What does this do?"

Flo looked at him. "I have no idea. I put the key in and turn it on. It goes."

"It says heat. Would you like me to turn it on?"

Flo glared at him.

"Yes, please," I said.

"Have you figured out that GPS yet?" Flo craned her neck around towards me.

I played around with the gadget in my hand. "I can turn it on that's about it. Why in the world did Oscar give you a GPS for Christmas anyway?"

"Because he wanted one."

"Let me take a look at it," Andrew offered. "What are those coordinates again?"

Flo told him and in no time flat Andrew had a map up on the screen.

"We won't need that 'til we get a lot closer," Flo insisted. "Right now we're stopping at this Dunkin' Donuts. I need a muffin."

She was about to turn into the parking lot when the Wicked Witch tornado music tore through the car and scared the crap out of all of us. Sammy and I both jumped and smacked our heads on the roof of the car. Flo swerved and missed the orange and purple sign by less than a foot.

"What in the world is that?" Andrew yelled.

"Flo's ring tone. Answer it already!" I ordered. The music stopped for a second and then started blaring all over again.

"I can't reach it. I can't move and I can't find a freaking parking space."

"Where the hell is it?" I asked.

"In the pocket of my sweatshirt under my other sweatshirt!"

"Geez-o-Pete!" I reached around from the back and fished under her sweatshirt till I found the phone. I unlocked it and put it up to her ear. "It's Oz."

"Hi Oz," Flo said calmly. "Nothing. We're on our way down to the Pine Barrens."

"Park the car already," Andrew pleaded.

"Wait a sec, I'm parking," I held the phone while she jerked into a space and then put the phone back against her ear.

"No, we're not crazy, we're just going to check something out."

Pause.

"Where I did my field research. You know, near Batsto."

Very long pause.

"Oz, we'll be fine. You worry too much. I'll talk to you when we get back. Bye." She waved her magic fingers at me.

I hit the end key and waved the phone right back. "Get a hands-free. It's a $200 fine," I warned.

"Why do I need a hands-free when I have you?" she laughed, taking the phone and stuffing it back in her sweatshirt.

We all extricated ourselves from the Mini and attacked the Dunkin' Donuts counter.

"What can I get for you?" the girl at the counter asked.

"You can get for me a pumpkin muffin," Flo said.

"No, no pumpkin."

"No pumpkin?"

"October," was the response.

Flo looked at me like she didn't understand English.

"They only have pumpkin muffins in October," I translated.

"That's ridiculous. Then I don't know what I want." Flo crossed her arms in front of her chest in a huff. "You go first."

Sammy and Andrew had switched lines and already ordered bagels. I asked for an everything bagel with light cream cheese and grabbed a bottle of unsweetened iced tea out of the cooler. This would be my lunch, I reasoned.

"Are you going to get something or not?" I asked. Flo was staring at the donuts and muffin racks in a trance.

"There's nothing else I want. I'm not getting anything."

I paid for my order. "Fine. We're outta here then. They're waiting for us outside."

We ate in silence for the next ten miles while Flo grumbled that she was starving. I swallowed the last bite of bagel and ignored her.

"Sammy, your mother wasn't by any chance a medicine woman in Costa Rica was she?" I asked.

"She was an herbalist," Sammy corrected me. "How did you know?"

"Oscar Stern. My boyfriend, remember?" Flo said. "He worked with your father right after he went back to Cambridge, after Costa Rica. They became close friends and Duncan told him about falling in love with a medicine woman in Costa Rica."

"That was my mother then. Evangeline Rousseau. It's a very romantic story. Poppy came to Costa Rica in the early eighties to study indigenous vegetation and their medicinal uses. He was married at the time and had two teenage boys in Scotland. My mother was his teacher. They fell madly in love and I was born two and a half years later."

"How long did he stay?" I asked.

"Poppy stayed on and off until his research was done. That was just after my eighth birthday. After that, he only came to see us once in a while. But he always kept in touch and supported us and put me through college. I believe he always loved my mother and he made sure that I always knew he loved me too."

"How long ago did your mother pass away?" Flo asked.

"Mama died seven years ago of dengue fever, just when I was starting at Princeton. When Poppy came to the Gardens I was already working on my doctorate at Columbia. So, he hired me to help ..." Her voice trailed off as she stifled a sob.

"I'm so sorry," Flo jumped in. "I know how you feel, my mom died five years ago. My dad's still alive but he lives in Florida now. I hardly ever get to see him. We both miss my mom."

"Well at least Mama and Poppy don't have to miss each other anymore. I'm bringing Poppy back to bury him next to Mama near San Jose. It's what he wanted."

I was afraid Sammy might start crying again, but luckily a buzz in my pocket saved the day.

"Sorry," I said. I checked my phone. QJack. I looked at Flo in the rearview mirror, she was shaking her head "No". I answered anyway.

"Hi."

"Hey, Clara. I'm back. I'm really sorry I had to leave like that. It couldn't be helped," QJack said.

"Oh, that's okay," I said.

"Can we get together tonight? I really want to see

you."

"Um, No, I can't. We're pretty busy today."

"Lot of clients?"

"Actually, Flo and I are on our way to South Jersey for the day. I don't know when we'll be back."

"Where in South Jersey? Maybe I could meet you down there."

"Not gonna happen. We'll be somewhere in the Pinelands. She wants to show me where she did her graduate mapping work. I don't have a clue where we're going. She's driving I'm just along for the ride."

"That's too bad. I miss you."

I didn't say anything.

"Well, watch out for the Jersey Devil," he laughed. "I'll call you later."

"Okay. Bye."

"That was Q wasn't it? What'd he want?" Flo asked.

"Dinner."

Flo turned to Andrew. "I've been meaning to ask you. You work with Zylanica right?"

"No, I work for Zylanica. I'm just located at the Gardens."

"You do?" I asked.

"Then you know Quentin Adams," Flo said catching my eye in the mirror again.

"I don't really know him. I've met him. He's the head of Discovery," Andrew answered.

"Quentin Adams was my father's main contact on the smallpox project," Sammy added.

"Then he knew Janice too?" I asked.

"Of course. It's Zylanica's project. He's overseeing the whole thing," Andrew said.

"Do either of you know a Jack Carrigan?" Flo asked.

Both of them shook their heads. My partially digested bagel began churning and making its way back up my esophagus. I fought the urge to vomit, cracked the window and leaned my head back against the seat.

Flo peered at me in the mirror. "He lied. A lot."
"No kidding." I moaned and closed my eyes.

TWENTY-TWO

"Andrew, would you please stop fiddling with that thing between your legs," Flo said.

"Why? Would you prefer to fiddle with it?" Andrew grinned from ear to ear and held up the GPS for Flo to see. He was fascinated with the device and had insisted on navigating every single turn for the last hour and forty five minutes. "County Route 542 will be coming up in exactly one mile. Turn left there and travel 8.75 miles east."

"I know," Flo said impatiently. "I told you, we really don't need that thing until after we get to Blaine's. Unfortunately, I already know how to get to…," she took her hands off the steering wheel and made little quotation marks in the air, 'Exotic Aquatics'."

"She's right Andrew. Give it a rest." Sammy leaned forward and lightly put her hand on his shoulder.

"What county are we in? Burlington or Atlantic?" I asked hoping to change the subject.

Andrew opened his mouth to answer, but Flo cut him off. "Atlantic right now. We'll be back in Burlington as soon as we turn off this road."

"Back? I don't get it." I thought we were going south

and Atlantic County is south of Burlington isn't it? I know I aced that fourth grade geography test. Johnny Boyle, the only native Alaskan I've ever known, was in awe of me in fourth grade because I got straight A's and tried to bribe me with watermelon Jolly Ranchers if I let him cheat on the state capitals test.

"Turn left here," Andrew directed.

Flo just shook her head and made a slow turn onto the county road. I pressed my face up against the window mesmerized by a floater on my eyeball that for some reason made me think of Q wearing a black tuxedo. I tried focusing on the twisted pines and stunted oaks that flew by the window, but I couldn't make Q disappear. The "barren" landscape and gray reality of the day mirrored my mood. Flo predicted rain but it felt more like snow. Either way, I was miserable.

"Are we close? I'm not feeling well." My stomach ached and I couldn't move my right leg. I wriggled around trying to get the blood circulating again.

"Patience is the key to Paradise," Andrew quoted holding up the screen over his head so both Sammy and I could see the road map. "Arnold H. Glasgow."

"Excuse me?" I said.

"Who is Arnold H. Glasgow?" asked Flo.

Sammy answered for him. "Who knows. It doesn't matter. Andrew quotes. That's what he does." Sammy's smile was an admiring one. "He's memorized thousands of them. He's got a quote for every occasion. Birthdays, weddings, bankruptcies…. He does fortune cookies too."

I laughed out loud. Amazing what you find out when you cram four people into a subcompact car for a couple of hours. "Hey Andrew, do you know the fortune about teeth?"

"The secret is in your teeth," he stated matter-of-factly.

"That's just not normal, I'm sorry," I laughed. "I'm just one of those people who has a tremendous amount of useless information rattling around in my brain."

TIFFANY BLUES

"He's wicked smart at data analysis though. He was top in his class at the University of Copenhagen. He even got his PhD in less than three years. ZylanicaSwiss snapped him up before his thesis was even published."

Andrew tried to turn around in his seat, but couldn't quite maneuver it. "Thanks Sam, but I'm not all that."

"Go ahead, you can ask him anything about anything. Ask him about football... I mean soccer. Like who scored the first goal in World Cup history, he knows that," Sammy said.

"Lucien Laurent of France, 1930, Uruguay. And, I can also count cards." Andrew winked.

"Too bad we're not going to Atlantic City," Flo said.

"Yeah. Too bad," I added.

We whizzed past a brown New Jersey historical site sign.

"What'd that sign say?" Flo asked.

"Batsto Furnace," Sammy answered. "What's a Batsto Furnace?"

"Part of Batsto Village. It was the blast furnace where they turned bog iron into cannonballs back in the 1700's." Flo sounded like a tour guide. "Some say it's the birthplace of the Jersey Devil. Damn! We just passed it!"

Flo did a sudden one-eighty and I went flying onto Sammy's lap. It was a miracle that the cannonball sitting in the pit of my stomach didn't end up there too.

"Was that absolutely necessary?" I complained pulling myself back over to my side with the door handle.

"I missed the sign."

We left the macadam road and bounced down the rutted dirt lane towards Exotic Aquatics. We headed downhill, crossed the stream with the tea colored water, maneuvered through the darkness of the cedar swamp and headed for the greenhouse complex. Flo pulled up to the front of the trailer/office. The place looked deserted.

"Who's going to go knock on the door?" Flo asked.

"I'll go," Andrew volunteered. He hopped out and

tried the trailer door. It was locked. He peered in the window, then disappeared around the corner. A few seconds later he was walking back towards us from the other end of the trailer.

Andrew opened the passenger door and leaned in the car to report. "It's cleared out. The door's locked. Place is empty."

"Are the maps still on the walls?" Flo asked.

"I don't remember," Andrew sighed. "I'll go back and check." He came back shaking his head.

"Empty, nothing on the walls. Doesn't even look like they're still in business." He picked the GPS up off the seat and slipped in next to Flo.

"*Now* we need the GPS," Flo said as she leaned over towards him checking the map on the screen. "We need to drive around behind the last greenhouse, where this dirt road ends. I guess we'll have to leave the car back there and walk in through the woods. That's the only way. Maybe there's a trail."

We bumped down the rutted lane at a snails pace making our way towards the last greenhouse.

"Flo, be careful," I warned. "Remember the dogs. If they're loose, we're out of here."

Sammy put her window down. "What dogs? I don't hear any dogs. I don't hear anything."

Flo stopped the car just before the last greenhouse, turned off the engine and we all held our breath, listening intently. It was eerily quiet.

She started the car again and crept around the corner, coming to a complete stop in front of the last greenhouse. The door to the locked greenhouse was gaping open. If there were any plants in there they must be frozen to death by now. Thank God, no sign of the dogs.

"I've got to check this out." Flo jammed the car into park and leapt out. Andrew and Sammy scrambled after her.

"I don't think this is such a great idea," I yelled to

them. "I'm staying here."

They disappeared into the greenhouse. I eyed the keys in the ignition and fantasized about making my escape. Who was I kidding? Chocolate, I needed chocolate. I ran my hand under Flo's seat. Three pairs of sunglasses and an empty coffee cup. Damn, not even one furry Raisinet. I squeezed my upper torso between the front seats and popped open the glove box. Another pair of sunglasses, identical to the other three, fell out. Assorted paper, a stack of Dunkin' Donuts napkins, tape, a hundred dollars in pennies and a good luck acorn. Not one freaking piece of chocolate in the whole car. What was wrong with this woman?

Flo opened the driver's side door and got in. "Nothing," she said.

"Nothing?" I asked.

"Nothing. Not a carnivore in sight. The place is totally vacant and... why is your head in my glove compartment?"

I flipped the glove box shut and struggled to sit upright.

Sammy climbed back in beside me. "All the plants are gone. It's just empty. Looks like everything was just packed up and moved out. Electricity's off," she said.

"Thousands of *Sarracenias*. Gone. Just like that." Flo snapped her fingers in disbelief. "Son of a bitch."

We drove to the back of the property where the dirt road ended and the wilderness began. Andrew didn't say a word, just kept shaking his head as he studied the map. When we reached the end of the road, Andrew handed the GPS unit to Flo.

"Okay, let's see." Flo held up the unit and pointed to a spot way down in the lower left corner on the screen. "We're here...and we need to be there," she said moving her finger to the middle top of the screen. "We have to park here and walk to there."

"How long do you think it'll take?" Sammy asked.

"Hard to say. Depends on the terrain. Looks like we have to start by going through these woods." Flo waved at the evergreens in front of us. "Then, I don't know, we'll just follow the GPS." Flo was excited.

I unfolded myself from the car and scanned the heavy sky. It was only slightly above freezing and the dampness seeped right into my bones.

"How about if I just wait in the car again?" I asked putting one foot back in the Mini.

Flo made a face and opened the hatch. She took out a pack of dayglo-pink surveyors flags and waved them at me. "No way, you're coming with us. You want to stay here alone in the car? The Jersey Devil might get you."

I had to admit neither prospect seemed appealing. "What are the flags for?"

"Hansel and Gretel. I want to make sure we can find our way back. Just follow me." Flo turned and started down the path with Sammy and Andrew right behind her.

I slammed the car door and reluctantly trudged after them sticking carefully to the narrow sandy path that led into the trees. The woods closed in around us the further we walked downhill and the trail became imperceptible and dark. I looked up and the sky was gone. The ground underfoot was covered with thick green moss, like a sponge. A very soggy sponge.

"Okay, we're in a cedar swamp now. Notice how the roots stick up out of the ground? You have to walk on the roots," Flo instructed sticking a flag into the mossy carpet.

I took one step and sank down about a half a foot. "Damn, these boots are useless." My ankle was soaked and covered with moss.

"See, if you walk in between the roots. That's what happens," Flo clucked.

Andrew graciously pulled me out, but didn't stick around while I inspected the damage. I held onto the shaggy bark of an ancient White Cedar, took off my duckboot and poured at least a half a cup of water back

TIFFANY BLUES

into the swamp. "Geez-o-pete, my whole foot is soaked."

"Stop whining," Flo called back over her shoulder without slowing down.

"Look who's talking about whining, Miss Pumpkin Muffin," I yelled to the back of her red porcupine head.

Andrew caught up to Flo, but Sammy turned around and came back to help. She reminded me of a tropical bird, flitting from tree to tree, blending into the background, then popping back into view. I was impressed. Sammy was maneuvering through this minefield like she'd been doing it all her life.

When she was within an arms length of me she perched herself out on a narrow strip of bark and offered me her hand. "You know, I'm having deja-vu," Sammy said as she helped me up onto the cedar stump next to her. "These woods remind me of the rainforests where I grew up. It's so lush, so green even now in January. Not even the moss turns brown here."

No wonder she was so comfortable in this quagmire. It reminded her of home.

"I don't know too much about rainforests, but I think it's pretty weird how green it is in here. And dark. In the middle of the afternoon."

"Maybe we should have brought flashlights," she said.

"Oh no, then the Devil would find us for sure," I giggled. I never giggle, now I was reduced to giggling.

"Why do you and Flo keep bringing up this Jersey Devil?" Sammy leapt to the next buttress marked with a pink flag, balancing easily with her outstretched wings.

I crept along holding on to the cedar trunks for dear life. "It's just a scary Pinelands legend, or at least I hope it is. Back in the 1700's a woman named Mrs. Leeds went insane when she gave birth to her thirteenth child. She gave the baby boy to Satan who turned him into this horrible creature that haunts all of South Jersey."

"I've never heard that story before. What's it supposed to look like?" Sammy nervously scanned the woods around us.

"Well, the Devil's supposed to be about four feet tall. It's got the head of a horse, dragon wings, cloven hooves and nasty claws. They say if you see it, it's an omen of disaster." I got goosebumps just talking about it.

"Has anybody ever seen it?" Sammy shivered.

"Lots of people but the last reported sighting was something like a ten years ago," I scanned the woods half-expecting the monster to swoop down out of the trees. There was no devil, but Flo's pink bouquet was almost out of sight. She and Andrew were getting way too far ahead of us. "Wait up!" I yelled at the top of my lungs.

Flo and Andrew finally stayed put while Sammy and I slowly made our way to their woody island. When we reached them, they had their heads together, scrutinizing the GPS and verifying our location.

"How much farther do we have to go?" I asked Flo. "I can't take much more of this."

"Looks like it's about a hundred yards ahead," Andrew said. Flo took off past him, hopping from root to root like a long-legged frog. Like Sammy, she was in her element.

Suddenly the trees were gone and we found ourselves standing on the narrow bank of a small frozen lake. There was still no sun, just steel gray sky hovering over black ice. The cedars had given way to frozen mounds of dried bent grasses and little thickets of leafless shrubs. Here and there a few red cranberries still dangled from their evergreen stems, souvenirs of autumn in the random pools of dark brown water.

"This is amazing," Sammy said with wide open arms.

"This is insane," I said. "So what do we do now? Walk across the lake?"

"No, it's a bog. We're going to have to go around it to the other side. Be careful, if you go through the ice it'll be like trying to swim your way out of a bowl of Jello," Flo warned.

"Great. What flavor?"

TIFFANY BLUES

She ignored me and pointed to low growing shrubs along the edge of the frozen water. "See these? They're huckleberries. Hold onto these and walk close to them. See that?" She pointed out towards the smooth black ice that was interrupted with the little frosty mounds. "Where you see cranberries there's peat moss. Bog. Step on that, you're in the Jello."

"You got to be kidding me." My breath clung like smoke around my face. I couldn't believe I was out here in this mess.

"Sweetie, don't worry, just stay close to the shrubs."

We inched our way along the bog. About a quarter of the way around, I realized I couldn't feel my toes anymore. How long did it take to get frostbite? Flo was ahead of me oblivious to everything except the GPS screen. Sammy and Andrew were close on her tail.

"Oh my God. I think I found them!" Flo shouted waving her pink flags wildly as she dropped to her knees at the water's edge.

"Where?" Andrew and Sammy sprinted to get to her.

"Down here," Flo was on all fours, frantically breaking away the thin sheets of ice that encircled the half hidden treasure.

Andrew almost pushed Flo right into the bog as he crouched down to get a look. Sammy knelt down next to him and together their bodies made a wall that completely blocked my view.

"Florilla, you are a genius. I can't believe we found them." Andrew was ecstatic.

"Look at them. They're miniscule," Sammy said.

I tried to peek around their shoulders, but I couldn't see a damn thing. "I can't see. Can I take a look?"

"Oh, of course, sorry." Andrew held Sammy's arm and they both carefully stood up and backed out of the way.

"Down here Sweetie." Flo pulled me down to the ground next to her and I flinched in pain as my right kneecap made contact with something very hard. I lifted my knee and saw the GPS pressed into the wet sand under me. I dug it out and held it in front of her face. "Flo, the GPS. It's soaked and covered with sand."

"Never mind the GPS. It's waterproof. Just give it to Andrew."

I sat back up on my knees and I handed it to him over my shoulder. Flo pulled me right back down again. "Sweetie, look at these *Sarracenias*!" She was pointing at a greenish-brown shriveled clump of nothing. "They're so tiny." Flo gently took a miniature, pale green, trumpet and held it between her two fingers. "Little tiny Kool-Aid pitchers. Like fairy plants. I've never seen anything like this."

Was this a joke? These itty-bitty bug catchers were going to save the world from a deadly smallpox virus? Not possible.

I heard a loud click behind my head followed by Sammy's voice. "Andrew, what the hell are you doing?"

We whipped our heads around. Andrew had a big ass silver handgun pointed at our heads with one hand and had a tight grip on Sammy's wrist with the other.

"Get up, both of you and hand me your cell phones ladies."

"What the ...?" we said in unison and held onto each other as we struggled to get up.

"Andrew what's going on?" I asked.

"Shut up and give me your phones." He waved the gun wildly back and forth between Flo and me. Sammy was twisting and turning trying to break loose. In one quick motion he pulled her in and wrapped her in a headlock. Her eyes filled with fear and confusion.

I grabbed my phone out of my pocket and threw it at him. Flo was rummaging around in her sweatshirts for hers.

"Flo, just give him the damn phone!" I said.

"I can't find it! I think it fell out in the bog." She turned towards me slapping her hands all over her body

TIFFANY BLUES

like she was swatting flies.

"Let me look." I put my hand in the left pocket of her outer sweatshirt and immediately felt the lump of phone. Our eyes locked. What was she thinking? Zero chance of cell reception out here in this godforsaken bog.

"Bitch. I'm going to kill you both if you don't give me the fucking phone NOW."

"Well I can't find it so just go ahead and kill us!"

"That's helpful Flo...very helpful." I turned to Andrew. His face was bright red, dripping with sweat. A cloud of steam radiated from his body. Stay calm Clara. Fear is not an option. "Look, she lost the phone. It's gone. Will you please tell us what's going on?"

"It's simple, Clara. I've been searching for these hybrids for over a year, they're worth a fortune. Now that you've found them for me, I have no further use for you." He looked down at Sammy. "Any of you."

"What are you talking about? They're not worth anything until we stabilize the volatile compounds. Janice said the smallpox antidote..." Sammy choked as he jerked his arm against her throat.

"Doctor Pearl doesn't know shit. She still thinks we're making fucking aspirin. Samantha, dear Samantha, I cannot believe that you never made the connection. These little Sarracenias," Andrew nodded towards the tiny pitcher plants, "can do much more than just kill insects. The chemical lure in the peristome of the hybrid has the molecular structure of a potent alkaloid. It is a simple task to create the derivative, a neurotoxin capable of causing muscle paralysis and asphyxiation. If it hadn't been for my sweet Samantha here sharing her little secret about your book," he sneered at Flo. "I would still be looking for them."

"Why didn't you just ask Duncan where they were? Or Blaine for heaven's sake?" Flo blurted.

"Shut up!" Andrew growled and steadied his gun. He adjusted his grip on Sammy's neck and added calmly,

"Blaine... is an idiot."

"You got that right," Flo said ignoring his warning.

"A couple of weeks ago I tried to make a deal with him," Andrew continued very quietly now, almost as if he was talking to himself. "Thought he'd jump at the chance. He gives me the hybrid, he gets millions. The bugger refused."

"He's lying," Flo whispered, slipping her hand into her left pocket. "Slimemold would never turn down a chance at something worth millions of dollars."

Right now I didn't give a rat's ass about Blaine. Andrew was wacked and we needed to find a way out of here. I glanced at Flo and saw her pocket moving ever so slightly. Even if she got 911, what good would it do? We'd be dead for a week before they found us.

Andrew was completely focused on Sammy now. He put his mouth close to her ear and whispered, "And then there was your father. I'd been working this angle for two frigging years already. Once I learned that he was your dear old Dad, I knew you were my golden ticket. I thought that if Duncan was going to tell anyone where the hybrid was hidden, it would be you. If it meant I had to marry you to get these little jewels, so be it. But the bastard wouldn't give me a clue even after we told him we were going to be married."

She froze. "What are you saying?"

"You're such a fool. Did you really think I'd want to waste away in a laboratory with you for the rest of my life?" Andrew's insidious laugh made my skin crawl.

"But we're going to Costa Rica to bury Poppy and get married on the beach."

"*We* are not going anywhere. Now that I've finally gotten what I need from the McPherson clan I won't have to listen to your sniveling anymore. But..." Andrew pulled Sammy's chin back towards him with the crook of his arm and kissed the top of her head. "I will miss this hot little body of yours." He paused and nodded towards the lake,

TIFFANY BLUES

"You know the water's so acidic here your flesh doesn't rot."

"Laurito! You are the Devil!" Sammy blindly kicked backwards at his shin and missed. She ripped at his face with her fingernails, but he didn't even flinch; just shifted his arm down so she couldn't move.

Okay, Universe, remember the good fortune wishes we made last week? Now would be a good time to make good on those. No way I was going to spend eternity as a pickled jello pop. I tried to make eye contact with Flo. If we moved closer to Andrew and got him to back up just three feet he'd go through the ice. Maybe we could knock the gun into the bog, or at least make a run for it. I mentally screamed at her "Look at me." She wouldn't look. I inched closer to her and nudged her with my elbow. Andrew saw it.

"Enough. You're wasting my time. Turn around both of you. We're going to continue our little trek all the way around to the other side. I hear the water's deeper over there."

Neither of us budged. Andrew dragged Sammy towards us. She was sobbing, trying to break free. "Let's go ladies, you're coming with me. Now."

"No, these ladies are coming with me."

A hooded, camo-clad figure in dark glasses stepped out of the line of evergreens with a big black mother of an automatic rifle pointed right at Andrew.

"What the fuck are you doing here?" Andrew screamed.

This was beyond surreal. The two of them stood there, guns pointed at each other.

"You know why I'm here," Camo-man said, steadying the rifle with both hands.

"Bullshit. The plants are mine. The toxin is mine. Fuck Zylanica."

"Do you really think I'm doing this for Zylanica?" Camo-man took one hand off the gun and popped his sunglasses up over his hood. He slid his eyes over to me for a microsecond. Cerulean blue. Damn it. "Now put the gun down," QJack said.

"Idiot," Flo murmured to me. Then for all the world to hear, "Why don't you two just kill each other and let us go. We won't tell anyone. Promise. Cross my heart and hope to die."

"Are you nuts?" I shook my head in horror. I swear to God, for a split second, there was a faint smile on QJack's face.

QJack moved a little closer to Andrew, weapon raised. "I understand why you want the plants."

"You have no idea."

"Oh, but I do. I also have people who want them and will do pretty much anything to secure them. What I don't understand is why you killed Duncan and Tracy."

Andrew released his hold on Sammy's neck, twisted her arm behind her back and held the gun to her head. Her eyes widened, her face contorted in excruciating pain.

"You...killed...my father?" she sobbed.

"I had no choice. After I made the offer to Winship, he went straight away to Duncan. Your father was going to turn me in. Tracy overheard everything. She was hiding in the lab, you know how she followed Duncan everywhere. That pitiful puppy was obsessed with him. *In so far as one denies what is, one is possessed by what is not, the compulsions, the fantasies, the terrors that flock to fill the void...* Ursula Le Guin. Such a shame that Tracy couldn't mind her own business. That waterfall was so icy, she really should have been more careful."

"And you did your own personal clinical trial on Duncan?" Q asked.

"Yes, but I thought the passionflower vine was a nice touch. Turns out we were right, Dr. Adams. These *Sarracenias* produce a highly effective and rapid toxin. They're priceless. We could still both make a fortune now." Andrew pressed the gun to Sammy's head.

TIFFANY BLUES

"Unfortunately, these lovely women are in our way."

Flo grabbed my hand and the chill reality set in. We were going to die out here. I thought about Spencer. He still needed me. I wanted grandchildren. And geez-o-pete, Delores would have a heart attack. This wasn't right. Pluto wouldn't even get to my seventh house for another year, my last hope for a decent relationship before I died. I looked at Andrew, then at QJack. I hated them both.

Q fixed his rifle squarely on Andrew. "You don't want to hurt anyone else. Put the gun down. This whole place is full of snipers. You don't want to die."

Out of nowhere the freaking Wizard of Oz tornado erupted out of Flo's pocket and ripped through the bog. Andrew threw Sammy to the ground and turned his gun on Flo. I think I screamed. Q lunged at Andrew. Two shots were fired and Flo went crashing into the water.

The cold seared through me. I could see a bright light and I was floating towards it. That's it. I must be dead. Suddenly, I was rising up...Rising from the dead! Arms were pulling me, carrying me up into the light.

"Clara? Clara? You back with us? I thought I lost you there for a minute." QJack's voice.

I was on my back in the grass now with QJack leaning over me, his face just inches away from mine. "My head hurts," I moaned.

"You hit your head pretty hard when you fell in the bog. You almost drowned."

"Where's Flo? Is she...?" I panicked.

"Flo's ..." An approaching helicopter drowned him out.

"What?" I yelled and tried to put my hands over my ears.

QJack said something I couldn't hear. I turned my head. NJ State Police and guys with "FCT" printed on their backs swarmed around us. Andrew was lying on the ground covered in blood. Very dead. QJack gently slid his arms under me and lifted me off the ground. I leaned my head against his chest. The helicopter hovered right over us and lowered one of those red rescue baskets.

"No way!" My teeth were chattering now. "I'm not riding that thing up there!" I said weakly.

QJack laughed, put me in the basket and waved as I disappeared up and into the helicopter. Flo was already inside, covered chin to toe in shiny aluminum foil. A Ranger guy made me lie down next to her and covered me up with another roll of aluminum foil.

Flo turned her head in my direction. "Sweetie! You're dead too?" she murmured.

"Yeah, I'm dead too."

TWENTY-THREE

The IV drip in my arm was annoying. I felt fine. I pressed the nurse button about a hundred times before anyone answered through the speaker above my head.

"Can I help you?" the voice said.

"You can take this needle out of my arm now please?" I answered.

"We can't do that without doctor's orders," the voice argued.

"If you don't take this IV out of my arm in the next five minutes, I'm yanking it out myself."

Flo was in the bed next to me sound asleep. A large nurse with a slight limp came charging into the room.

"You know how much trouble I could get into for this?" she asked ripping off the tape around the needle.

"Don't worry, my brother is chief of surgery in Princeton. He'll vouch for you." I rubbed my sore hand where the tape had been.

"We know all about your brother."

"You do?"

"He's been checking up on all of us every two hours since you got here. That huge basket of yellow mums over there is from him, I think."

"No, his wife picked them out. I hate yellow mums."

"Yeah me too. It's starting to look like a funeral parlor in here, what with all these baskets and flowers all over, there's even one there by Ms. Munrow from Cayo Hueso," she answered, slowly removing the needle from my hand. "Here, just hold this a sec."

"Must be from Cody, her twin brother. She'll be happy. What's your name?" I asked the nurse.

"Maggie." She taped a band aid over the cotton pad. "You seem much better now. No more hypothermia. And your head CT scan came back negative. You hungry? I can have a tray sent up."

"Hungry?" Flo was awake.

"Hey, Sweetie! It's about time you woke up," I laughed. "You've been sleeping for almost twenty-four hours."

"Where'd all the flowers come from? Looks like a funeral home in here."

"Everybody. The birds of paradise next to you are from Cody," I said.

"Can you take that thing out of my arm too? I want to look at the card," Flo asked Maggie who obliged.

"Owww! That hurt," Flo complained when she ripped off the tape.

"Sorry. Food should be up real soon." Nurse Maggie left us alone.

"Maggie, please, no more Jello," I said.

"You had Jello? What flavor?" Flo asked reading the card from Cody.

"I don't know. I didn't eat it. I never want to see any gelatin like substance again."

"He said *Heard you were frozen, come warm up in Paradise. TTY soon, love Cody.*"

"Sounds good to me." I kicked off my blanket and dangled my bare legs over the edge of the bed. Things started spinning. Oooh, a little dizzy. I laid back down and watched the door hoping someone would walk in with a turkey club.

Instead of a food tray, another giant bouquet of flowers walked in. Red roses, white hydrangeas and ferns. Behind them was Q, or Jack, looking ever so delicious in jeans, boots and a slightly frayed Annapolis sweatshirt. He came in with a smile and set the flowers down on the bed table.

"That's some sexy gown you have on there," he grinned and sat on the side of my bed facing Flo. "How're you feeling?" He patted my hand.

"Ridiculous. But very, very grateful. Thank you for saving us from the..."

"I saved you from yourselves. You didn't make it easy, you know. Florilla, how are you doing?"

Flo sat up. "Well, they covered us with aluminum foil blankets and put us in the easy bake oven. Made us suck in hot air, then stuck us with needles. Now we're starving."

"After twenty four hours of no solid food, that's understandable," QJack laughed.

"So, how did you find us at the bog anyway?" I asked.

"Your cell phone."

"You were tracking me? Everywhere I went?"

"No, not everywhere," he smiled.

"Who are you? Really?" I asked letting go of his hand.

He took an official looking badge out of his pocket and held it up for me to see. FCT, Counter Intelligence Unit. His name was Jack D. Carrigan.

"I was working deep cover at Zylanica."

"See I told you it was terrorists all along!" Flo said.

"Is Jack Carrigan your real name?"

"If I told you, I'd have to kill you." The blue eyes danced and he laughed a real laugh.

"Sammy, is Sammy okay?" Flo asked.

"She's a fighter. She was shot, bullet just missed her heart, didn't hit any vital organs so she'll make it... she's downstairs in ICU. Poor girl, what a mess with her father and Andrew. The physical wounds will heal, I don't know about the emotional scars."

"My God. Flo, maybe we can help her. I feel awful." I said.

Flo made sad eyes at me and nodded in agreement. "Do you know anything else about Tracy Bennett?"

"Apparently Duncan made the mistake of getting involved with her. She ended up in the wrong place at the wrong time because she was, or she thought she was, in love with him. At least that's Janice Pearl's version. She died from a traumatic brain injury when she was pushed off the waterfall."

"He really was a monster. Who was Andrew anyway? What made him go bonkers?" I asked.

"Zylanica had a contract with the U.S. government for a secret project to do research for an antiviral. Andrew was working, through a middleman, as a spy for another European pharma. We've been investigating them for a while for corporate espionage. When Andrew discovered the toxin, he was ready to sell to the highest bidder, especially our enemies."

"An antiviral for the new strain of smallpox, right?" Flo asked.

Jack raised his eyebrows and nodded.

"So that part was true," Flo said.

"Yes, no one but a few researchers like Dr. McPherson and Dr. Pearl and one other microbiologist at the Zylanica sterile site knew the extent of the research. Only Dr. McPherson and Dr. Winship knew the locations of the plants with the most promise for the antiviral."

"So, this really was a national security thing?" I asked. "Did anyone let NYPD know that?"

"Not initially but once Duncan was killed and you both got tangled up in this we had to let them in on it. They did most of the forensic investigation."

"Tangled up? Now that Blaine's dead you wouldn't have found the plants without us," Flo frowned. "He is dead right?"

TIFFANY BLUES

"Almost. He was delivering a sample of the plants to Dr. Janhairy at Kew Gardens for safe keeping and was kidnapped. We rescued him a little worse for wear." Jack turned to me, "That's why I had to leave so quickly the other night Clara. His death was just a cover story we used to try force Andrew to move on this. We had a general idea of where the plants were from Blaine but needed Andrew to lead us to them."

"You mean you left Clara *to go save Blaine*?" Flo was incredulous.

"My job gets in the way sometimes. Makes a personal life difficult."

"So, how much did the great Dr. Winship really know anyway?" Flo asked.

"He was just the supplier of the plant material for the research. He knew where the plants were growing in the wild and was trying to figure out how to reproduce them in the greenhouse. Once we determined that one of the hybrids Blaine discovered could be a potential nerve toxin it became critical to secure the plants."

"Is the toxin D43?" I asked.

"You know about that too? You guys are good. Want to come back to the government?"

"Been there done that. No thanks," I answered.

"Where is Blaine now?" Flo asked.

"Operation Madagascar."

"Good." Flo sank back into her pillow happy as a clam.

"Okay, something's not making sense. When you tripped over the Tiffany Box at the Plaza, none of this had happened yet. What made you come to Dolly's Ferry for an astrology reading?" I asked.

"You told me you'd had a private meeting with Duncan after the lecture. I needed to know why. But then Duncan was murdered. I'm sorry to say, I was actually investigating you two when I came for my reading. It seemed very strange that Duncan would have taken time to give you two a private lesson on aphrodisiacs."

Flo jumped in, "Well you didn't know Duncan very well then did you?"

"And then we found out you both paid Dr. Winship a visit after Duncan was murdered. Once Blaine went MIA, it looked like you two were the only ones who had a clue. Why did you go to see him anyway?"

"Aphrodisiacs," we both said smiling.

"I ran background checks on both of you. When I discovered you had both been feds yourselves it sent up a red flag for me...and that gave me a good excuse to see you again." He reached out for my hand.

"So, you left the bug and had me followed," I said.

"Yes to the bug, sorry. But I didn't have you followed. We think that was the same crew that trashed your shop. Andrew's people," Jack answered.

"Speaking of Andrew, you never would have nabbed that devil without us. We should get a reward or something," Flo demanded.

"Very true. Sorry, there's no reward, but how about my undying gratitude?" Jack took my hand in his.

"Forget the gratitude, what I want to know is are you really a Leo? Is July twenty-third really your birthday?" I asked.

"No, Capricorn, January eighteenth."

"Good," I smiled.

Flo changed subject. "So Janice Pearl really wasn't involved at all?"

"No, she was just doing her job. She didn't have a clue."

"So it's over and the good guys won?" Flo asked.

"Yep, looks that way. At least the plants are secured and it looks like we'll be able to actually make the antiviral from that hybrid. The research is being moved from the Gardens to a top security international lab."

"And you?" I brushed one of the rosebuds with my finger.

"I move on to my next assignment."

TIFFANY BLUES

"Why didn't you tell me what was going on? I would have kept it a secret," I asked.

Q looked over at Flo.

"What?" Flo said.

Q just grinned and continued, "I was undercover, remember. I couldn't tell anyone. Not even... uh, um... my wife."

"Your wife?" I pulled my hand away from his and took a deep breath. "So the woman on the refrigerator isn't your sister is she?" I asked quietly.

"Clara, I'm so sorry. I really do care about you. I wish things were different. You have no idea."

I shrugged my shoulders and fought to hold back the tears. I could hear Flo muttering under her breath and making a fuss with her sheets and blankets. She was pounding her pillow into shape.

"Wait a sec," Jack pleaded. "I'm not a complete idiot. We're getting a divorce. When you first met me at the Plaza, she was giving me the divorce papers to sign. She gave me that picture years ago. It's very messy. You don't want me right now, trust me."

Jack stood up and kissed me on the forehead.

"I have to go. You take care." He lifted up my chin. "Maybe someday," he said. In your dreams I thought.

He nodded to Flo, who had turned her full attention to the *Local on the 8's* on the TV over the bed, and left.

"Damn, he had such potential. Maybe he'll come back after he's divorced," I said with a lump in my throat.

"Sweetie. He is not available. Maybe you should just work on changing Phillip."

"Phillip's never going to change."

"I'm never going to change what?" Phillip asked from the doorway. Oscar was right behind him looking a bit disheveled.

"Oh, Oz!" Flo held her arms out to Oscar like a little girl wanting to be picked up. "I almost died!"

"I know Red. Promise me now, no more of this

283

craziness. I can't take it anymore." Oscar kissed her and hugged her for dear life.

I sighed. Phillip leaned over, his long hair brushing my cheek lightly, and kissed me hard, on the mouth. "Coco." His eyes welled up. "Are you finally going to stop falling for idiots?" he asked.

"Are you finally going to commit to a relationship?"

"Touche," he laughed and hugged me tight.

"Has anyone checked on the Elvi?" Flo asked.

"Abbs has it covered, no problem. Oh, I forgot something," Oscar exclaimed. "Be right back." He nodded to Phillip and left the room.

"Where's he going?" Flo asked Phillip who just shrugged his shoulders.

A minute later in came a familiar blue box so big it completely hid Oscar's face. He was carrying it as if there were a ticking bomb inside.

Flo looked at me. "A soup tureen!"

He carefully put it down on Flo's bed table. I'd recognize that box anywhere, it had the same little smudge on the side of the lid. Flo's mother's vintage Tiffany box. Oscar had had it all along.

I jumped out of bed to look just as she opened the lid. Inside was a silver platter with two crystal glasses, a rocks glass and a martini glass, alongside two little airplane liquor bottles. Jack and Grey Goose. And, perched in the martini glass was a little robin's egg blue box, the words Tiffany & Co. barely visible under the perfectly tied white satin ribbon.

"That ain't no soup tureen," I said.

Magical Intentions™ Scorpio Moon Passion Charm

To make your own charm for Passion, gather together the following materials:

- Vanilla scented candle – symbolizing passion

- Piece of red cloth(about 8 in. square) – to make your charm

- 1 ft. length of thin red ribbon – to seal your charm

- A red colored gemstone, i.e. ruby or garnet – symbolizing passionate love

- A small bowl for mixing herbs

- ***Herbs and their symbolic meanings:***
  Rosemary: Ruled by the Sun; Helps heighten feelings of passion
  Cinnamon: Ruled by the Sun; Helps to increase passion
  Rose Petals: Ruled by Venus; Help open our hearts to love
  Basil: Ruled by Mars; Increases feelings of passionate love
  Lavendar: Ruled by Mercury; Helps communicate true feelings ***Vanilla bean or Real Vanilla Extract:*** Ruled by Venus; Heightens passion and increases sexual attraction

Directions:
- Choose a time when it is quiet and you can focus your energy. Place your gemstone near you, fill your mind with loving thoughts and visualize your intention.
- Place the candle in a heat resistant candle holder and set it safely away from all flammable materials. Light the candle.
- Take a small amount of each of the herbs (a tablespoon or two is enough), place in the bowl and mix them together with your hands.
- Lay the cloth out flat and scoop the mixed herbs onto the cloth. If using vanilla extract, add two drops of vanilla to the herbs.
- Make a charm by gathering up the 4 ends of the cloth around the herbs. Put the ribbon around the cloth ends and tie up the bundle by making three knots in the ribbon. Say the following meditation (or a similar one of your own) as you tie each knot:

    "Hearts entwined, two beat as one. Our passion burns brightly, like the light of the sun. I (We) ask this out of love for the good of all."

- When you are done, say "***thank you for bringing passion into my life***" as you ***blow out the candle!***
- Carry the charm bag and the gemstone with you or leave it in a special place like your bedroom. Occasionally hold your gemstone to receive its energy.

Making this charm can help you crystallize your needs and desires. Have patience, keep thinking positive thoughts, and be open to the possibilities that may present themselves.

What happens next is always up to you!

Made in the USA
Lexington, KY
07 June 2013